PROMISE ME

Always

RHONDA SHAW

PROMISE ME ALWAYS

ISBN-13: 978-0-9962538-3-3

Copyright © 2018 by Rhonda Shaw

Edited by Jenn Wood / www.facebook.com/editingproofingbeta

Cover Design and Interior Formatting by Tugboat Design / www.tugboatdesign.net

Acknowledgements

Many thanks to Diana Gardin for her support and belief in *Promise Me Always*, and for loving Danny and Gabrielle's story as much as I do. *Promise Me Always* wouldn't be what it is today without her invaluable support and guidance.

Prologue

I walked along the deserted streets, riding the shadows to remain unseen, the white puffs of my breath against the black night the only sign of my presence. My mind raced, the constant whirling making me sick. But I had no answer. The expectations of me tonight were clear, but there was no way I could go through with it.

Refusal meant death, but conformity guaranteed a life sentence. If I ever wanted a chance at having a life—to be someone outside of this godforsaken place—I needed to walk away. But, my ticket to freedom wasn't there yet, and if I backed out now, I would have to look over my shoulder, more than I already did, until that day came—if they even let me live through the night.

No matter what I did, I was fucked. Everyone expected me to take this path, so why the hell not? Acceptance provided the family—the belonging—I never had, even if it wasn't the family I'd dreamed of.

But this wasn't what I believed in. There was no trust, no security, no unconditional love in this family. Only constant fear, distrust, and death.

Always death.

At the end of the sidewalk, I paused. A trail of sweat rolled down my back and my heartbeat jackhammered in my ears. My fate waited for me in the alley and I had to decide.

It was now or never.

The choice I made in this moment would forever follow me. It would decide my success or failure. It would determine whether I escaped this hell-hole of a life or remained imprisoned.

It would define me.

I took a deep breath and rolled my shoulders before pulling the hood of my black sweatshirt over my head. Even though my insides twisted and turned, I refused to let anyone see that. I'd remain calm and composed, like always. The heavy weight of my piece stuffed in the waistband at the small of my back provided a boost of confidence, but, decision made, I prayed I didn't need it.

With all emotion wiped from my face, I continued forward, my muffled footsteps announcing my arrival. A small group, hovering around a prone body sprawled on the ground, turned at my approach. Terrell, the leader of this sorry ass gang, broke away and sauntered toward me.

"Hey, my man, D." Terrell slapped my hand in greeting, along with a one-armed hug. "It's about time your ass got here. We're all freezing our balls off waitin' on you."

"Sorry, man. I got held up."

"No problem, dawg. No problem."

The circle opened, providing me an unobstructed view of the body they'd been surrounding. He shuddered from the beating he'd received, and a dark hand reached in to roll him over before pressing on his head, exposing the small black cobra tattooed on the side of his neck, the sign of the rival gang in the area.

"You know what you need to do."

I swallowed hard. "Terrell—"

"No excuses, D. If you want to be a part of this family, then you know what you gotta do. How you gotta earn our trust." He stood to his full height and narrowed his eyes. "And if you don't, then you know what happens."

I took a sharp breath through my nose and pulled out my gun, releasing the safety as the bystanders nearby stepped back. I aimed at his head, averting my gaze from the dark eyes staring at me, daring me to shoot.

"Fuck you," the guy spat.

"Come on, man. What you waitin' for?" Terrell said from my side. "He wouldn't have waited to pull the trigger on you. He don't deserve you thinkin' about him, D."

I closed my eyes, fighting to ignore everyone and everything around me, and strained to hear the voice over the noise invading my mind, the one to guide me to the right choice and get me the fuck out of this. But I was lost, so lost, and had no idea what to do. When a hand gripped mine, intending to squeeze the trigger, the answer became clear. Anger replaced any confusion that had been clouding my thoughts.

My heart leapt into my throat, and I spun in the opposite direction at the last second, as the gun went off, firing into the corner and causing our audience to scatter in cover.

I reeled on Terrell. "What the fuck?"

He held up his hands in a gesture of peace. "I was just givin' you a little help, my man. It looked like you needed it."

"I don't need your fucking help." I backed away as I reset the safety and shoved the pistol into my waistband. At my retreat, the rival gang member's expression filled with shock and disbelief.

Terrell narrowed his beady eyes at me. "Where you goin', D?"

"I'm out." I shook my head and crossed my arms. "I'm not doing this."

"*I'm not doing this.*" Terrell's tone mocked before he dropped his sneer. "What? You think you got a fuckin' choice?"

I held out my hands. "Do whatever you've got to do."

Terrell stepped in front of me as the others flanked behind their leader in support. Noting my defiance, he snorted. "I don't know whether to laugh or be impressed."

"I'm not here for your fucking amusement." My insides churned as I waited on his reaction, but I refused to throw away my dreams.

He chuckled, his breath showing on the air in bursts. "Well, well, well. I see how it's gonna be now, D."

"This is how it's going to be."

"And we're just gonna forget everything I've done for you? Everything I've gotten for you, so you can follow this fuckin' dream of yours?"

"I never asked you to—"

"No, you didn't!" Terrell's eyes flashed hot before he took a deep breath. "But I did it because that's what family do. But you seem to want to forget that. You seem to want to forget *we're* your family. The only one you have, my brother."

Silence passed as Terrell continued to size me up. Then he relaxed and smiled, a gold tooth gleaming in the one flickering streetlight struggling to stay lit. "So, I'll tell you what I'm gonna do." He waved his hand, signaling his men to stand down when the click of a gun hammer sounded behind him. He stood close, and I was thankful we were the same height, eye to eye. "I'm gonna be watching you. Very closely." His voice dropped to a threatening whisper. "And when you finally have something you can't live without, something you want more than fuckin' life itself, I'm gonna be there and I'm gonna take it."

The threat hung in the air between us before he backed away and led his family out of the alley, soon disappearing out of sight into the dark, seedy corners of the city. I let out the breath I'd been holding and dropped my head, very thankful to be still alive.

But Terrell's final words were cemented into my brain, and I knew from this point forward, neither me nor anyone in my life would be safe.

Chapter 1

~ *Danny* ~
Present Day

The stark white room drove me fucking crazy. My eyes darted around, desperate to find a hint of color somewhere. The walls were white, the drapes over the bolted window also white—well, more of a musty yellow with age and smoke from cigarettes—and the vinyl floor gleamed white under the bright lights. The fluorescent light fixture on the ceiling buzzed and flickered, the effects of which, combined with everything else, gave me a pounding headache.

"Do you know why you're here, Danny?" The counselor's voice pulled me back to my miserable reality.

My eyes flicked around at the others in the room, staring at me, curious about my reasons for being here and desperate for juicy gossip. But each had signed an agreement to keep their damn mouths shut about everything discussed within these walls, and each one of them knew I wouldn't hesitate to sue their ass if anything leaked I hadn't disclosed to the media.

There were other programs I might have gone to that were more like a resort than a prison, such as this one, but I didn't want the fluff. I needed fucking help, not a goddamn pampering vacation. I chose this center back in my hometown because of its notoriety for hard-fought results, which was most important if I had a chance in hell of turning my life around. It made it even harder when everyone only saw me as a celebrity and kissed my ass, rather than a person who needed support and deserved privacy. But if dealing with the unwanted attention led to getting clean, then I'd deal.

I scratched at my hair and met his gaze. "Uh…yeah."

"What happened?"

I cleared my throat and struggled to take a deep breath, the reality of my situation weighing on me. "I OD'd. Almost died."

"And now?"

"Well, yeah…I want to be clean."

"Of course, that's why we're all here." He smiled at me. "But why do you want to be clean?"

He asked me the same question every day since I'd first arrived, and I still wrestled with answering it.

"Because…" I trailed off. Today wasn't any different.

I stared right into the counselor's pale gray eyes and almost said what was on the tip of my tongue. But if I voiced it, he would lecture me again about how I couldn't think that way. I can't change for someone else; everything needed to be for myself.

I understood that, I did, and I *wanted* to change for myself, but if I were being one-hundred percent straight, I also wanted to be someone she would be proud of. Not this sorry ass drug addict who'd almost killed himself by taking too many Ativan before chasing with bottles of whiskey. She would hate that person, wouldn't understand the pull, the need for the drugs to make it through the day—to even face the day—and she would have turned away from it all…away from me.

He understood what was going through my head and nodded. "Take more time, Danny. We'll try again next time. Samantha? How about you?"

With the attention off me, I rubbed my hand over my now short hair and leaned against the back of the chair. I closed my eyes, not bothering to listen to anyone else's sad, pathetic story. Mine was fucked up enough; I didn't need the added misery.

Gabrielle.

Just thinking her name caused my chest to ache and my heart to thud. Six years, and I still wasn't over her—far from it. I thought about her every day, never missing one since the horrible night at The Sanctuary. Countless times, I'd wanted to cave, determined to find her. But I'd stopped myself, knowing she likely hated me and would refuse to give me the time of day. Even though I didn't blame her, not one bit, her rejection had the power to slay me. From anyone else, I could deal, but not her. Instead, I'd turned to drugs and alcohol, desperate to dull the constant pain deep in my bones, to chase away the hallowing loneliness inside of me. My life since that night had been nothing but a fucking mess.

To any outsider, looking back with remorse probably seemed fucking ridiculous since the stars had aligned for me as soon as I'd reached L.A. with my boys, Dollar and Big T, and had lucked out with a connection to an agent. After securing a contract, it seemed only months later I was a huge star, almost a household name. But I'd lost all that time to a drug-filled haze.

"Okay, everyone. Thanks for all the sharing. We're done for today." The torment was finally over as the counselor ended the session.

I hopped up and booked it out of there before anyone tried to stop me. I kept my gaze low to avoid eye contact, and almost made it back to my room without interference, until I turned a corner and smacked straight into one of the other participants. Gary, or something.

"Hey, DOA! I wanted to ask you—"

"Oh, hey, man." I cut him off, sidestepping him. "Yeah, no, that's cool, but maybe later, all right?" I shoved a thumb over my shoulder as I kept walking. "I've got…something to do."

"Oh, yeah. Sure. No, that's cool. I'll catch you later."

With my teeth clenched, I let out a breath through my nose and prayed for patience, and when I reached the door to my room, I slammed it behind me. This was the last place I wanted to be, but it was the only place I found peace. To sit in one of the common rooms meant just that; I would have to socialize with others in the program, the absolute last thing I felt like doing. It was always the same, incessant questions about my music, my personal life. Then they'd bring up the stupid fucking rumors—who I was sleeping with, how I'd ended up in rehab—about anything that wasn't their damn business, and I wasn't in the mood to ward it off.

So instead, I grabbed my journal with an embossed "D" on the cover from the white Formica desk, and sat on the bed with my back against the wall. I had to work through this fucking block, write ideas for new songs, and somehow get my mind off my problems. But as I sat there struggling to come up with something, even just one motherfucking word, I had nothing. After a half an hour, a blank page blared at me with only doodles in the margin.

"Fuck!"

I tossed the journal onto the floor and it landed with a smack, loose papers spilling out the side, each one of them with nothing but fucking scribbles. Words were out of reach, which worried me more than anything. The inability to produce a mean quip or a clever verse just wasn't an option. I had to come up with something.

Being famous at almost twenty-five years old was a concept still hard for me to grasp. My songs climbed to the top of every hip-hop chart known to man, a surprise to me each and every time, and they earned me more money than I knew what to do with. Everywhere I went, people recognized me because of the interest my music garnered, both good and bad. I laughed when my songs showed up as examples of what was wrong with the people of my generation by the stupid fucking politicians and public interest groups. But I was humbled whenever they were declared a prime example of pure talent in the hip-hop world.

With the popularity came women, lots of them. I could have a different choice every night, if that's what I wanted. Sometimes I took up an offer, needing to find release outside of a bottle, but other times, I only wanted to go back to my room—alone—to wallow in my grief.

Every one of my dreams had come true, everything I'd worked so hard to achieve, but I struggled to enjoy any of it because I was fucking miserable. I longed for the one real thing ever to exist in my life, resulting in me walking around with a black hole in my chest for the past six years. My only means to surviving the time without her was to numb the pain wracking my body, and then even my escape of choice turned on me when I'd collapsed. Dollar found me, only hours from death, and called 911, but I almost wished they'd left me to end my misery.

The phone in my room shrilled, threatening to cause a relapse of the headache that had finally relented. I debated not answering, but then whoever it was would keep calling, and if I *still* didn't answer, there'd be a knock on my door. A welfare check, as they liked to call it.

"Yeah?"

"You have a visitor, Mr. Anderson."

"I don't want to see anyone."

"Tell him it's me...Dollar," I heard on the other end, and I sighed. He'd been trying to visit me, and I'd turned him away each time, not ready to face him and hear his lectures, but I'd put it off too long.

"All right. I'll be down in a sec."

Dollar was already there when I arrived, and he jumped up from one of the chairs.

"D, my man." He pulled me into a one-armed hug.

"Hey, man. Good to see you." It was, even if I had been avoiding him.

If there was anyone who had complete confidence in me, it was Dollar. Ever since day one, when he first heard me in a freestyle battle at The Sanctuary, a club from our old stomping grounds, he'd become dedicated to doing whatever he could to get me on the path to stardom. He'd hounded me to cut recording after recording, and to rework quips so they were cutting as well as lyrical. Because of him, I'd made it and would never forget all he'd done for me. Not only was he still one of my closest friends, he was my manager as well.

There was only one thing we'd ever disagreed on and that had been Gabrielle; but in the end, it hadn't mattered because he'd gotten what he wanted.

"How are things going?" he asked.

"All right. Still working through things." I sat in the chair across from him.

"When are they going to let you split this joint?" He smiled, displaying multiple gold teeth.

"When I'm ready, man."

"We need you back out there. We need to start some new shit."

I slouched in my chair and hissed out a breath, not ready for this conversation. "I need fucking time, Dollar. Let me get my shit together. I can't think straight yet."

"That's cool, man. That's cool. I get it. I'm just curious is all." He eyed me. "Do you need anything, man?"

My eyes narrowed. "What do you mean?"

He shoved his hands inside the waistband of his jeans and pulled out a small plastic bag, tossing it into my lap. I picked it up and, recognizing the long, white bars of Xanax, threw it back at him.

"Get this shit out of here, man! What the fuck are you doing? How did you even get that past the search?"

He chuckled. "I have my ways." He leaned toward me, holding the bag out. "Come on, man, take it. Just in case."

I stared at him. How could he not understand what in the hell was going on with me? How did he not get that those pills in his hand were the reason I was here?

I jumped up. "What the fuck, Dollar? Why are you shoving that shit on me when *that's* what almost killed me? You're the one who found my ass!"

He stood and held up his hands. "Okay, dawg. I'm sorry! I'm just trying to help. You say you're struggling, so I wanted to give you something to help, soothe away the stress, whatever concerns you got. That's all, man." He shoved the bag back into his pants. "No need to get fucking hyped. You don't want it, you don't want it. Simple as that."

He sat down and waited for me to do the same. When I did, he asked, "What are you stuck on, dawg? What's stopping you from doing your thing… besides this place?"

My gaze held his, contemplating whether I should tell him the truth or make up some bullshit, but after a minute of saying nothing, disbelief covered his face.

He swiped a hand over his dark shaved head and rubbed his eyes. "Are you fucking kidding me, man?"

My elbows rested on my knees as I leaned forward and stared at the floor. "I didn't say anything."

"You didn't fucking need to. You thinking about her, and I know it. It was six years ago, man. *Six* motherfucking years ago."

He would never get how she'd been my world; the only thing I wanted more than the game. She was everywhere. She was in my head, in my heart, and even in all my songs. He didn't get it, and I didn't have the energy to explain.

I stood and headed toward the door.

"You know, Dollar… I need to go. We'll talk later, all right? I just need to go."

"D, come on, now…"

I ignored him and walked out before he could stop me, unable to believe he'd pulled that shit on me. He was desperate for me to get back my mojo—fuck, so was I—but to pull that? It only proved he didn't understand what I was going through. He didn't understand that I still wrestled with the decision we'd made six years earlier, and didn't understand how badly I needed closure.

Back in my room, I sat on the bed, rapping my head against the solid wall, the dull thud echoing. I needed to write something and get past this fucking block.

I closed my eyes and, as always, the first picture to pop into my mind was her. It had taken only one look into her big, green eyes to trap me, despite knowing she was way outside my league. Her vulnerability, her stunning beauty, and her surprising strength had pulled me in, demanding me to reach out to her, to talk to her, to be with her; even when it was the last fucking thing I wanted. But I hadn't been able to resist, had fallen under her spell, and we'd been happy, had loved each other, and believed we could have forever, until…

An image flashed inside my head of her prone body on the sidewalk, her skin so pale and cold, with her jacket in shreds a short distance away and splatters of blood staining the cement, and my eyes flew open, my stomach souring. I couldn't go back there and relive that horrible night.

I often wondered if she listened to my music on the radio or downloaded any of my songs, and if so, did she recognize the mentions of her or our relationship. I would never know, but I hoped she did. I hoped she understood it as the olive branch I intended it to be, and that I hadn't meant what I'd said all those years ago; that there'd been other reasons for what I'd done. Everything had been to save her.

I continued thumping my head until inspiration hit, surprising me, and I jerked upright. Leaning over, I grabbed my journal off the floor, and thumbed the "D" on the front. The night she'd given it to me, I remembered her being so uncertain I would like it and unaware that nothing else could have been more perfect. I'd carried the notebook with me every day since then, had refilled the paper countless times, refusing to use anything else. The scuffed cover was beat up and worn with abuse, the embossment faded, but I didn't care. I would carry it with me until the day I died.

I turned to an empty page and picked up my pen, hoping my hand could keep up with the verses flying through my mind.

"Even in the beginning, it was because of you,
Every joy, delight, and happiness was due to you,
I've lost so much, but in my heart, my head, my soul, I always have you,
I'm alive because of you, I survived because of you,
If only you knew, simply by the mere thought of you..."

Chapter 2

~ Gabrielle ~
Present Day

Whipping into the parking space in front of the dance studio, I hopped out of the car and swung open the door. I smiled at the older woman manning the reception desk.

"Hi, Gloria. How did they do today?"

"They're still finishing up. It sounded like they had a good time in there." She pointed at my head. "I love your hair."

"Thanks. I got it colored, so it's got all these different shades of blonde going on."

"Well, it looks fabulous. You look gorgeous, like always." She eyed the white peasant blouse and slim cropped jeans I wore and shook her head. "What I wouldn't give to wear something like that."

"You're such a charmer, Gloria."

I moved toward the viewing window on the opposite wall of the small waiting area. Inside the room, a group of young girls—all wearing pink ballet leotards and tights with white tutus—stood in a line, listening as the instructor demonstrated the correct positioning of their arms. I smiled, remembering when I was their age and learning the proper positions. I had been determined to get everything right the first time, and without a doubt, the little girl standing right smack in the middle of the line with her brows bent in concentration was doing the same thing.

9

As if feeling my eyes on her, she lifted her gaze from her teacher and spotted me peering through the window in the mirror. She gave a little wave before turning her attention back to the position of her arms as she tried to mimic the instructor. My heart swelled with pride.

I loved that my daughter shared my passion for ballet, so much so that the one day a week I took her to the studio was a big event. I only wished I could enroll her in more classes, but the one would have to do for now, as it was all I could afford on the small wages I made doing medical transcription part-time out of my home. Maybe if I talked to Brad about some extra money…but he would say one class was more than enough. Perhaps I could figure out a way to stretch something to make it work, wanting to do whatever, sacrifice anything, to make my baby happy.

The instructor gave a final bow, teaching everyone to follow her lead, before the door next to me flew open, banging against the wall. Earsplitting chatter surrounded me, along with excited bodies, as the girls rushed into the small waiting room in search of their parents.

"Hi, Mom!"

I leaned down and pulled my daughter into a hug. "How was class, baby?"

"It was so much fun! We twirled!" She wound her finger in demonstration.

"Wow! I bet you did a terrific job too," I said, and she nodded in agreement. "Okay, let's find your shoes."

As we searched under the chairs for her sneakers, the instructor, Ms. Wendy, walked out of the room and smiled at me. "Dani did wonderful today. Her turnout and her center are really improving."

"She's been working on it at home a lot."

"She has a natural talent for ballet." Ms. Wendy eyed me. My long, trim figure wasn't something I could hide, and she was obviously wondering if that's where Dani's innate ability came from. "Are you sure you didn't dance? You certainly have the body for it."

"No, not really. Just a little bit as a child." I gave a quick smile and turned my head, pretending to be doing a thorough search for Dani's shoes.

"Oh well, that's a shame. Perhaps you'd be interested in one of our adult classes?"

"Oh, I don't know. I'm not sure it would fit in my budget at this point."

"Well, take a schedule and if it works out, we'd love to have you." Ms.

Wendy gave my arm a squeeze before greeting another mother.

Once her back faced me, I closed my eyes. I hated lying, but I didn't want to open the door to the still painful subject. I hadn't danced in many, many years, and planned to keep that time where it belonged—in the past. Dani didn't even know I once dreamed of dancing professionally. That part of my life remained locked away, along with the other significant occurrences, and I'd swallowed the key in order to move on.

Tucking Dani into the backseat of the car, I climbed into the driver's seat of my trusty Honda Accord and pulled out of the parking lot. The small used car was a major step up from the Ford Fiesta held together with duct tape. It had taken awhile, with a lot of hard work and persistence, but Dani and I could finally spread our wings a bit.

We'd lived hand to mouth for so long that it was refreshing not having to count every penny all the time. We were still on our own, so to speak, but ever since moving in with Brad after we'd been dating for six months, he helped where he could, at least monetarily. In other areas, he still needed work.

It frustrated me that he refused to be a father figure for Dani, reminding me how he wasn't biologically her father. Despite his resistance, however, I hoped that one day he would get past it and treat Dani as his own, especially since her real father declined to be involved in her life. He'd made that perfectly clear by saying nothing.

I glanced in the rearview mirror and smiled at Dani, who sat facing the open window, enjoying the warm summer air blowing across her face. Her bun sagged, allowing tendrils of her dark hair to blow around, and her sharp blue eyes held a sparkle in them. She may be the spitting image of her father, but her happy demeanor was all her own.

Seeing him every day in Dani's face made the road to getting past my life with Danny much more difficult. Adding additional insult to injury, everywhere I turned, I either saw him or heard him; his songs playing on the radio or one of his videos showing on TV.

In the paper or on the news, people blasted him for his music, calling him everything from a bigot to some form of the devil. I thought the accusations were ridiculous and understood his lyrics didn't reflect his personal beliefs, but rather the culture. Others didn't seem to see it that way. After hearing about one of his songs discussing domestic abuse, which I had recognized as being about his father, my own mother had expressed outrage over me being with someone who sang about such things, going so far as to ask if he'd abused me when we'd dated. I reminded her that she had liked him before the demise of our relationship, which she conveniently ignored.

His face was now plastered on multiple billboards around the area, announcing his plans to tour again after a hiatus, and it took everything within me to avert my eyes from his piercing gaze, the only way to escape the hollow pain in my chest that crept in whenever I saw him. Rumors of him being in rehab had swirled around, and being such a private and stubborn person, I was happy to hear he'd sought help and was now on the mend, free to go back to one of the many models he supposedly dated. Now, if only I could mend myself.

Everyone was proud of their homegrown star, ecstatic about his return to his roots. I was proud of him too, and happy for him and his success, but all the constant reminders of him didn't help to plug the gaping hole in my heart.

To everyone else, I was content with life. I loved my daughter, enjoyed being a mother, and was in a pleasant, if not terribly exciting, relationship with Brad. He helped to support us so I didn't have to work full-time, which allowed me to be there for Dani at all times, and I was thankful for the freedom. What I wouldn't tell anyone, however, was not a day went by where I didn't think about Danny.

Over the years, I'd come to recognize how all-consuming our relationship had been. I'd almost loved Danny *too* much, allowing much of myself to become lost, wanting only him as the center of my life. Despite that, I believed the love we'd shared had been genuine and our emotions very real. He, apparently, hadn't felt the same way, and had made it obvious that horrid, painful night at The Sanctuary.

I shuddered. That night had been a nightmare.

Yet, even with the negative past, I missed him, even though he'd made it crystal clear how he felt about me. To this day, I still didn't understand the drastic change in his feelings, seeming to transform overnight, and regardless of what I told everyone else, I would never get over that night—or him. I was still so angry, shocked, and hurt by his words, followed by him snubbing his daughter. In spite of everything, deep down, I still loved him and forever would, as wrong and twisted as that seemed. My feelings didn't matter, though. I would continue living without him, and without closure, as I had for the past six years, telling myself to be gratified with my life. I had to remind myself that even though everything with Danny had started out beautifully, it hadn't always been that way, and things could have been worse. Much worse.

But, six years ago, meeting Danny had transformed one of the worst times of my life into one of the best, if only for a short while, and I would never forget that.

Chapter 3

~ Gabrielle ~
Six years earlier

I froze with my hand on the cool metal door handle. I dreaded the next step, the one thrusting me into a foreign environment, with unknowns and uncertainties facing me at every corner. There was no turning back now; I understood I had no other choice. But the realization didn't stop my heart from pounding or a cold sweat from breaking out.

Squeezing my eyes shut, I took a deep, steadying breath and pulled hard on the door. On the other side, I stopped short, letting it close against my back. I glanced around, looking for any indication I wasn't alone, but the hallway was empty.

"Jesus, Gabby. Will you just come on?" My younger sister, Monica, rushed back toward me and grabbed my arm to tug me down the hallway toward the front office, as indicated on the small, almost illegible sign hanging over our head.

No matter how much I tried to put it off, we were now in new territory and the teasing was eminent, but I squared my shoulders and soldiered on. I refused to cry today. I was through with the tears since they didn't change our circumstances. No, I was determined to get through the day and then the week, and eventually become a wallflower. But when we passed two girls on the way to the office, their inquisitive glances passed over us. Monica's fashionable skinny jeans and cropped sweater passed their approval test, but their eyes widened at my tight bun and buttoned-up white blouse under a black sweater, tucked into straight black jeans, and they giggled, whispering to each other as they strolled in the opposite direction. I reluctantly admitted my invisibility would not happen overnight. Like always.

"Just ignore them," Monica muttered as she opened the door to the office and pulled me in.

We entered and grimaced at the assault on our hearing. Multiple conversations were happening at once, in raised voices in order to compete with the hum of the copier, the buzzing of the overhead lights, and the constant ringing of the phones. We stood at the chest-high counter, cluttered with papers stacked haphazardly, in a variety of colors and sizes, waiting. Taking in the chipped, ice blue paint on the walls, the worn laminate tops of the counters and desks, and the incessant flickering of one light bulb struggling not to burn out, the reality of our situation hit me hard—again. We were a long way from the clean, modernized surroundings of our old high school.

"Hello?" Monica called out over the noise.

"Oh, I didn't see you there, sweetheart. What can I do for you?"

A friendly, but tired face with bright blue eyes, surrounded by over-washed blonde hair—the color only found in a bottle—greeted us. Her gravelly voice sounded as if she smoked three packs a day.

"Today's our first day." Monica held her head high and spoke confidently.

"You two are new here?" She rifled through some papers. "Let me find your information. What are your names, sweetie?"

"I'm Monica Wells, and she's Gabrielle."

"Gabrielle? What a pretty name." The woman's eyes narrowed as she took me in. "Pretty name for a pretty girl."

I caught her scrutiny, but only smiled in acknowledgement.

"Well, you can definitely tell that you two are sisters, even with…well, whatever." She waved her hand.

I didn't miss her meaning. The disbelief at the drastic differences between Monica and me was old news and nothing I hadn't dealt with before. It wasn't breaking news that my sister appeared more her age than I did. In fact, "Ms. Prudy" had been my nickname at my old school because of my preference for long-sleeved tie-neck blouses. Maybe this school would come up with something just as clever.

The only other attire I was content in was a leotard and ballet skirt, but those were hardly appropriate to wear outside the studio.

"Okay, I've got your schedules." The clerk handed over a slip of paper and went over Monica's with her, and then she turned to me. "Your first hour is—" she pulled out another piece of paper and pointed to a corner, "—right here. Here's a map of the school, and your lockers are here. I'm Ms. Thomas, if either of you girls need anything or have any questions."

Armed with the stack of papers, we left the office and headed off to our respective classes, but not before I overheard the woman's remark to her co-worker. "That poor girl is going to get eaten alive out there, and she's the older one."

Yes. She was probably right.

Bidding Monica good-bye, the last friendly face I would likely see all day, I made my way down the long hallway as a bell trilled overhead, followed by doors banging open left and right to emit swarms of bodies rushing toward me. The mass swallowed me up and I hitched up my shoulders, trying to push through. Some glanced my way, some ignored me, which I was thankful for, and others stopped and stared. My face flushed and my body trembled, but I kept my focus trained forward and continued walking, trying to mold myself against the wall in order to stay out of the way.

The crowd pushed and pulled me in multiple directions, and I fought to keep my ground. People yelled around me as if I wasn't there. Papers, books, and other objects were tossed into my path, causing me to duck, but I persisted, fighting the crushing wave, and refusing to stop or make eye contact with anyone. The bell rang again, and the hallway cleared out as quickly as it had filled, leaving me alone again. I stopped and leaned against the cement wall, grateful to be able to take a deep breath.

Reaching the classroom, I paused and tried to steady my pounding heart.

"Let the fun begin," I mumbled and opened the door.

The teacher turned at the sound, his expression puzzled, but friendly. "Yes?"

It all became real with several pairs of eyes following my every move, and I tried to swallow around the sudden tightening of my throat. "I'm in your class." My voice wobbled and my hand shook as I handed him my schedule.

His smile broadened, trying to put me at ease, which I appreciated, even if it didn't help. He glanced at the paper he took from me. "Welcome, Gabrielle. I'm Mr. Watson." He turned to the classroom. "Class, this is Gabrielle. Let's make her feel welcome, okay? There's an open desk right there." He pointed toward the back corner of the room.

I rushed down the aisle and slumped into the seat with an inward sigh. I only had to survive through seven more classes and then the day would be over.

Mr. Watson restarted his lecture and I recognized the topic of the Civil War, something my old school had covered the year before, so I let my eyes roam over the other students sitting around me. Not one resembled me—a straight-laced, conservative white girl from the suburbs, although I wasn't the only white person present.

The area, known for its high number of factories, was home to many blue-collar neighborhoods, and I lived in their world now; not by choice, but by events out of my control. All I cared about was getting through the school year, my last one. After graduation, I could follow my dreams to Juilliard and put this whole mess behind me.

"Please pass this back to Gabrielle." Mr. Watson handed a book to the student in the first chair.

I was startled at hearing my name, turning too late to catch the book tossed over the shoulder in front of me, and it landed on the floor with a loud, heavy thud. Before I could pick it up, another hand beat me to it.

My heavyset neighbor held the hardcover over his head, out of reach, and his dark brown eyes smirked at me. "Fifty dollars, and I'll give it back to you."

My eyes flitted to the front of the classroom, but the teacher's attention was on the blackboard, unaware of the happenings. I swallowed, unsure of what to say or how even to handle the situation. The last thing I wanted was to get the teacher involved, especially on my first day, forever labeled a snitch. But then a low voice spoke, saving me from having to do so.

"Don't be an ass, Kris. Give her the fucking book back."

I scanned behind me and spotted the owner of the voice leaning back in his chair. His black hoodie kept his face in shadows, but as he leaned forward, his sharp blue eyes came into view, shocking me with their intensity.

"You gonna give me fifty, D?"

He glanced at me before scowling and slouching in his seat, looking bored. "Nah, but I'll give you a foot up your ass if you don't give her the book."

Kris sighed and tossed the book on my desk. I gave him a fleeting glance before looking back at the boy in the corner, who had turned his attention to the window. I studied him with interest for a second, and, as if he felt my eyes on him, his head turned my way.

"What?" he mouthed with an annoyed frown.

I jerked and dropped my gaze to the floor by his feet, but whispered, "Thank you" before turning around. Believing I'd found a compassionate heart, I'd been hopeful, but very wrong.

The day progressed without another incident, and I got used to the stares, nudges, and points in my direction. I only had to keep my focus on my goal at the end of this battered road. I could, and would, make it through.

Stopping at my locker after my last class, I tried the padlock, but someone had taken a hammer to the dial, and there was no hope in using it. I leaned against the beat-up metal cubby, with a huge dent in the bottom preventing the door from closing, and dropped my backpack with a defeated sigh. I glanced down the now silent hallway, taking in the strewn papers, food wrappers, and whatever else thrown everywhere, as if the hall was one big garbage can. The clock on the far wall didn't even work, forever on straight up twelve, and more than one burned out light hung overhead, throwing long stretches into darkness. Graffiti marked the walls, some of which still showed, the attempts to cover with paint failing. I didn't belong here, but it didn't matter. There was no way out.

~ *Danny* ~

I stood in the shadows, watching. She looked breakable and overwhelmed standing there, fighting with her locker and forcing back the tears. The circumstances bringing her here were a mystery, but, without a doubt, it was clear she would rather be anywhere else. She stood out like a sore thumb, like royalty among the servants, and thinking about how she most likely expected the world to kiss her ass when she walked by made my blood boil. She should expect fair treatment when playing with the commoners, and I was no different. I was sick and tired of feeling like I was nothing, simply because I hadn't been born into the same opportunities as others; that I had to work for everything I had.

As I continued to watch her, however, I couldn't help but feel sorry for her. She was obviously upset, and, if anything, had tried to keep her head down and blend into the walls. An impossible feat, in my opinion.

She was beautiful, no question about it. I had no idea what the story was with her clothes, but whatever. I wasn't one to talk. Even though she wore her hair pulled back into a tight bun, the honey blonde color was silky and stunning, with white and golden streaks throughout. Her skin was fresh and clear, her pink tinted cheeks giving her a fragile appearance, but her eyes stood out most. They were big, round, and the shade of bright emeralds mixed with a rich bronze. I found myself wanting to talk to her in order to see them up close, which only made me irritated again.

School hadn't been in my plan this year, intending to drop out and focus on my ticket out of this hellhole, which didn't require a diploma, but something had pulled at me to show up, and now I wondered if I was looking at it. I didn't question fate; I believed in destiny or predetermination, but the last thing I needed was some stuck-up chick interrupting my plans. I struggled to harden myself against her, but watching as she sunk against the locker in defeat, the desire to reach out, to shelter and comfort her, was too overwhelming.

Pushing away from the wall, I stepped out of the shadows. I would help her one more time, and then I would forget her and this place.

"You don't want to be here alone for too long." My voice was harsher than I meant it to be, but she needed truth more than she needed a friend.

Her head jerked up. I half expected her to cower away, but she surprised me by reaching for her bag and rushing forward to get in step with me. "Thank you."

I glanced at her out of the corner of my eye, but didn't stop.

"It was nice of you—"

"I'm not nice." I snorted at the ridiculousness of that description.

"Oh. Well, I appreciate that you—"

"Look." I stopped, turning toward her as I lowered my hood. "You seem like a nice girl; maybe a little uptight, but whatever." I waved at her, standing there all buttoned up. "But watch your back, all right?"

Her eyes watered. "Watch my back?"

Jesus. I hadn't meant to make her cry, so I bent toward her, forcing her gaze to mine and tried to soften my message. "Look, I don't know who you are or where you come from, but you don't belong here. We all know that. I'm just trying to give you some pointers, so I don't pass your body along the side of the road somewhere."

She nodded as a tear fell down her cheek.

I sighed and shifted my weight, at a loss as to what to say. I was obviously going about this all wrong. "Fuck it." I grabbed her arm and pulled her down the hall with me. "Let's go."

She let me tug her with zero resistance and that worried me. If she wanted to survive in this hood, she needed to have some fight in her.

Once outside, I jogged down the cracked cement steps, giving acknowledging nods to those who still mingled around the front of the school and were glancing our way, curious about what was transpiring. When I reached the crumbled sidewalk, I stopped and let go.

"Now get out of here. Go home and don't stop until you get there."

"Can I at least know your name?"

"Jesus Christ, girl! What's your deal? Just get out of here."

She scowled, tears forgotten. "I can't even know your name? What? Am I not good enough?"

My brows lifted, surprised at her change in tone. I studied her a minute, before shaking my head. Maybe she did have a backbone on her. "D."

"D?" she repeated with a look of disbelief.

"My name is D." Maybe she wasn't as smart as she looked.

"Your name is D? Like, as in the letter 'D'?"

I nodded as I pulled my hood back up. "Yep." I started down the sidewalk before turning and walking backward. "And you're not in Kansas anymore, Dorothy."

Chapter 4

~ Gabrielle ~
Six Years Earlier

Giddy that I'd been able to convince my mother to let me try out for the local ballet company despite not having the money, I skipped down the front steps of the school, my duffel bag containing my dance apparel hanging over my shoulder, and set down the sidewalk. Three miles stood between the high school and the studio, and the walk would take me through some of the rougher neighborhoods, but I hoped being in broad daylight would afford me some protection. Otherwise, I was out of luck. The only bus route available arrived too late and I didn't have money for a taxi, if one was even to be found.

I kept my eyes forward and my shoulders back. Maybe if I appeared comfortable and used to my surroundings despite unease lurching within me, I wouldn't draw any attention, but that was probably too much to ask for.

Over the past week, I still suffered through the stares and snide remarks behind my back from the other students. I ignored them as much as possible, determined not to let anything affect me, even though my face heated and burned with each comment overheard. It took everything I had to keep my head down and pull away from the hands groping my behind as I walked down the hallway, while the owner whispered in my ear that he wanted to help me "unwind" before cackling with his friends. For some unexplained reasons, the males of the school believed their duty was to loosen the "tight-ass librarian;" my new nickname. I could endure the long school days know-ing afterward, my sanctuary awaited, which was what dance was for me.

Exposed to ballet at a young age, I'd fallen in love with the art. Every day as a little girl, I only wanted to wear my leotard and tutu, and I'd twirl around, pretending to be a prima ballerina. My family had attended endless recitals and shows over the years, as I took part in every performance I could. With each one, I strived to be better, perfecting my form in order to achieve the lead role.

I'd finally accomplished my dream of landing the principal in *Swan Lake* when my world had fallen apart. Now, it was time to pick up the pieces and return to where I'd left off; back at having to prove myself, but I savored the challenge, excited to show my talent. I needed this if I had any chance at trying out and getting a scholarship to Juilliard, which was my one ticket out of this hell in which I found myself.

Despite its less than desirable location, the studio was renowned for its classical ballet intensive and its connection to the local company in the city. I hadn't considered myself lucky at all since our move to this downtrodden area, but if there was a positive anywhere, this was it. My hopes and dreams hinged on being able to start over again at this studio.

A hand landed on my shoulder, throwing me off guard, and I stumbled. Catching myself, I turned, my eyes widening at the sight of the group of boys following me, and I took a hesitant step back.

"Hey, baby. Where you goin'?"

Five guys surrounded me, and they all appeared to be around my age, if not a few years younger or older. All of them eyed me as if I was a succulent piece of candy, and I started to shake.

I tried to take another step back, but bumped into one of them. His smile was lewd and my skin crawled. When another hand reached out, I spun out of its reach, hyperventilating as panic took over.

"Please. Please just leave me alone."

"Now come on, sweetie," the first guy said, who seemed to be the leader of the group. "We just wanna get to know ya, you sweet thing." He licked his lips as his gaze traveled down the length of my body.

Circling me, they all murmured in agreement, and my head became fuzzy and dizzy from lack of oxygen. He noticed my bag on my shoulder and yanked on the strap. "Whatcha got in your bag, sweetie?"

I jerked out of his grasp and smacked into someone else, and then they swarmed. What felt like thousands of hands grabbed at me from every angle, and I couldn't get away from them. They tugged, pushed, and pulled me in multiple directions. Someone knocked me in the head, causing my hair to spill out from the tight bun and fall over my face, temporarily blinding me. I fell to the sidewalk, cracking my elbow on the hard cement and stars swam in front of my eyes from the pain.

"Please," I pleaded again, my voice small from terror. I tried to yell louder, hoping someone in one of the many small, dilapidated bungalows lining the street would hear and come to my aid, but my tight throat squeezed off any sound I would have made.

There was a sudden *bang* and my assailants flinched, some of them starting to run. I rocketed upright, the quick movement making me lightheaded, and I lowered my head until the dizziness passed. Pressing my hands to my ears, which ached from the loud explosive noise, I peeked around the wall of legs of those still in front of me and a surge of hope flooded me. Once again, my savior was coming to my defense, and relief mixed with elation almost had me smiling despite the situation. Maybe I'd found a compassionate heart after all.

~ *Danny* ~

Terrell chuckled when he spotted me.

"Damn, D. You scared the shit out of me."

"That was the point." I stuffed the gun back into the waistband of my jeans and covered the grip with my shirt.

When I'd come around the corner and spotted Terrell's gang, I'd retreated, not wanting to be noticed as we weren't on the best of terms, but when the flash of blonde hair had glistened in the sun, I'd known instantly who was in the middle of the pack. My heart had stopped, and before I realized what I was doing, I was rushing over as I pulled out my gun. I had to get them away from her or she wasn't going home in one piece tonight, if she went home at all.

23

Even though I wanted to forget this girl, I couldn't stop thinking about her, wondering and hoping she was okay. A couple of times, I smelled her soft, powdery scent and turned, thinking she was there, but there was no one. At night, her big green eyes often starred in my dreams, making me curious to learn more about her. Things would be better for her if she had nothing to do with me, but fate appeared to have different plans. Everywhere I turned, I crossed paths with her.

I strode over and pulled her to her feet, passing a critical gaze over her to assess the damages. There was no sign of blood or injury, only the stark fear shining brightly in those beautiful eyes, along with her pale complexion, which made my pulse quicken and my blood pound through my veins.

I nudged her behind me and stood facing the group, my hands fisted at my sides. "Leave her alone, Terrell."

Darkness gleamed in Terrell's eyes. "Oh, I'm sorry, dawg. I didn't realize this was your lady."

"Just back the fuck off." I stared at each one of them, ensuring they all got the message. I wasn't fucking around.

Terrell stood in front of me, toe to toe. "I think you better watch your tone there, white boy."

I matched his glare, not backing down. "I said, back the fuck off, punk."

Terrell's crew held their collective breath, waiting on his next move. He continued to glower at me. I heard his unspoken threat, but it didn't matter. I wasn't budging.

He snorted and stepped back. "All right, all right. I see how it is. Always playing the fucking hero."

He strolled away, his gang following him, before he glanced back over his shoulder. He pointed two fingers at his eyes and then at me. "Remember, I'll be watching you, boy. This ain't over yet. Not by a fuckin' long shot."

Terrell paused, letting his gaze linger on Gabrielle behind me, and his lips curled. She lifted a shoulder, attempting to shield herself from him. When he licked his lips, slow and deliberate, I saw red and lurched forward, my right fist lifting before I realized what I was doing. I jerked to a halt, restraining myself seconds before his crew would have jumped me, and Terrell chuckled before sauntering away.

Once the group turned the corner and was out of sight, I spun around and put my hands on her shoulders. "Are you okay?"

She gave a stilted nod of her head and took a deep breath, but didn't say anything.

"What the fuck did I tell you?" I leaned down to grab her bag and shoved it at her. "You shouldn't be walking out here alone." My tone was sharp, but my adrenaline was crashing, making me edgy and irritable. Plus, I was still unsettled on her behalf at what had happened and what I knew could have happened had I not intervened.

But at the fright and panic all over her face, I regretted my tone and fought against the urge to pull her into my arms in order to soothe her, to make everything right.

~ *Gabrielle* ~

I stood rigid, holding my bag, and my entire body quaked, my fear working its way to the surface. The tears that had flooded my eyes found their way out of my tear ducts and flowed down my cheeks, but I didn't move or make a sound, frozen in place. My elbow throbbed without any signs of relenting, and scratches burned on my arms and face, but I could do nothing more than stand there and break down.

D hissed in a breath and let it out before pulling me against him. I stiffened, but then settled into his warmth, soaking into the refuge he was providing, if only temporary. My cheek pressed against his hard chest, his heart beating just beneath my ear, and my hand bunched into his thin t-shirt. Fresh soap overlaid by a light scent of car oil filled my nose.

"Come on, don't do that. You're okay." He rubbed my back in slow, soothing circles.

I hiccupped as I fought for control, but then only fell apart more. It was all too much, and I had no idea how to handle any of it. I felt sick and scared, and out of my element.

I peered up at him through bleary eyes. "Thank…you…." I gasped, trying to pull much-needed air into my straining lungs.

He shrugged. "It's nothing."

"I…don't…know…" I stopped, trying to steady my staggered breaths. It took a few moments before my breathing was somewhat under control, and he patiently waited me out. "I don't want to know what would have happened if you hadn't showed up."

He gave a small nod in agreement and his eyes softened from their usual hard intensity. "You're right, you don't want to know." Then every muscle in him braced and he jerked back, setting me away from him. The air around me was instantly cold, and I shivered.

Embarrassed that I'd let myself get comfortable in his arms, becoming too clingy and making it awkward, I busied myself by brushing off my pants. Sharp pain in my elbow made me wince when I pulled my hair back into a low ponytail.

"Where are you going?" he asked.

"Parks Boulevard."

"Parks? You were going to walk all the way to Parks?"

"Yes."

His eyes widened. "Jesus, girl. You're asking for trouble."

"I don't have any other options."

"You can't get a ride? Take the bus?" he asked, and I gave a quick shake of my head.

Standing with his hands on his hips, he dropped his head, appearing to be thinking something over. His fingers tunneled into his shaggy, jet-black hair, long enough to brush against the back of his neck, and he tugged before dropping his hands. He gave a short huff of what sounded like laughter and set off down the sidewalk, his hands jammed deep into the pockets of his jeans held up by a black belt, but low enough so the waistband of his gray boxers peeked out just under the bottom hem of his sweatshirt. "Let's go."

I studied his back, unsure if he meant for me to follow, but seeing he was going in the direction I wanted, I hurried to catch up with him. He gave me a sideways glance when I fell into step beside him, but didn't slow.

We walked together in silence before he broke it.

"How often do you have to go to Parks?"

"Um, well, if they accept me, every day."

He glanced at me, surprise quirking one of his eyebrows and lighting up his vibrant gaze. "Accept you? Where are you going anyway?"

"It's a dance studio. You have to be accepted to join the company."

"Dance?" He turned his shoulders toward me and gave me steady eye contact. "What kind of dance?"

"Ballet."

He stopped and his lips curved. "Ahhh. So that's why you look the way you do."

I tugged on my ponytail to keep myself from staring. It was the first time I'd seen anything close to resembling a smile on him and it was disarming. "I guess." My shoulder lifted in a slight shrug as I studied the ground, uncomfortable under his intense gaze, which bore through me, all the way down to my toes. The vivid vibrancy of his eyes always amazed me.

"You guess." He gave another snort as he set off again.

"So, who was that guy?" I asked when I caught back up with him.

He didn't stop, only shaking his head. "Someone you'd be smart to stay away from."

"How do you know him?"

"Look, just stay away from him and his buddies, all right? That's all you need to know."

D kept walking without a further glance at me or another word. I grumbled in frustration. Trying to get information out of him was like trying to climb to the summit of the highest mountain in one day.

"I haven't seen you in class lately."

He shrugged.

I glanced at his profile, waiting for some further explanation, but seeing I wasn't going to get any, I pressed. "Did you switch classes or something?" He stopped without warning and the top of my head almost crashed into his nose before he ducked out of the way.

"Sorry," I said lamely as he scowled at me.

"Look, I'll walk with you every day since I need to come this way anyway, but that's it. No questions, no talking, no nothing. Got it?"

My mouth dropped open. "You don't have to be rude about it. I was only curious."

He smirked. "There it is."

"There what is?"

"That hidden fire I've been waiting for."

"I don't know what you're talking about." My eyebrows knitted together as I stared at him, at a loss as to what he meant.

"Then let me spill it plainly. You and me, we're nothing alike. We have nothing to talk about, nothing in common. So, let's not pretend otherwise, okay?"

"How do you know that?"

"What?" His tone grew tired, exasperated.

"That we have nothing to talk about? You never even try. You're just rude all the time. You just assume." I poked his chest and he eyed my finger, raising his brow at me, but I didn't stop. "If anything, you're the one with the snotty tone. Acting all as if you're better than I am and I'm a pest. At least I try."

Respect swept over his face before his permanent scowl replaced it. "Whatever. I know how things are around here, and how they are from where you came from."

I lifted my chin, refusing to back away from his presumptions. "Where did I come from, since you know so much about me?"

"Not here."

"Well, duh!" I threw up my arms. "That's obvious since I'm *new!*"

He stepped forward, a menacing expression on his face. "Then let me explain it like this. I know me and I know people like you. We don't get along."

I rolled my eyes and moved away from him, continuing down the sidewalk. Rescuer or not, I wasn't listening to this anymore. "Whatever. This is a stupid conversation. You're obviously rude and not worth my time. Just like everyone else, jumping to conclusions about me without even getting to know me."

His mouth fell open in shock as I turned and walked away, but D was smiling when he caught back up to me. "You're finally getting it."

"Oh, I get it," I huffed in frustration. "You're a jerk." I stopped and turned to him. "But explain something to me. If you're such a jerk, then why do you keep helping me?"

"I'm not cold-hearted."

I considered him, trying to make sense out of this complicated guy standing in front of me looking smug. No, he wasn't nice, but he wasn't the complete jerk he wanted me to believe either. Something else hid underneath the surface, and I was about to give up and walk away when it flickered in his clear eyes—anxiousness. He feared me as much as I did him, and was attempting to put some distance between us for whatever reason, which I would respect…for the time being. He had me curious about him.

"Fine." I strode past him toward the studio, which was now in sight. When I glanced over my shoulder, he remained, watching me with his hands still jammed in his pockets. "Thanks again, D."

I didn't miss his small smile before he turned and disappeared out of sight.

Chapter 5

~ Gabrielle ~
Present Day

On the passenger seat next to me, my cell phone chimed from inside my purse. I reached over to pull it out, reading the display before turning on the speakerphone.

"Hey, girl. What's going on?" Kat's voice called out.

"Hi, Aunt Kat!" Dani yelled from the backseat.

"I just picked up Dani from ballet and we're heading home. I need to get started on dinner. What are you up to? Studying?"

I listened as she ranted and raved about her schoolwork. After working as a paralegal—even though I'd always said she should model, with her dark, sensual look and tall, curvaceous figure—Kat had returned to school for her law degree, which meant her life was now all about going to class and homework. That also meant we didn't spend as much time together as we would like, but I was thrilled for her. My one dear friend, who had been there when the bottom dropped out on me all those years ago, and had stuck with me through it all, helping with Dani in more ways than I could count, was achieving her dreams and proving many people wrong. Everybody had expected Kat to be the one who ended up pregnant and a high school drop-out; not me, the school's "tight-ass librarian."

I remember when she'd shown up at my ballet class and I'd been terri-fied, afraid she would continue making fun of me as her friends had done in school, but Kat wasn't like that and we became good friends soon after. I don't know what I would have done without her during those bleak days; I doubt I would have survived.

Turning into our neighborhood, I noticed more cars than usual parked along the sidewalks of the quiet street lined with small, modest bungalows. Not only were there more than usual, but they all were expensive cars—a Hummer, Mercedes, and a Bentley—extremely out of place and all in front of my house.

"Uh, Kat, I'm going to have to go. There's something going on at my house."

"What? What's happening?"

"I don't know, but there are a lot of cars parked outside of it." I glanced around as I pulled into the driveway, and breathed a sigh of relief when I spotted Brad's car sitting in the detached garage. "Brad's here, so maybe he knows what's going on."

"Be careful. Let me know, or else I'm going to worry about my girls." Concern colored Kat's usually cheerful tone.

"I will," I said as I hung up and climbed out of the car. I walked to the back door and held it open for Dani. When we stepped into the kitchen, the deep rumbling of multiple voices greeted us from the front room.

"Stay in here, Dani."

She shrugged as she headed toward the fridge in search of a snack. "Okay."

I laid my purse on the counter and moved through the small dining room attached to the kitchen when Brad came barreling around the corner, almost running me over.

"I thought I heard you come in." He put his hands on my shoulders to steady us both.

I gave a puzzled smile as I studied him. His face held a flush of color and his brown eyes sparkled. "What's going on? What's with the fleet of cars out front?"

He grabbed my elbow and guided me back to the kitchen, out of earshot. "You're never going to believe what's happened. One sec." He hurried back to stick his head around the corner and called out, "I'll be right back, guys."

There were several murmurs of "Yeah" before he popped back into view. Tall and slender, the clothes fit as if made only for him. His short dark hair was always perfect, not a single strand out of place, and his chiseled face was the epitome of classic good looks. He was also the complete opposite of Danny, which was what had attracted me to him.

He grinned, showing perfect, white teeth. "Okay, so I'm in my office and a call comes in."

I nodded and sat at the table, forcing myself to ignore my annoyance over his lack of acknowledgement of Dani, who sat next to me listening. He was thrilled about something, so I would overlook his inattentiveness—again.

"You'll never guess who is going on a world tour, and they want my company—me—to work with them on marketing and everything."

I smiled and shook my head, eager for him to get to the point. "I'll never guess."

"DOA."

Cold alarm spiked at my scalps and drained down my face, and my heart skipped a beat. I had to have misheard. "Who?"

"DOA. You know who he is. Danny Anderson, the big rap star who grew up around here. He's putting out a new album this year, and he wants to tour with it."

I shot to my feet, causing the kitchen chair to scrape against the linoleum floor and almost tip. "I know who he is." The hair on my arms prickled and my heartbeat tripped when the hum of voices from the other room reminded me there were other people in our house, one of which might be Danny. I strained my ears, trying to recognize anyone. "Who's here?"

"That's the thing." He grinned, oblivious to my distress. "They wanted to get started right away, so I suggested coming here rather than some restaurant or stuffy conference room. I wanted to show them this side of me. Fun, relaxed, all that stuff, since they haven't officially signed yet, wanting to get to know me more. To make sure we can work together—"

"Who's here, Brad?" My voice rose and tremored. I only wanted the answer to one question.

"Everyone." His eyes narrowed when he finally realized I wasn't happy with his announcement. "What's your deal? I thought you'd be happy for me. This is a huge account. Huge money."

"Is *he* here?"

"Who? DOA? Yeah, he's in there. He wanted to be personally involved, like he always is. Make sure everything is to his liking, since he wants to kick things off here at home."

"Omigod." I covered my mouth with my hand and began to pace around the kitchen. I needed to move, to get away.

"What's your problem, Gabby? And don't get on your high horse about swearing. It's not like he's going to drop the f-bomb or whatever."

My eyes dropped to Dani, and I tried to figure out how to get her out of the house. I couldn't believe this was happening. After never hearing from Danny when Kat and I had tried to inform him of my pregnancy, we'd assumed he didn't care and didn't want to be a part of her life. If that wasn't bad enough, I never told Brad the identity of Dani's father, and had never intended to; explaining he was gone and out of our lives for good, so it didn't matter anyway. But now he was back and sitting in my house, by some unbelievable coincidence. There was no way I was ready to see him up close and personal after all these years.

I reached down and pulled Dani out of her chair as I grabbed my purse with the other hand. "We'll get out of your way then, and get dinner out."

He stepped in front of me when I started for the back door. "No, I need you both here. That's why I brought them here; to meet you guys, meet my family."

I snorted and tried to step around him. "Trust me, I don't think they care."

He seized my arm, turning me back toward him. His eyes were hard and his jaw tight. "They might not, but I do. You're not leaving."

"Please. You don't know what you're asking of me."

"You're right. I don't understand what the big deal is. Most people would welcome the opportunity to meet a big star."

"Please, Brad, don't do this. I'll explain everything later, but just let us go," I pleaded with him, my eyes filling with moisture as I stared into his unfeeling ones.

"Hey, Bradley boy!" a voice shouted from the other room.

"Stay here," he hissed. I watched as his long legs carried him out of the room. "How are we doing in here?" Brad's voice was saccharine, the sound almost making me gag.

"Mom?"

I peered down at my daughter, whose eyes, so like her father's, were wide with concern after catching on to my distress. There was no way Danny would not recognize himself in her. Anyone who saw them together would see the similarities.

How the hell had this even happened? I didn't know what to think, what to do. Part of me wanted to rush in there and throw myself into his arms. I wanted to tell him how much I still loved him, admit how much I missed him. The other half was horrified. How could I face him after all this time? After what he'd done to me? After he'd turned his back on his daughter and forced me to raise her all alone? What would I even say to him? I never believed I would ever see him again, so unprepared for this moment wasn't even close to describing it.

"It's okay, honey." Leaning against the counter, I pressed my palm against my forehead. "I just need to think."

I needed to calm down and think. There was no reason I couldn't be civil to him. I could hop in there, say hi, and be gone. That was all, and Brad could keep up his farce of being a family man and get the job. None of it required Dani being involved. There was no need to put her in the middle since Danny didn't care about her to begin with.

And I had to make him believe I didn't care anymore either, somehow convincing him that our past was behind me and I'd moved on, that I didn't think about him every day and wonder. Hiding in the kitchen wouldn't prove that. I would say hi, then leave, and continue to bury the ache, the same as I always had for the past six years. I needed to remember he hadn't cared then, and he wouldn't care now. He would be just as uncomfortable seeing me and would be grateful once I left the room.

My heart battered itself against my ribcage, my palms were sweaty, and my stomach was a churning ball of nerves, but I could do it.

"Okay, okay." I took a steadying breath before leaning down to put my hands on Dani's shoulders, forcing her to make eye contact with me. "I'm going to go into the other room and you need to stay right here, okay? Do not move from this spot."

She nodded, and I took another deep breath, standing upright. I tugged my blouse and tried to calm my racing heart, despite being about to face the one person I worked to forget on a daily basis.

What would his reaction be? He probably hoped never to see me again after shredding me to pieces in front of an audience. He was going to be shocked at my sudden appearance, giving me the upper hand since I knew what I was about to walk into. I would be nothing but cordial. I refused to let him see the grief I still carried around, the pain I still fought to ignore.

Squaring my shoulders, I set off with a purposeful stride, uncertain what to expect, so reminiscent of the early days with Danny. I was hesitant to test how strong Danny's hold on me still was. But I only had to do this once, and then perhaps I could move on—the one thing everyone had wanted to begin with, all those years before, warning me that his world was nowhere I should be. I hadn't listened, blinded by love and promises of always. There were times when I wished I had, for it had almost cost me everything.

Chapter 6

~ Gabrielle ~
Six Years Earlier

The day after my tryout, I walked out the front door of the school, unsure of what to expect. Would D keep his word to walk with me every day? He hadn't attended our class—in fact, I hadn't seen him in school at all since the first day—so I couldn't tell him I would indeed be walking to the studio daily, having been accepted.

For the first time in a long time, a thin thread of happiness weaved back into my life. The ballet master, Ms. Greiger, hadn't thought twice about accepting me once I'd laced up my toe shoes and stepped through the instructions relayed to me, despite some rustiness. Getting back on my toes after being off them for so long had been wonderful. I regained a sense of peace, albeit fragile, and one I only found through dance.

When I reached the last of the cement stairs, I didn't have to wonder any further if I had an escort when I found him leaning against a tree, waiting, his head down as if he was listening to something. Draped over his head was his standard hoodie, and his low-riding, worn jeans dragged on the ground around his scuffed tennis shoes.

D glanced up and our eyes locked, causing thousands of butterflies to take flight in my stomach. His gaze lingered before he broke the connection and pushed off the trunk, starting down the sidewalk as he removed his head-phones from his ears. I took a deep, steadying breath and picked up my pace, thankful for my long legs, in order to match my stride with his quick one.

"Hi, D."

He glimpsed down at me before returning his gaze straight ahead.

I ignored his sullenness. "How are you today?"

"So, you were accepted?" he asked.

The fact that he remembered sent pleasant tingles of surprise dancing along my skin. "Yep."

"So, what? Do you want to be a famous dancer or something?"

I was at first worried he was being sarcastic, but he actually seemed curious. "I don't know about famous, but I want to be a dancer, yes."

He nodded as if he understood this.

"What about you?"

His lips quirked. "No, I don't want to be a dancer."

I chuckled. "That's not what I meant. What do you want to do?"

He gave me a narrowed, speculative look before turning away and shaking his head. "Nothing."

"Come on! Nothing? You don't dream of anything?"

"You wouldn't understand."

I rolled my eyes. "I wish you would stop saying that."

He shrugged, unconcerned. "Well, you wouldn't."

Not wanting to go down that road with him again, I switched gears, happy I'd been able to get him to open up, even just a little. "What's your name, really?"

"You don't believe it's D?"

"No. I'm sure all your friends call you D, but I'm guessing it's a nickname and your mother didn't actually name you after the fourth letter of the alphabet." I looked at him and smirked.

His lips twitched, and he appeared to be trying not to laugh. When he glanced back at me, though, all humor dropped from his face. "Do you like, stand on your toes and stuff?" He mimed the action with his fingers.

My brow arched, wondering at the change of subject, but I let it pass. "Yes, I do. They're called toe shoes."

"Does it hurt?"

I shrugged as I glanced around the worn-down neighborhood. Years of neglect showed on the houses with broken doors and windows. Others were half destroyed by fire, but the city had yet to tear them down. It was a depressing scene. "Sure, but you get used to it after a while. Plus, you can use gel pads or lamb's wool, or something to help cushion your toes. Sometimes you lose a toenail."

He grimaced, but didn't ask anything else. We walked in silence for a bit before he said, "I rap."

I frowned. "You wrap what?"

He shoved his hands in his pockets and hunched his shoulders. "I rap. You know, music."

"Oh," I said as understanding dawned on me, and was immediately fascinated. "Really? Is that what you were listening to? Are you any good?"

He shrugged, but said nothing.

"So, is that what you want to do? Rap?"

He lifted his shoulders again as he peered up at the sky, clearly uncomfortable.

"Rap something for me." I was almost begging, the urge to hear him perform his craft so strong I couldn't fight it.

He laughed, a nice, low rumble, and the light expression brightened his face. "No, I'm not going to rap something for you."

My heart stuttered, and warmth pulsed through me. I wanted to hear his laugh again. "Why not?"

"Why don't you dance for me?"

I dropped my bag and set myself in fourth position, praying I didn't twist an ankle on a pebble, before rolling up to balance on one foot while lifting the other to my knee. I spun around twice before landing into a lunge with my arms in third position.

"What was that?"

I leaned down to pick up my bag. "A pirouette."

His mouth opened and his eyes widened before a stony expression fell into place. He turned and we continued walking.

"I'm waiting," I pressed.

"Waiting for what?"

"My rap."

We stopped again, and he glanced at me before staring straight ahead over my shoulder, preparing the rhymes in his head as he nodded to a beat only he could hear. His voice was sharp as he snapped out the words, bending them in a way where I could almost hear the music that might have been playing along with it. He told me a story about a girl who was white-faced and straight-laced, and, like Dorothy, was totally out of place.

When he finished, I smiled. He'd been trying to offend me, but I found his lyrics funny. "That's good."

His gaze lingered, as he'd most likely expected me to get insulted and stomp off in a huff, but when I didn't, he shrugged. "It's the best I could do on short notice, considering the material I have to work with."

My grin widened. "Are you saying I'm boring?"

"Not too many skeletons in your closet, I'm guessing."

"And you do?"

"You have no idea," he murmured.

"Why are you always doing that?"

"Doing what?"

I walked over and stood right in front of him. He was only a few inches taller than I was, but appeared as if he towered over me. "Make me scared of you, or try to make me believe you're some evil person."

"I'm trying to make it clear you shouldn't trust me."

"And why shouldn't I trust you?" I crossed my arms.

"Because it would be better for you if you didn't."

"Isn't that for me to decide?"

"Sure." He shrugged. "If you weren't so naïve."

I threw up my arms. "Well, then help me to not be naïve. Help me learn what I need to survive here. Don't just tell me I'm naïve and walk away."

His gaze held mine before a beautiful smile broke out on his face, completely transforming it. "You're a funny girl, Gabrielle."

I was ready to lash out at his condescending comment, but stopped when he said my name. I'd been positive he hadn't remembered it, me being nothing more than a small blip on his radar, and hearing his low voice say it caused goose bumps to break out over my skin and a shiver to roll through me. God help me, but there was something about this rude and impolite guy I liked.

"You should do that more often," I said instead.

His eyes narrowed, the hardness returning to his face. "Do what?"

"Smile. It looks good on you. Thanks again for the escort."

I stepped past him, but paused when he called out.

"Hey!"

I turned my head and raised an inquisitive brow.

"It's Danny."

I smiled. "It's nice to meet you, Danny."

Chapter 7

~ Gabrielle ~
Six Years Earlier

I shoved through the throngs of people crowding the school hallway and wished time would move quicker. Each day, I found myself looking forward to the time I spent with Danny on our walks. Kat had ended up in the same ballet class as me, and had even offered me a ride, but I'd declined, not wanting to lose the alone time with Danny.

Even though he was difficult to talk to under the best of circumstances, and sometimes it was like pulling teeth to get him to say anything, I still got something out of him, and from the little I'd learned, I was fascinated. Something about him drew me in. He wasn't nice; if anything, he acted like a jerk on purpose. But there were those brief glimpses where he wasn't hiding behind his armor and he was quite charming. When he smiled, his face lit up in such stunning contrast to the usual hardness, revealing how handsome he was when not perpetually scowling. I could tell he had a good sense of humor, but didn't show it for some reason, choosing rather to act aloof and tough with a mammoth-sized chip on his shoulder. And despite his off-putting manner, I wanted to learn more.

But after the warning from Ms. Thomas not to hang around him after she'd spotted me walking with him after school, and then from Kat, explaining Danny had once run with the wrong crowd who might now be looking for paybacks, I decided to ask him about what I'd heard. I was unsure how to do it, however. I didn't want to lose him as a chaperone, and the last thing I wanted was to upset one of the only people who'd treated me as a human being. How Danny could be dangerous, I didn't understand—standoffish, yes, but not dangerous. He did carry a gun, but it wasn't as if he'd pointed it at me or threatened me with it. In fact, it had come in good use and I was thankful he'd had it on him at the time. If what Ms. Thomas and Kat said was true, that picture didn't mesh with the Danny I was getting to know. Not that he was open and friendly, but he didn't appear dangerous or scary; or a walking target, for that matter.

Plus, Kat told me the garage he worked at wasn't anywhere near the studio, so he'd lied about that in order to walk with me. While unusual, it didn't seem like someone I needed to avoid. There seemed to be a hidden motive at play, and what exactly, I was determined to find out.

Danny waited outside the school when I emerged after the last bell. And, as with every day before, once he caught sight of me, he started walking, not bothering to give me a moment to catch up.

Just when I got up the nerves to say something, always discomfited at first by his intense silence, his hand clamped down on my arm, shocking me mute, and he pulled me closer to his side, shielding me from view with his body. I frowned and was about to ask what was going on when I noticed a car on the street slowing down as it passed. All I caught was a quick glimpse of the driver, but what I saw was an older man with wild hair surrounding a haggard face. The ancient car's muffler rumbled, the vibrations palpable. I jerked when it backfired as the car slowed almost to a stop, and glanced at Danny for a clue about what was happening, but he kept his eyes forward as if he detected nothing out of the ordinary.

"Hey boy!" the man from the car yelled.

Danny ignored him and continued walking, the car creeping next to us.

"Don't you fucking ignore me! I know you fucking stole my stash!"

Danny closed his eyes and steeled his jaw, the only acknowledgment of the man shouting at him, but he didn't stop moving, pulling me along with him.

"Are you going to answer him?" I whispered.

"Ignore him."

A chill of unease slithered through me. "Do you know him?"

I bit off a shriek when the horn on the vehicle blasted. The noise drew people to their doors, curious about the spectacle on the street in front of their houses. The man changed from short, sharp beeps to laying on it without yield. Danny finally stopped, yanking me to a halt with him.

"Go home!" he yelled.

The blaring ceased, but the man continued to glare at us. Nervousness crawled along my skin. I didn't like the unstable look on his face.

"Go on! Get the fuck out of here!"

When the car still didn't move, Danny cursed and let go of my arm as he stomped over to it. He leaned in the passenger side window, and while I couldn't overhear everything, I caught "Get out of here" again, along with "You're high." Whatever else he said worked, and he strode back to my side, watching the vehicle amble its way down the road.

"Who was that?" I asked when the show was over.

He took a deep breath and set his icy blue eyes on me. "My father."

"Your fath—" I snapped my mouth shut, unsure of what to say. What kind of man drove around during the day, yelling at his son for no apparent reason? And Danny said he was high. I wasn't sure what to think, but I felt sorry for the man and Danny.

Danny, studying me, misread my reaction as disgust. "I know, I know. Your father is probably the perfect daddy with his perfect little job, and he comes home every day to his fucking perfect little family."

Resentment shone in his eyes and bitterness colored his tone, and I jolted. Heaviness settled over me and my limbs felt like they were made of lead. "You have no idea—"

"Oh, I'm sure I do. You wouldn't understand—"

"He's dead. He killed himself." I swallowed hard. Those words always ended up clogged at the back of my throat.

The anger plunged from his face replaced by shock. "I'm sorry," he said.

"Life sucks, you know?"

He let out a breath. "Don't I?" He closed his eyes and shook his head. "I'm an asshole. Forget I said anything, okay?"

He started to walk away, but I put a hand on his arm to stop him. It was now or never. "Why are you doing this?"

He glanced down at where my hand rested before raising his gaze back to mine. "What?"

I fought through the rising panic, his hard expression making me uncomfortable, and I almost told him to forget it, but I didn't. If I wanted answers, I needed to push through. "This. Walking with me every day."

"Because I said I would help you out." He frowned. "If you don't want me to, just say so."

"No, it isn't that. You told me you worked by the studio on Parks, not five miles in the opposite direction."

All expression fell from his face. "I said it was on Parks, not right next door. What does it matter anyway? What a way to make someone feel fucking appreciated."

His retreat, always his immediate reaction, frustrated me and I lost it, not caring if I made him mad. "I don't understand you. Why are you doing something nice, but want me to believe you're a jerk? You act like you're put out, but *you're* the one who offered! What do you want from me?"

"What do I want from you?" He ran his hand through his hair and scoffed. "What the fuck do I want from you?" he murmured. He paced around before spinning back to face me, his hands jammed in his pocket. "What do I want from you? Gabrielle, you have no idea how much I fucking want from you."

I gasped and my heart rate tripled. "What?"

He took a step toward me. "Since the first second you walked into that classroom, all scared and nervous, I haven't been able to get you out of my fucking head. You're all up there and no matter what I do, you won't get out and it's driving me nuts."

I shook my head in denial, unable to process what his words meant. No way would I have ever guessed he was interested in me when he acted as if I was a piece of lint, stubbornly refusing to come off his sweatshirt.

He smirked at my apparent disbelief. "Now, I know you're thinking I must be crazy because there is no way a guy like me and a girl like you could ever like each other, let alone get along, and believe me, I've told myself that a million times. We're not just opposites; we're like motherfucking polar opposites."

"No. No, that's not what I'm thinking."

"No?" One dark brow rose. "What are you thinking then?"

"Wouldn't it have just been easier to ask me out?" I braved, even though my heart threatened to pound out of my chest.

Danny grinned and let out a huff of laughter before turning serious again. His throat moved as he swallowed, and one hand reached out to cup my face. My eyes fluttered at the contact, but opened again when he closed the distance between us. His intensity deepened the blue of his eyes and they bore down on me when he rested his forehead against mine, and I melted. "You don't want to get messed up with someone like me. I'm bad news for you. Please believe me when I say this."

"Isn't that for me to decide?"

He moved in to nuzzle his nose close to my neck and inhaled. "You smell amazing, G." His voice was a low rumble against my sensitive skin.

I jerked my head back so I could see his face. "G?"

He chuckled, and his breath warmed my cheek. "You don't like the nickname? I've got others—G Girl, Double G, GE."

"GE?"

"Yeah, like the light bulb." His gaze deepened. "You're the only brightness in this bullshit life of mine."

I sucked in a shaky breath. How could he make a corny nickname after a light bulb sound romantic? Somehow, he had, sweeping me away with his sweet words. I searched for signs he was pulling one over on me, but his expression remained serious with no hint of amusement. Instead, he looked uncertain as he waited, anxious for my response.

His lips were so close that I wet mine, aching for him to lean in and kiss me, wrapping his arms around me as he held me tight against his long, hard body, but he stood his ground, unmoving. My skin flushed from my scalp to my toes, and my whole body tingled, every nerve on high alert. My lungs tightened, making it difficult to take a deep breath.

"I had no idea."

"I didn't want you to." He stepped back and let his hands drop from my face, holding mine in each of his. "So, what do you say, G? Do you want to go against your better judgment and go out with a guy like me?"

I couldn't stop myself from smiling. "I say it's about time you asked."

One corner of his mouth lifted. "I have one condition. Don't let anyone else try to tell you anything about us."

I raised my brows. "Even you?"

He chuckled and shrugged. "I'll only tell you the truth, G. You have to decide if you can handle it or not. Simple as that."

I studied him. "Okay. Then I have one condition as well."

"Oh yeah?"

"Stop making assumptions about me and what I'm thinking. And I get to call you Danny," I added quickly. "I guess that's two conditions."

He nodded his head before reaching out to trail his fingers along my jawline. "Sure, G. It's a date then?"

I leaned into his hand, feeling as if I was glowing from the inside out, and smiled. "It's a date."

Chapter 8

~ Danny ~
Present Day

"I don't know, man." Big T, who was now head of my security teams and my personal assistant, rubbed the back of his neck with his big hand. "I'm not loving the theme."

"What did you have in mind?" Brad flashed a bright salesman grin.

I tried not to sigh. I didn't trust the guy and I didn't like him. He was fake and trying too hard, but Dollar wanted me to work with this firm, so I would deal.

I studied the paperwork in front of me, the words blurring, and I fought to concentrate on what it all said. I widened my eyes, forcing myself to read it over again as I couldn't blow this off. This tour was important for me to get my career back on track. It had to be perfect.

"Holy shit," Big T murmured, and for some reason, the hair on the back of my neck prickled.

"There you are." Brad glanced to the doorway. "Come in here and meet everyone."

"Sorry. There was something I needed to take care of." The soft, familiar voice sent goose bumps floating over my skin. "Hey, Teddy Bear."

"Oh my, my, girl." Big T stood with a deep chuckle and enveloped her in a big hug.

I didn't need to be told who was in Big T's arms. One whiff of her powdery fragrance, the same she'd worn years before, stopped my heart before launching it into a skittering beat. I froze, drinking in the sight of the love of my life materializing before my eyes, appearing out of thin air like a ghost.

Gabrielle looked amazing, still so beautiful and stunning. She'd filled out some, but she was still long and slender. One glimpse at her and the lie I told myself every day, about being able to find someone else who made me feel the same way she did, slapped me hard across the face. There would never be anyone but her, just as I'd always told her.

She took a big breath as she prepared to meet my eyes for the first time in six long years. When they landed on me, trapping all the air in my lungs, it was suffocating. Her green eyes were huge and glowing, reminding me of how they had always sparkled, just for me.

"Hi, Danny." Jesus, that voice. The mere sound of it did things to my body that no drug had ever been able to do, no matter how many I tried.

"Danny?" Brad repeated, confusion coloring his tone. I wanted to tell him to shut up.

I stood slowly, clenching my hands into fists in the pockets of my loose jeans so I wouldn't reach out to touch her. "G. You look good, girl."

"G?" Brad asked, but everyone continued to ignore him.

"Thanks." Faint rose circles bloomed on her cheeks. "You do too."

I nodded, but couldn't get any other words to come out, feeling like a tongue-tied idiot. She smiled at me before looking down at Dollar, who still stared at her in amazement.

"Hi, Dollar. It's good to see you."

Snapping out of his shock, he shoved his chair back and rushed around the table, giving her a quick one-armed hug. "Oh yeah, girl. Yeah. Good to see you too. Real good, yeah."

Her eyes landed on the two large men sitting in the corner watching, but no one introduced her to them.

Brad let out a huff of exasperation. "Is someone going to tell me what's going on here?"

"Oh, sorry. I actually lived in the same neighborhood as these guys. I knew them from before they were famous, as the saying goes."

Her dismissal of what we'd had felt like a knife to my heart and had me reaching for my chest to rub away the pain. If only things had been that simple, but I wasn't going to correct her.

48

"And you didn't tell me?" He didn't bother trying to hide his irritation.

Her spine stiffened at his tone, but she kept her smile easy. "I didn't realize I had to. I didn't know you would be working with them until I came home five minutes ago, remember?"

"You live here?" I made myself focus on her so I wouldn't punch the asshole in the face for talking to her like that.

She turned back to me. "Yes. Brad and I live together."

"Are you married?" I struggled to ignore the jealousy bubbling up inside me. That she was with this slime made me sick.

"Uh…no, we're not." She refused to make eye contact with me, and her eyes flitted toward Brad.

"Gabby and I recently decided to take our relationship one step further." He whipped out another a bright, toothy grin, attempting to connect to us man-to-man. *Why rush into marriage*, he seemed to say.

"But, you said you had a kid?" Big T said.

"Oh, well, *I* don't actually have a child. Gabby does, but of course, I think of her as mine."

All eyes came back to her, and her face flamed.

"G?" The only thing that gave away my shock was the small tremor in my voice.

She narrowed her eyes at me. "Like you didn't know."

Her tone made me take a step back, as if she'd slapped me. "What? What are you talking about?"

"Now isn't the time to lie, Danny."

She was clenching her teeth so hard that my mouth ached looking at her tight jawline. I didn't understand why she was so angry.

"G, I'm not lying. I didn't know you had a kid."

"Okay, fine. You didn't know."

I frowned. "So, were you married to someone else before?" I attempted to fill in the gaps since she wasn't being free with the information, especially since she thought I already knew. "Since you're not…"

Her gaze flew up to the ceiling as she fought the tears swimming in her eyes, and an awkward silence settled over the room. "This isn't happening. You have to have known…"

"I don't understand why this is so upsetting to you, Gabby," Brad scolded.

"These gentlemen don't need to be a part of whatever drama happened between you and her father."

"Her?" I asked. "You have a daughter?"

She pointed at Brad and ignored me. "I want you to remember this is all because of you. I asked you to leave me out of this."

Gabrielle turned and left the room, leaving everyone watching after her thoroughly puzzled. I noticed Dollar slouched down further in his chair with a pained expression, the same one he'd had the whole time I was with her. But he also looked like he had a bad feeling about what was about to go down, and I did too.

I couldn't explain why, but all the hairs on my body stood in anticipation of something. What, I had no idea, but I had my answer when she strode back around the corner with a little girl trailing next to her, reaching up to hold her mom's hand, dressed for ballet and her black hair in a loose bun.

I didn't need a mirror to tell me I was setting eyes on my daughter for the first time. My breath clogged my throat and my blood roared like a tidal wave through my head, as my mind reeled, struggling to supply explanations to what I was seeing.

She stepped into the room and the little girl glanced around with big, blue eyes. "Everyone, this is my daughter…Dani."

Dollar chuckled from where he sat. "She even has his name. Damn…"

She eyed me, waiting for me to say something, but I was at a loss for words. It was as if everything drained from me, and then came roaring back in out of control. When I continued to stare at Dani in shock as she gazed back at me, twin blue eyes inspecting each other, Gabrielle broke the silence. "I don't need to say anything more, do I?"

I shook my head and tried to swallow. "No." My throat tightened, making my voice hoarse.

"Good." She shifted toward Brad. "Do I need to clarify anything further, now that you see them together?"

He wasn't stupid. The resemblance was obvious. "He's her—"

"Yes."

"Holy…" He slumped down into his chair.

She glanced down at our daughter and her tone gentled. "Dani, honey, I'd like to introduce you to some people. This is Big T, but Mom always called him Teddy Bear."

He stood to his full height and grinned at her. "You can call me Teddy Bear too."

"Okay," she said in a soft voice, her eyes wide at his size.

Gabrielle pointed. "That's Bill over there, but everyone calls him Dollar."

Dani frowned. "Dollar?"

"Yep. It's a silly name, isn't it?"

"My name ain't silly," he said with a mischievous smile. "Nice to meet you, Dani."

Gabrielle turned so they faced me, and I couldn't move, everything in me frozen. "And this…this is, uh…oh, God."

Her eyes pleaded with me, snapping me out of my stupor. I knelt so I was eye level with her, my little girl, and my voice quivered. "I'm Danny…Dani."

"Hey!" She giggled. "That's my name!"

Her laugh was like sunshine and everything within me thawed. I smiled at her. She was beautiful. "Yes, it's your name. Just like mine."

"That's funny because you're a boy."

"I had my name first, so it's funny because you're a girl," I teased.

"No!"

"No, you're right. It's a beautiful name for a beautiful girl." I looked at Gabrielle, her eyes glistening at our exchange. "She's…amazing."

She nodded and pulled her closer to her before clearing her throat. "Tell everyone nice to meet you, Dani, and see you later."

"See you later!" She waved before her mother turned and walked them out of the room.

I remained rooted in place, watching them walk away, until they disappeared around the corner. I turned back to my two best friends in the world. "Did you know about this?" I asked Big T.

"No idea, D. I would have told you, you know that."

I turned to Dollar. "You?"

He shook his head as he sat back in his chair in a lazy fashion, but he couldn't quite wipe the disgusted look off his face. "Nah, man. No idea."

"She said she tried to tell me." I pushed to remember receiving any messages from her that I hadn't read, or any phone calls I hadn't returned, but nothing came to mind. Despite the last six years being nothing but a blur for the most part, I was certain I would've recalled being told I had a child.

When she came back, I stepped up to her, unable to stop the anger suddenly flowing through me, having lost so many precious years with her and now, my daughter. "Why didn't you tell me?"

"Why didn't...?" she started to repeat, flustered. "Danny, I did tell you."

I tried not to blow up, but my blood was boiling. "I'm telling you, I had no fucking idea," I gritted out, trying to keep a tight rein on my control, even though I wanted to rant and rave at all that I'd missed. "Do you honestly think I wouldn't have said anything to you about this? That I wouldn't have wanted to be involved in her life? After everything I went through as a kid?"

She crossed her arms over her chest, unaffected by my anger. "I have no idea what you might have wanted, Danny, since you made it perfectly clear how you felt about me," she yelled at me, momentarily forgetting about our audience before clearing her throat and lowering her voice. "I don't know what to tell you. I tried."

"Well, you didn't try hard enough." Chest heaving, I put my head down and my hands on my hips, grappling with everything, before pulling my keys out of my pocket. "I'm fucking out of here."

"Now, wait, DOA." Brad jerked out of his trance and rushed around the table. "I appreciate this is a lot to take in, but we haven't finished going through the contract yet."

I caught the glare he threw Gabrielle out of the corner of my eye, but when I turned back, he gave me a big, bright smile. Prick.

"Nah, man. I'm done here. We'll be in contact."

Opening the front door, I glanced back at Gabrielle and our eyes met for a split second, and the old, yet familiar, pull pulsed between us, but I was too angry to appreciate it. I stepped out and Andre', my security guard, was right behind me, closing the door in Brad's face.

The door opened again, and Dollar and Big T followed us out.

"D, hold up," Dollar said as he jogged over to my side.

I stopped and jingled the keys in my hand.

"What you thinking, man?"

"Honestly, Dollar." I turned to face him. "I'm so fucking mad right now that I can't think straight, so I don't know what the fuck I'm thinking. I have a little girl in there that I knew nothing about, and she knows nothing about me. I missed six years of her fucking life, and now I have to figure out how to get that back, which I can't."

I was shouting as I pointed at Gabrielle's house, and I stopped myself, not wanting to make a scene. Taking in a deep breath, I rolled my shoulders. "Look, I just need to process this, and then I'll do…something, I don't know." I glanced back at Dollar and Big T. "But this stays quiet, all right? Nothing is said until we get a fucking handle on it."

"D," Dollar said. "You can't possibly be buying into this right now. This isn't the time to start playing—"

"Are you fucking kidding me right now? I just learned that I have a daughter and you're going to tell me this isn't the fucking time?"

Dollar held his hands up. "That's not what I'm saying. Hear me out."

"Nah, man." I shook my head and turned toward my car. "Nah, I'm not listening to your bullshit right now. You're just going to have to fucking deal, Dollar."

And just like that, we were right back where we had started.

Chapter 9

~ Gabrielle ~
Present Day

My cell phone rang a few days later, and when I didn't recognize the number, my stomach pitched, but I answered anyway, despite the likelihood of it being Danny.

"Hey, girl. It's Big T. How's it going?"

I squeezed my eyes shut. Even though I'd been dreading this call, I made myself sound calm and pleasant. "Hi, Teddy. What's up?"

"D was going to call you, but he got tied up and asked me to since he didn't want to put it off any longer. He wants to meet you and the little squirt for lunch."

A lump formed in my throat, making it difficult to swallow. Somehow, Danny was right back in my life, whether I was ready for it or not. This was his daughter, though, and he was attempting to get to know her. I couldn't deny him that, regardless of how hard the situation might be on me. "Uh, okay. When?"

"Tomorrow around noon."

So soon. Based on his reaction, this was bound to happen, but I hadn't expected it so soon. I figured he had places to go and people to see, given his celebrity status now, giving me time to prepare and build up my defenses, but that didn't seem to be the case. My heart would continue to be battered, but I'd endure the pain for Dani. Everything was for her. She deserved to have her father in her life, and if he wanted to be there, then I wouldn't deny either of them. I knew firsthand what it was like to have a father around, and then not.

I agreed and took down the restaurant information before hanging up, right as Brad walked through the back door.

"How was your day?" I asked him.

He heaved a deep sigh. "I still haven't heard from DOA or anyone."

Despite his goading, I refused to feel guilty. He was the idiot who brought everyone here so he could put his "family" on display without discussing it with me first. "Well, I'm sure they'll be in contact soon. I just got a call from Big T, in fact."

"He called *you*? For what?" He huffed and propped one hand on his hip.

"Danny wants to meet Dani for lunch tomorrow."

"He wants…lunch…what? Why would he call you, and not me?"

I straightened and scowled. "She's his daughter, Brad, and he wants to be a part of her life. You're going to have to get used to that."

"I don't have a problem with that," he said, clearly not caring about what happened between father and daughter. "What I have a problem with is the fact I haven't heard anything from them about signing the contract. That's what's most important."

My eyes widened. Could he really be so selfish? He seemed to be taking his slightly inflated ego—something I'd been able to ignore in the past, and had even thought was cute at first—to new extremes in light of recent events.

"You're unbelievable." I pushed past him and out of the room, ignoring when he called out.

For the rest of the night, we avoided each other, and even when we got into bed together, both facing opposite walls, an ocean of space laid between us, but I refused to relent. He was the one who should apologize, not me.

The next morning, silence still loomed over us while he got ready for work, and I went downstairs to fix breakfast. Dani's attention was glued to the small television at the table, still dressed in her pink princess pajamas and her hair mussed from sleep. I smiled at the sight of my still sleepy daughter before clearing my throat, figuring now was as good a time as ever to fill her in about her father.

"Honey, you remember the man you met the other day, who had the same name as you? Danny?"

"Uh huh." Her focus remained riveted to the screen.

I turned off the TV before walking around the counter and sitting across from her.

Her eyes rounded, affronted by my behavior. "Hey! You always let me watch my shows in the morning while you make breakfast!"

"It's only for a minute. We need to talk." When I was sure I had her complete attention, I took a deep breath. "There's something you need to know about him. He's your father." When Dani continued to gaze at me with a glaze over her blue eyes and no change in expression, I wondered if she was sleeping with her eyes open. "Hey, did you hear what I said?"

"Yes."

"And you have nothing to say?"

She pondered for a moment before she shrugged. "Nope. Can you turn the TV back on?"

"No, I can't turn the TV back on. Dani, do you understand what I'm telling you?"

"Yes."

I wasn't sure she did, even though she'd asked in the past about having a dad after meeting some of her friends', but she'd talk when ready and only then, just like her father. "He wants to meet us for lunch today. Okay?"

Dani's eyes veered back to the television as if willing it to turn on by itself. "'Kay."

I sighed and hit the remote. Brad strode in and reached past me as I scrambled eggs in a bowl, to fill up a mug with coffee.

"What time is your date today?" he asked with a testy tone, breaking the standoff between us.

I fought the urge to roll my eyes. "It's not a date."

"Whatever. What time is it?"

"Noon."

He jerked his head in Dani's direction. "Did you tell her?"

I glanced over. "Yeah, I just tried. She said she understood, but I'm not sure."

He nodded, taking a drink of coffee before dumping the rest in the sink. "I'd appreciate it if you could ask them to give me a call."

I didn't lift my focus from the bowl, and this time, I did roll my eyes.

Again, he showed no concern for anyone but himself. "Sure, Brad. I'll ask them to call you," I mumbled to his back as he walked out the door, not bothering to stay for breakfast or even say good-bye to Dani.

Later, after showering and dressing us both, we got in the car and took off for the restaurant, running a few minutes late. I'd taken longer than anticipated, fretting over what to wear, like it was our first date, before telling myself to get over it; that this was about Dani, not me. I eventually decided on a white halter summer dress covered in small yellow daisies, with white strappy mules. Afterward, I'd helped Dani select a simple jean skirt and pink t-shirt with tan Mary Janes, and styled her hair in a Dutch braid.

I struggled to ignore the butterflies in my stomach and reminded myself, again, Danny wanted to see his daughter, not me. I was only background and had no reason to be nervous.

"Are you okay back there?" I eyed Dani in the rearview mirror for any signs of discomfort or nerves.

"Yep."

Well, at least someone is. I pulled into the parking lot and took a deep breath. *It's now or never.*

Grabbing Dani's hand, we entered the small restaurant. The family-style atmosphere reminded me of the Italian place he had taken me on our first date. He'd always preferred the smaller, local restaurants rather than the bigger, trendier chains.

The hostess smiled at us. "Hi! Can I help you?"

I removed my sunglasses and surveyed the room. Few of the tables sat empty, but I recognized no one. "Uh, yeah. We're supposed to be meeting someone here." I stepped closer to the podium, lowering my voice. "It's Danny Anderson, or DOA, I guess. Is he here yet?"

The girl flushed at the mention of his name, apparently a fan. "Are you Gabrielle?" she asked, and at my nod, she smiled. "He's in the banquet room. Right this way."

We followed her to the back of the restaurant to a closed door. She held it open and waved us in. "Go ahead."

I nodded in thanks before the door shut behind us. Danny sat at a table, studying his phone, while Big T and the two giants conversed in the back corner. Dollar's absence didn't escape me. It seemed he still hadn't gotten over his issues with me from the past, whatever they were.

Big T strode over with a big grin on his friendly face. His calm and tranquil presence soothed my nerves, and I was grateful he was there.

"Hey, girl. Looking good."

"Thanks, Teddy."

He smiled down at Dani, who peered up at him with interest, still holding my hand. "And how about you, little D? How you doing?"

She giggled. "Good."

~ *Danny* ~

I trailed Big T with my hands shoved into my pockets, trying to calm my racing heart. I didn't want to be nervous, but I was venturing into new territory here. The last thing I wanted was to screw things up with Dani, especially since I had no clue how to be a father, my own being the perfect role model of a complete fuck-up, but I was determined to do my best and give her the life I'd always wanted.

Gabrielle looked so beautiful that I couldn't stop staring at her, but then I turned my attention to my little girl smiling up at Big T, and I lost my breath. She turned her blue eyes on me, and took a tentative step closer to her mother.

I knelt in front of her and smiled. "Hey, Dani. Remember me?"

She nodded, but said nothing as she stuck close to her mom's side. Gabrielle lowered to her level to put a reassuring arm around her.

"This is Danny, remember? We talked about who he is earlier. He's your dad."

She glanced at her before looking back at me with a slight bob of her head.

My heart stopped with fright at the word "dad" before filling with pride that I'd been a part of creating this beautiful girl. I wanted to be the hero in her life; I wanted her to be daddy's little angel. I'd missed her first six years, and even though I was still so fucking angry about that, I wasn't going to let it discourage me. I was going to try to make up the lost time. But first we needed not to be so afraid of each other.

I held out my hand to her. "Can you shake my hand hello?"

A timid smile broke out on her face as she eyed my hand before tentatively placing her smaller one in it. I gave it a light squeeze before purposefully giving a hard shake, causing a bubble of laughter to escape from her lips.

I caught Gabrielle's eye and smiled, which she returned, and my heart swelled. "Come on, Dani. Let's sit down."

Big T patted my back. "I'll be back, D."

Hearing this, Gabrielle glanced over her shoulder. "You're leaving, Teddy?"

"Oh, yeah, girl. Things to do, you know. Besides, I think you guys have lots of catching up to do."

I tried to ignore the trepidation in her eyes, even though her anxiety gnawed at me. I was the cause of her unease, my actions putting us in the situation we were in, but I hoped over time, I could remove it as well.

"Oh, okay. We'll see you later, I hope."

She sat Dani between us, but she refused to meet my eyes as she took her seat. Uncomfortable silence fell around us, no one knowing where to start, before I cleared my throat.

"What's your favorite thing to eat, Dani?"

"Salad."

I frowned. "Salad?"

She nodded, and Gabrielle laughed. "Yes, your daughter has very unique taste for a child. Although she does have a weak spot for French fries and chicken nuggets."

I feigned relief. "Phew! I was beginning to wonder about her. Is that what you want? A salad?"

"With ranch dressing, please."

"All right, I think we can manage that." I looked at Gabrielle. "What about you?"

She picked up a menu, the trembling of her fingers revealing her nerves, just as they had on our first date, making me want to take her hands in mine, like I had then, and tell her everything was okay. But it wasn't, and I couldn't. At least not yet. "Oh, I don't know. I'm not really hungry, but I could probably do a salad as well."

After the waitress took our orders and left the room, silence fell across the table again. I kept trying to draw Dani into conversation, but she only gave me one-word answers until Gabrielle threw me a bone.

"Dani, why don't you tell your father what your favorite thing to do is?"

When her brows creased, her mother leaned in and whispered in her ear. Her eyes widened in excitement and she turned to me. "I love ballet," she gushed with a bright smile.

"Is that right? Do you take classes?"

"Uh huh, but only one." Her lower lip protruded into a slight pout.

"And why's that?"

"Because—"

"Because that's all we have time for right now," her mother interrupted before taking a drink of water.

She'd obviously cut Dani off on purpose, but I didn't push. "Do you dance with your mom?"

Gabrielle blanched as she took another sip, but Dani didn't notice and shook her head. "No. Mommy doesn't dance."

It was my turn to be confused as I eyed Gabrielle over Dani, which she avoided. But then the waitress arrived with our order, preventing me from asking anything further. I couldn't understand why she would keep something like that from Dani, when she had been magnificent and destined for the stage. But I was the last person to comment, since it was most likely my doing.

We eventually fell into easy conversation, and I explained the art of rapping to Dani and even free-styled a few lines for her.

She clapped her hands when I finished. "More!"

I chuckled. "Another time, and I'll teach you how to do it." I glanced at my watch and shook my head. "I hate to do this, but I've got an appointment I've got to get to."

"Oh, that's okay. We need to be getting back anyway." Gabrielle stood and gathered her purse.

I walked around the table to her side. "Can I talk to you for a second?" I gestured to a far corner where we could speak in private.

A wary expression fell over her face and she glanced down at Dani. "I don't want to leave her."

"Yo, Andre'. Come here," I called to one of the security guys sitting at the back of the room. "He'll sit with her. He's one of my bodyguards, so he's cool."

She eyed the enormous man as he lumbered toward us, uncertainty still etched on her face, but she didn't push it further.

"Dani, baby, this is Andre'. He's going to hang with you for a sec while I talk to your mom, okay? We'll be right over there."

Dani nodded as her eyes widened, taking in Andre's huge biceps and thick neck. He smiled at her, softening his demeanor, and somehow, he didn't appear as intimidating anymore.

"Dani and I will be cool. I've got a few tricks I can teach her." He pulled out a couple coins from his pocket.

I gently steered Gabrielle by the elbow to the opposite corner of the room.

"About the other day…I wanted to say, I don't know what happened or whatever, but if you say you tried to tell me about her, I believe you. I know you wouldn't lie about something like this."

"No, I wouldn't."

"Right…I want to make sure that was clear, so things are cool between us, you know, for Dani, because I want to start spending time with her."

"Of course." She gave me a false smile, which I saw right through, telling me I had a lot of work to do before things were truly "cool" between us, but I was up for the challenge. "Just let me know when."

"I'll have to check my schedule and see when I can meet you guys again."

Her shoulders sagged, but she smiled again. My G, always so willing to please. I hated to take advantage of it, but at this point, I would take what I could get. "Sure, no problem. I can do that."

"Okay, good. I'll be in touch then."

I started to walk away, but once we were shoulder to shoulder and her soft scent tickled my nose, I turned, unable to resist. Stepping close to her, so close I could almost kiss her neck, I leaned in, and she stiffened, her chest starting to heave.

"You look amazing, by the way."

She swallowed and turned, finally meeting my eyes and gave me a small smile.

Reaching out, I tugged on one of the waves spiraling down from her head. "I like your hair down like that."

Her eyes widened, and she gasped when I leaned in to brush my lips against hers before walking away.

Chapter 10

~ Gabrielle ~
Six Years Earlier

I ran a brush through my hair for the umpteenth time, fighting the urge to grab an elastic band and pull it away from my face. Left down for my date, it hung in rolling waves past my shoulders, the light picking up the streaks of golden and honey blonde. Always in a bun, this felt foreign and heavy, irritating me whenever loose strands floated across my face. But I was determined to stick it out. I wanted to look pretty for Danny and had a feeling he would like it; a drastic change from the every day.

Despite her less than enthusiastic opinion about the date, and the fact that she considered Danny a thug, Monica had helped pick out my outfit. I had to admit the deep blue of the boat neck sweater selected by her framed my long neck and sculpted shoulders like one of my leotards, and wasn't too revealing. The color highlighted the soft rose of my cheeks and made the color of my eyes appear greener. I'd applied minimal makeup, more than my usual nothing, and I liked how my eyes popped. The rest of my face was simply too long and thin for me to do anything about.

The only piece of my wardrobe still in question was the dark rinse hip hugging jeans. Monica assured me they fit as they should, but, tighter and lower than anything I'd ever worn, I worried my underwear would peek out every time I bent over or sat down. After some experimental tries, however, everything stayed covered with no panty shots, much to my relief.

I stood and took a deep breath. I could do this.

A knock rapped against the bathroom door. "Gabby? You okay?" Monica's tone was concerned.

I opened it and Monica's gaze trailed over me. She did a little jump on her toes and clapped her hands. "Omigod! You look amazing!"

"Really?" I turned back to the mirror and tugged at the hem of the sweater.

She stood behind me and I studied our reflections. It was weird that we were almost identical in appearance, even though our personalities were so different and there were a couple years between us.

"I'm serious, Gab. You look awesome. I haven't seen you look like this in years."

"Thanks for telling me I look like crap all the time."

She laughed. "Well, not crap, but definitely not like this." Her eyes softened and became thoughtful. "You shouldn't hide behind the bun and buttoned up clothes, Gabby." Before I could respond, she glanced down and scowled. "What are you wearing for shoes?"

"I don't know, actually."

"I've got the perfect pair. Don't go anywhere." She dashed out of the bathroom and returned a split second later, thrusting brown leather ankle boots with low heels into my hands. "These will look awesome."

I frowned at them. "I don't need to be taller, Mon, and tower over the guy."

"You won't. He'll still have a couple inches on you." Seeing the doubt on my face, she rolled her eyes. "Oh, come on! They're perfect and you have nothing else to wear, admit it."

Running out of time to come up with another option, I sat down on the side of the worn, beige bathtub and pulled the boots on. "Fine, but if I twist my ankle in these, I'm going to kill you."

"What's going on in here?" Our mother appeared in the doorway.

"Putting on the final touches," Monica answered as I stood.

"Oh my." Her hand went to her mouth. "You look beautiful, honey. He better be a special boy to deserve someone like you."

I caught Monica's sneer and interrupted her before she formed a retort. "Don't say anything. Leave him alone."

A knock sounded from the front of the apartment, and I gave myself one last critical examination in the mirror, trying to ignore the thudding of my heart and the giant ball of fiery nerves in the pit of my stomach. I hoped he didn't expect me to eat anything.

"Here goes nothing," I muttered.

Wobbling in the heels, I crossed the room to the door without tripping, and yanked it open. Danny stood in his trademark stance, shoulders hunched forward as he leaned against the doorjamb, wearing a black T-shirt under his black hoodie and his hands shoved in the pockets of his jeans. His head lifted when the door opened.

"Hi!" I cringed when it came out like a screech.

His eyes bugged before he could stop them, as he took in my appearance and straightened. I was happy to see he still stood taller than I did, even with the stupid heels.

I stepped back and opened the door further. "Come in."

He entered and glanced around, his sharp blue eyes landing on my mother and sister, who hovered in the back hallway. He tensed when he spotted them.

I smiled and laid a hand on his arm, trying to reassure him. "Danny, this is my mom and my sister, Monica."

He stepped forward with his hand outstretched. "It's nice to meet you, Mrs. Wells. Hey." He lifted his chin toward Monica. "I didn't know there were two of you walking around."

"Well, if you showed up…" Monica broke off when she spotted the deadly glare I shot her from behind him.

He caught her meaning and his lips twitched. "You're right, I probably should."

"Do you live around here, Danny?" Mom asked.

He rubbed his hand over his hair and looked down. "Oh yeah, not too far from here. On Bonaventure."

"With your family?"

He shrugged and shoved his hands back in his pockets. "Just me and my dad."

"What does your father do?"

"Not much."

She faltered when it was apparent he wasn't going to elaborate. "Oh…"

I gritted my teeth in a tight smile, the tension in the room smothering, and picked up my purse from the table, eager to get out of there.

"Are you ready?" I reached for my gray sweatshirt hanging on the hook by the front door.

Monica made a squeak of a sound and gave a quick shake of her head. She rushed to our bedroom and returned with a jean jacket in her hand.

"You left your coat in our room, Gab." She tossed it to me.

Once Danny and I were out in the hallway and the door shut behind us, I sighed as I sagged against the wall. "I'm sorry about that."

He smiled. "It's only going to get worse."

I straightened, now happy for the added height since my eyes were almost level with his. "Wait a minute! What about my condition? You agreed to it."

He chuckled. "Baby, I agreed I wouldn't assume what you were thinking, not what others were."

"That's not fair. You—"

He stopped me by grabbing my hand and pulling me closer, touching his lips gently to mine. "You look amazing, G."

"Thanks," I breathed. He'd caught me off guard by the kiss—my first one—and my lips tingled from the feel of his.

"You ready?"

I nodded and let him lead me down the hallway, and out the front door of the apartment building. Once outside, I regained my senses from the surprise kiss and tugged on his hand. I smiled when his eyes met mine. "Smooth change of subject, D."

He gave one of his rare full laughs and a burst of warmth filled me.

"I thought it was Danny?" he said.

"Oh, it is, but that was a D move."

He jerked to a stop and stared at me, unfiltered amazement crossing over his face. "You think there's a difference?"

"I know there is. I just need to learn where one stops and the other begins."

Danny studied me for a moment before shaking his head and turning away. "You'd be the first," he murmured. He walked over to an old rusted red Buick parked along the curb and opened the passenger door. "Most only want to know D."

I stopped on the opposite side of the door from him. "I want to know both, but mostly I'm interested in Danny."

~ *Danny* ~

I shut the door and shook my head again as I passed in front of the car toward the driver's side. "You're better off not knowing either of them," I muttered.

I drove to the restaurant, located outside of town and picked on purpose, not wanting to go anywhere we might run into anyone. I wanted us to be able to talk without interruption and without any speculative looks. People were already talking about us, and I didn't want to give them any more ammunition. Things with her needed to stay on the down low.

I snuck a sideways glance at her sitting across from me, watching the world pass by outside her window, and wondered what lottery I'd won. No way in a million years would I have ever imagined I'd be so lucky to have this amazing looking woman beside me. Not only was she gorgeous with an incredible body, which I'd suspected was hidden beneath the clothes she wore, but she was straight and clean. She wasn't a fucked-up mess like most of the girls I'd grown up with, who only wanted to party hard and get laid.

Nobody had any ambition to leave this godforsaken town, just like their parents. Once out of high school—if they even graduated—they would be next in line for a job at the local factory, and soon they would become alcoholics who worked during the day, drank when they got home, and got shit-faced over the weekend, only to start the process over the next week. The tradition would continue, but not for me. I was determined—no, I was *unyielding* in my plan—to get out of Dodge as quick as possible, and hip-hop was my ticket.

Focused on my goal, I ignored everything around me, resolute not to let anything stand in my way. I would have continued that way if one girl hadn't wriggled her way into my field of vision, leaving me helpless to get her out.

I wasn't an idiot; I realized Gabrielle was too good for me. She deserved so much more than I could ever give her, even if I did manage to make it big. She was smart, gorgeous, and had goals for herself. She didn't deserve the cynical, contemptuous bastard that was me. But no matter how much I told myself to back off and stay away, I couldn't.

I tried to be placated with the daily walks and simply being around her, refusing to talk much, not wanting to discover anything more about her;

knowing if I did, I wouldn't be able to ignore my growing attraction toward her. I'd been hard on her at first, but the coldness had served as a means to keep some distance between us. The last thing I wanted was for her to learn about me, and laugh at the pathetic and depressing reality of my life. But when she'd told me about her dad, a glimmer of hope formed that perhaps this girl from the other side of the tracks would understand me, even if only a little bit. At that point, there was no choice. I had to have her.

And now she sat in my car, looking like an angel sent down from heaven, and I was a tongue-tied loser. I didn't know what to say and words were rarely a struggle for me. So, I went with what was forefront in my mind.

"Hey." I reached out and tugged a strand of her hair. "I like your hair down like that."

Her lips twitched, and she dropped her gaze down to her hands folded in her lap. "I've already heard from my mom and Monica how I look like crap most of the time."

"That's not what I meant."

"I know." She had a teasing glint in her eye. "I'm only giving you a hard time."

I smiled and shook my head before glancing back at her. "I told you what one of your nicknames was."

"G?"

"No, the other one. Double G."

"Oh, right. What does that mean? It sounds like a bra size."

I chuckled. "Nah, it's not a bra size. Gorgeous G."

She gave me a big smile as the color rose in her cheeks. I loved it when she blushed.

"So, where did you get the car?" she asked, trying to deflect the attention from her. "I didn't know you had one."

"I've been working on it at the garage and finally got it running. It's been dead for a while, but I was able to save up the money to buy the spare parts I needed."

"I wish I could get a car."

"You don't need one. I can take you wherever you need to go."

She stared at me before shaking her head. "You can't take me everywhere."

"Why not?"

"Well, I don't know. It doesn't seem reasonable."

"I don't see a problem with it."

I parked the car in a large lot and walked around to open her door. Once inside, we followed the hostess to a blood red vinyl booth in a corner of the dark Italian restaurant. The dining room was dim, with tea lights in red plastic bubble candle holders lighting each table, and the heavy scent of garlic, onions, and tomatoes filled the air. Everyone spoke in hushed tones, and quiet operatic music played in the background from speakers hung here and there around the room.

"I hope you like Italian food," I said as we studied the menu.

"Yeah, I do. It's great."

"I figured you can't go wrong, but you never know…" I stopped, aware I was chattering from nerves, which I never did. This girl had thrown me off.

"Its fine, Danny. Really."

"Sorry." I gave her a sheepish grin. "You got me nervous, G."

"You? I'm sweating bullets over here." She lifted her menu and it trembled.

I reached across the table and, taking one of her hands, threaded my fingers through hers and squeezed. "You're perfect. You've got nothing to worry about."

"And neither do you."

We smiled at each other before laughing, which helped the nerves to fall away. After placing our orders with the waitress, silence fell between us, neither of us knowing where to begin.

"Tell me about your songs," she eventually said. "What do you rap about?"

"Anything and everything."

"Yeah, but what inspires you?"

I paused, taking a moment to formulate my answer because I was distracted by my chest expanding and filling with gratitude at her genuine interest. I couldn't recall the last time anyone took the time to ask, or was curious about me. "Life. My life. The things I see and go through. The people I meet." I paused, considering, and then cleared my throat. "It's hard to explain, but it's difficult for me to just…talk about things, but I find if I can jot down phrases, a rhyme or whatever, and put a mean mix to it, it all comes pouring out."

"I'm impressed. There's no way I'd be able to rap anything. My mouth and my brain don't work that quickly." She laughed, the soft sound doing weird things to my stomach.

"I'd never be able to dance on my toes."

"I could teach you."

"Hell, no. I'll leave the dancing to you. So, that's what you want to do, huh? Dance?"

"Yeah, I hope to make it into Juilliard."

"What's that? Some sort of dance school?" She nodded. "Why wouldn't you?"

"If I don't get a scholarship, then I won't be able to afford it. I may not even get in."

"Again, why wouldn't you?"

"I may not be good enough."

I scoffed. "I doubt that."

"How would you know? You've never seen me dance."

"I know because I know. I can see your passion for it. That's what counts."

She smiled at me, and at that moment, I wanted to do whatever she asked of me, give her everything she desired. "You're going to make it big, aren't you, D?"

I smiled at her over the steaming plate of pasta the server placed on the table between us. "That's the plan, G."

And right then, I hoped she might become part of it.

Chapter 11

~ Gabrielle ~
Six Years Earlier

We sat in the car in the parking lot of the restaurant after dinner talking, bouncing from one topic to another, sponging up everything about each other. We hadn't meant for it to happen, but the conversation continued to flow and neither of us wanted the date to end, wanting to continue discovering all there was to know about the other.

Danny grabbed my hands in his. "I want to ask you about your dad, but I'll understand if you don't want to talk about it. Okay?"

I swallowed and nodded.

"Do you think about it a lot?" His thumbs rubbed small circles on the back of my hands.

I took a deep breath and gazed out the dirty front windshield. I liked the feel of the strength in his hands as they grasped mine, and it somehow helped me to gather the courage to discuss what had happened.

"Yeah, I think about it. I try not to, but it's hard." I gave a wistful smile. "But it isn't like what everyone probably thinks. They probably think I'm sad and upset."

His brows bent in surprise. "You're not?"

"Well, I am, but mostly I'm angry." My eyes tightened on his. "How dare he take the easy way out, you know? He got himself tied up in all these bad deals and got us in more debt than you can imagine, and then just left my mom to bail us out. He didn't trust her enough to tell her, or that she would stand by his side through it. It isn't fair to her, and isn't fair to Monica and me to have to completely change our lives because he couldn't deal with it himself."

"So that's why you moved here?"

I nodded. "We couldn't get anything from insurance since his death was a suicide, so it's all we could afford and close to where my mom was able to find a job. This is the only place willing to give her a chance since she didn't have any work experience. She was a stay-at-home mom right out of college before this."

"Where did you live before?"

"In Rochester."

He chuckled. "Damn. *Way* on the other side of the tracks."

I smiled, but it quickly fell from my face. "But you know what, Danny? I know you're thinking I want to go back because that's where I fit in, but you're wrong. I didn't fit in there either. They made fun of me there too. I don't fit in anywhere."

"Hey." He scooted closer on the bench seat and ran his fingers through my hair. "Don't think like that. You don't want to just 'fit in,' you know? Because that means you're conforming, and that's not you. You're your own person and you know what you want. You know exactly who you are and that's what I like about you. Hell, I respect the fuck out of that. Who cares if you don't run with the crowd? I hate all these posers who go along with everyone else because they can't fucking think for themselves."

"You really believe that?"

"Yeah, I believe that."

"Thank you." I glanced down, embarrassed by what I was about to say. "Can I tell you something and you promise you won't laugh at me?"

"I will never laugh at you, baby. Never."

I bit my lip and squirmed before blurting out, "This is my first date. Ever."

Disbelief washed over his face. "You're kidding me, right?"

"Nope. Eighteen years old and first ever."

"Well," he said, and started the car. "It's their loss, sweetheart. That's all I've got to say."

"Where are we going?"

He grinned at me as he turned out of the parking lot. "I'm about to pump up this date so it will be the only first date you remember."

* * *

Danny parked and came alongside to open the passenger door. When I stepped out into the shadowy night, the cool wind stirred up my hair and I shivered. "Where are we?"

He took my hand in his. "Come this way."

We walked through a dim park, lit by a spattering of tall lampposts, only a few of which were working. We had crossed a bridge, which ended on a small island, and all around us, only the dark expanse of water was visible. Off in the distance, the buildings of the city shone brilliantly, casting a white glow against the black backdrop of the sky; but here, the bright lights barely reached us. The wind was brisk off the water, and I picked up my step in order to snuggle closer to him as I held my jacket closed.

We came to a wood bench at the point of the island, and he sat, pulling me down next to him and draping his arm across my shoulders. Heat poured off him and I turned into his side.

"You cold?" His mouth hovered over my ear, his warm breath tickling my neck.

I shook my head. "Not anymore. Where are we?"

"I come here a lot. The quiet helps me to think, figure shit out. I've thrown down some mean lyrics here."

"It's nice here," I murmured, enjoying the calming influence of the water as it lapped against the rugged shoreline, the sound occasionally breaking through the silence around us.

He nodded as he stared straight ahead. Even in the darkness, I recognized the edge in his eyes. "I've never brought anyone here."

I sat up in wonder, reading between the lines. He was a guarded person, and for him to let someone else into his private world showed trust. The dynamics between us were changing at warp speed, and while this excited me, tiny vines of anxiety crept in, threatening to crack the fragile hold on my level-headedness.

"Thank you." My words were simple, but I hoped they conveyed the enormity of my feelings.

He shook his head as he turned away. I thought I'd said something wrong, but then he chuckled. "What?" I asked.

"That's why you're dope, G. You fucking get me. No one else would ever understand the importance of this place for me."

I scooted back, putting some space between us. "Can I ask you something?"

"Anything."

"Why do you trust me? You don't know me."

Danny's eyes traveled over my face before they came back to mine. "Why do you trust *me*?"

I frowned as I struggled to put into words what I'd innately understood from the second I'd laid eyes on him. Everything felt right with him. How I knew, however, I couldn't explain.

He waited for me to answer and when I could not find the words, he smiled. "I feel the same way."

"I don't understand...how...."

"Maybe we're not supposed to." His shoulders hitched up. "Maybe we're just supposed to believe in it."

"But you didn't want to. You said so yourself, opposites and all that."

He sat back, considering me, before rising and walking a few steps away. Standing with his back to me, he stood straight, the lines of his body tense, as he worked his way over something in his head.

His shoulders dropped and he returned, sitting next to me as he grabbed my hands with his. "You're right. I didn't want to believe it." He stopped and shook his head. "No, it's not even that. I resisted because I knew if I gave in, it would be the end of the game for me."

"What do you mean?"

"You could destroy me, Gabrielle. Easily." Seeing my confusion, he pressed on. "I know I walk around like I don't give a shit, like I got a fucking boulder on my shoulder and that nothing fazes me, but you've somehow gotten past all that. Now I'm open to you. Exposed. I knew once we started, there was no turning back. Ever."

"You could hurt me just as much, if not more. Remember? First timer here." I tried to joke, if only to keep from suffocating. So much was swirling around inside me that I was having trouble not becoming overwhelmed.

"Never. I would never hurt you. I would hurt myself before I hurt you."

I broke eye contact and let out a shaky breath, unable to breathe under his penetrating gaze. I never would have believed I would find a boyfriend in my new life, but that's exactly what happened. It was exhilarating and nerve-wracking, all at the same time, but I'd never felt more alive. "God, this is intense."

"I'm sorry, baby, but that's the way I roll. I don't do anything half-ass."

"I'm not complaining." I gave him a timid smile as I turned back toward him, emboldened by his words. "But it would really help things if you would kiss me."

His eyes darkened in the hazy lights before he drew me to him, his fingers tangling in my hair, and his mouth pressed against mine. He held me there before angling our heads and parting his lips, encouraging me to open to him, teaching me what to do.

My arms wrapped around his neck to pull him closer. The heat rushing through me from the warmth of his lips and the gentle slide of his tongue was startling, and I craved more. I wanted his hands all over me and my hands on him, needing to feel everything. Caught up in the rapture, I forgot my usual apprehension. It was as if an eruption had exploded when we touched, and there was no way to bring the rush under control.

I ran my fingers through his unruly hair before moving to relish the strength of his shoulders and down his back. But when my hands bumped into something hard and cold at his waistline, I shoved away. The jagged edges of reality pushed through, reminding me of where I was and how everything was different, dampening all desire within me.

"What's that for?" I asked on a panted breath.

His eyes were bright and dazed, but he held his hands up as if in surrender. "It's okay."

I shook my head, my chest heaving as I fought the clogged feeling of alarm in my lungs. I couldn't stop imagining the gun accidentally going off. "Why do you even have the gun on you? It's a date!"

"It's okay, baby. Really. I carry everywhere I go."

"But why?"

~ *Danny* ~

I gave her an apologetic smile, but one that also conveyed she was still green to her surroundings. "Because I have to. You just don't understand yet."

Her eyes widened with a fearful expression that tore at me. She took in a haggard breath and stood, walking a few feet away as I had done moments before. I hung back, watching as she dropped her head and hunched her shoulders, hugging her arms around her torso as if to shield herself, before I could take no more and strode over, pulling her against me. She came willingly, for which I was thankful.

"You're safe with me, baby. I'll never let anyone hurt you."

"It just scares me that you have to carry a gun. I'm not worried about me."

My heart expanded at her words. When had someone else worried about me, let alone cared? Never.

I reached down and lifted her chin to meet her eyes. "I'll be fine." I kissed her lightly. "But thank you for caring."

I tightened my hold on her, and she rested her head on my shoulder as her arms circled my waist. We fit together like two puzzle pieces.

"Can you not have it on you when we're together?" she asked.

"Sure, baby. Anything for you."

"Thank you."

We stood wrapped in each other's arms before I began to rock back and forth.

"Alone in mistrust, I wasn't looking for much,
Until one day it changed and a bright light showed me the way,
It glowed and flamed, before taking my breath away."

I rapped softly in her ear, telling her a story about never believing in love until an angel appeared, bringing love and light to a world that was dark and mistrustful, and how things could never go back to the way they were.

She raised her head when I finished. "What was that?"

"Some lines I threw down about finding you."

Her eyes shone, and my chest expanded and filled. I felt like a hero. "They're beautiful. Thank you."

"You're beautiful." I leaned in for another kiss.

When we pulled away, both of us a little breathless, I stopped her from putting her head back on my shoulder. I had to tell her. Everything.

Her expression shifted to worry. "What is it?"

My mouth went dry. I struggled to swallow, my tongue feeling too big. "I'm falling in love with you, Gabrielle. I've never felt anything like this before."

She hesitated, and my heart tripped in panic, fearing I'd revealed too much, had misread everything, but then she smiled and everything was back to perfect. "I know this sounds crazy, but I'm already in love with you, Danny."

I caught her lips with mine. "Forever."

"Forever."

Chapter 12

~ *Gabrielle* ~
Present Day

"I don't know what to tell you, Brad."

He loomed next to me while I stirred dinner on the stove, demanding a word-by-word replay of what Danny said about signing his contract.

"I don't understand. How can you have lunch with the man, spend an hour with him, and never have the subject come up in conversation?"

Because not everything is about you. I stepped around him to retrieve the salad from the fridge. "It didn't. I'm sorry."

"What *did* you discuss then?"

"Oh, his daughter, maybe."

"Of course." He huffed in annoyance that I might dare to insult his intelligence. "But that couldn't have taken the whole hour."

"Jesus, Brad. Drop it. It didn't come up, okay? Can you tell Dani dinner's ready?"

Gritting my teeth, I turned back to the stove and turned off the burner. He hissed a breath out of his nose, but respected my wishes, for once, and let the matter drop. I waited for him to leave the kitchen and pound up the stairs before letting out the breath I was holding, rather than the scream threatening to break loose.

He was becoming impossible. These new dynamics with Danny were casting him in a different light, revealing his true, unfavorable colors. Despite my feelings for Brad never coming close to the depth of those for Danny, he had once been charming and pleasant, had promised a stable life for Dani and me. Now…now, that didn't appear to be the case.

Over dinner, conversation was minimal, and I thought we would get through the meal without Brad uttering another word about Danny, when he cleared his throat.

"When are you going to see him again?"

Willing for patience, I strove to keep my tone neutral. "I don't know. We don't schedule things in advance. He calls when he has time."

"That's rude. There appears to be a pattern here with him."

I frowned. "A pattern? What does that mean?"

"He expects everyone to wait around until he beckons, like we have no life of our own."

"He's busy and probably doesn't want to break any promises to Dani."

"I can see you're wrapped around his finger again." He took a drink of his wine.

I sat back with my mouth hanging open. Was he picking for a fight? I glanced at Dani, who sat listening to us. "Dani, if you're done, please go up to your room."

"Oh, no. Let her stay. Let her learn who her daddy really is. All the skeletons in his closet."

"Stop," I hissed. "Dani, please go to your room."

I waited until she scampered out. When the door shut upstairs, I whirled back to him, my face heating. "What's your problem?"

"My problem is my girlfriend is only thinking about herself and doesn't care one damn thing about me while she's out parading around with her ex-boyfriend."

"Jesus, Brad. You act like Danny and I are hooking up or something. I go because of Dani. That's it. Besides, we've only met one time."

"That I'm aware of." He sat back in his chair, leveling a challenge with his eyes.

I shot up and gathered the dishes. "You know, I'm not even going to respond to that. It's your issue if you think I'm out there cheating on you."

His eyes followed me as I stalked to the sink. "Why not? Daddy's back, and now daddy's rich and famous; not the white trash loser he used to be.

Why wouldn't you try to jump on that bandwagon?"

Fury pulsed through me, and I dropped the dishes on the counter with a loud clatter. "You're a real jerk, you know that?" I whipped around to face him. "Danny was never a loser. Even back then, he was more of a man than you'll ever be." I skirted the counter and stood in his face. "This just shows me you know nothing about me. It's always been about you, Brad. Never about me or Dani, always about you."

He shot up, making me step back. "Oh, you're right. I'm such a prick for taking in a single mom and letting her live here so I could support her and her daughter. Excuse me for believing I wanted to make a life with you, for falling in love with you."

I glared at him. "I was a package deal. You knew that from day one. Maybe you provided us a place to live, and provided money, but you've never been supportive, Brad. Not of me and definitely not of Dani. You never once acted like she was anything more than an annoyance to you. You never tried to make a life with us."

"What was I supposed to do? Roll around in the grass and play with her? She's not my kid!"

"It wouldn't matter to a real man!"

He jerked back and his eyes narrowed, his nostrils flaring as his breath came hard. "Only a needy whore would get knocked up by a loser who wanted nothing more than to forget about her while he left to make a name for himself."

I gasped at his words, but refused to let him make me cry. It didn't matter what he said; I was right. He was a selfish jerk. "You're an asshole. You never loved me. You can't love anyone but yourself. I'm getting Dani and getting out of here."

I brushed past him and rushed up the stairs to pull two duffel bags out of the hall closet. Opening the door to Dani's room, I tossed one on the floor. "Put as much as you can in there. We'll come back for the rest later."

Dani sat up on her bed. "Mommy, what—"

"Just do it."

With my breath coming hard, I hurried to the master bedroom and threw everything from the dresser and closet into the bag. I wanted to get out of there as quick as possible before Brad decided to flap his lips some more.

Rushing into the adjoining bathroom, I tossed everything into a backpack before going into the small bedroom we used as an office. I wrenched open the file cabinets and pulled out anything related to Dani and me. When I had everything, which wasn't much, I dashed back into Dani's room.

"Come on, Dani. Let's get going."

I opened the closet door and yanked things off the hangers, tossing them into the bag without bothering to fold them. Dropping to my knees, I grabbed her shoes until no more would fit, and tugged the zipper closed.

"Mommy, what about my stuffed animals?" She pointed to the pile on her bed.

"Grab one for now, and we'll get the rest later." I stood and pushed her toward the door, eager to leave. "Let's go."

When we passed back through the kitchen to the back door, Brad blocked the way. "I'll get everything else when you're not around, and I'll leave the key on the counter," I told him.

He didn't respond, and remained fixed where he stood with his arms crossed. I raised a brow at him, but placed my hand on Dani's shoulder, unsure of his intent. "Nothing to say, Brad?"

He stepped out of the way of the door, letting his actions speak for him, and I let out a humorless chuckle as I ushered Dani out. "Have a nice life. I hope you don't get Danny's contract."

Slamming the door behind me, I opened the trunk and tossed the bags in as Dani climbed into the back seat. I peeled out, driving without a destination in mind, my goal only to get as far away from him as possible. Once I'd put some distance between us, however, I realized we needed a place to stay for the night. Monica had moved to Chicago, my mother had remarried, moving a few hours away, and I didn't have money for a hotel, so that only left one option. I reached for my purse and pulled out my cell phone. After dialing Kat's number, I glanced in the rearview mirror and caught Dani's eye.

"It's okay, baby. We'll be okay." I hoped she missed how my lips trembled and my hands shook, or how I needed to pull over and fall apart.

The truth was, I had no idea what to do. We needed a place to live, but to have that, I needed a full-time job. Who would help with Dani while I was at work? I took a deep breath. One thing at a time.

The call went into Kat's voicemail. "Hi, Kat. It's me. I hope you don't mind, but Dani and I are on our way to your place. It's a long story, and I'll explain everything when I get there, but we need a place to stay for the night, and then I'll figure out something tomorrow. I'll see you later."

Feeling better with somewhat of a plan in place, I headed toward Kat's. I pulled up in front of the building where she lived and parked in a visitor's spot. "Come on, baby."

I opened the door with the spare key Kat had given me, and seeing she wasn't home, turned on the lights as we walked through the apartment. The place was spotless since Kat was never home. She had taken pains to create a masterpiece with sleek lines and lustrous colors of black, silver, and gold, but she was never around enough to enjoy it.

I stepped into the guest bedroom and threw our bags on the bed. "You can sleep here. Get your pajamas on and get ready for bed."

"Mommy?" Her eyes were big and tearful.

I stopped, sunk to her level, and pulled her into a hug. "I'm sorry, baby. Everything's okay. I'm here and I'm not going anywhere. We're just not going to live at Brad's anymore, okay?"

"Why not? Does Brad not want us to live there anymore?"

"Oh, honey. It's much more than that, but no. I didn't want us to live with Brad anymore. He will miss you so much though." I hated to lie, but I wanted to ease her uncertainty. She didn't need to know the true extent of how much of a jerk he was.

The front door opened and closed, and then the *click-clack* of Kat's high heels on the floor tiles filled the apartment. She appeared in the doorway, concern filling her brown eyes. "What's going on? Is everything okay? I got your message."

I glanced up at my beautiful friend with Dani still in my arms. "Yeah, everything's okay. We're going to crash here tonight, if that's all right with you."

"Girl, you can stay as long as you want, you know that."

"See?" I brushed Dani's hair out of her face and wiped the dampness away from her cheeks. "We'll stay with Aunt Kat and everything's going to be fine."

After seeing Dani to bed, I collapsed on the couch next to Kat, who'd curled into a corner with a glass of wine. "Everything okay in there?"

"Yep, she's better. Thanks again."

"Of course. So, what happened?"

"I finally realized what a jerk Brad was, that's what happened."

I filled her in about my lunch with Danny, and then the argument with Brad; from how he badgered me about Danny signing the contract to him calling me a needy whore.

Her mouth dropped open in horror. "He didn't!"

"He did, but you know what, it doesn't matter. I don't care." I leaned back and closed my eyes.

"What did D say?"

I lifted my head and frowned. "Danny? What does he have to do with this?"

"You called him, didn't you?" She twirled her finger around. "Told him about all this?"

"No. Why would I do that?"

She gave me an exasperated look. "Girl, he's the reason for this, and now that he's in Dani's life, he will want to know what's going on with his little girl."

I flipped my hand at her. "He can still get a hold of me on my cell phone. This isn't because of him. This is all Brad and the asshole he is."

"This has *everything* to do with him! Why do you think Brad started acting the fool?" When I only stared at her, she rolled her eyes. "Because he knew he couldn't compete with D, and if you guys are the same way as you were in the past, no one can."

"What are you talking about?" We were nothing like we were back then. We were both very different people. At least, I was.

"The way you looked at each other, like you could never get enough of each other. Like no one else was even around. You only had eyes for each other. I'm sure it's the same way now."

"What? Did you forget what happened in that stupid club?"

"Of course, I didn't forget," Kat said in her matter-of-fact tone. "But, it doesn't matter. He could have tossed you in front of a train, it wouldn't have changed the way you felt about him."

"Oh, please. I'm not that pathetic." I scoffed, embarrassed to admit the pitiful truth.

The sad fact was, however, even before the horrid night at The Sanctuary, there had been many signs I needed to remove Danny from my life, and I ignored all of them, even at the expense of my safety.

Kat sat up and grabbed my hands. "Gabby, it's okay to have feelings for him, because I know you do, and I know one day hasn't gone by all these years where you haven't thought about him. And you know as well as I do that he still has feelings for you. There's no way you guys could go from inseparable one day to a clean cut like you did. Something went down."

Restless and twitchy, I got up, needing to move. "I don't want to go through this again. He made his choice, and now we've both moved on, whether you want to believe it or not." I pinned Kat with a narrowed look. "Now, we have a shared interest in Dani, but she is still *my* responsibility, and he doesn't need to be dragged down into the day-to-day business of it."

Kat sighed her disagreement before she took a sip of her wine. "Okay. It's your decision, but just do me a favor, all right?"

"What?"

She stood and took her time walking into the small kitchen to dump the rest of her Pinot Grigio. She returned to the living room and wrapped me in a hug. "Don't lie to yourself anymore, honey. Let yourself be happy."

"What does that mean? I *am* happy," I insisted, even though I was lying through my teeth.

She pulled back and gave me a sad smile. "You'll know when the time comes. There's a lot to work through and get past, but you will, and you'll know."

Chapter 13

~ Gabrielle
Six Years Earlier

Danny and I left the restaurant holding hands, and walked to his car. Getting in, he started the engine before sitting back.

"Where to?"

"I don't know. Let's go to the park. It's nice there."

He glanced out the window at the light snow falling, signaling the soon approaching winter. "It's too cold to sit by the water."

I smiled. "I didn't say we had to get out."

He put the car into drive. "Okay. Your wish is my command."

Crossing the bridge, he drove around until he found a space hidden from view, something he did every time we parked out here. It was rare for the police to cruise the island, their attention needed in higher crime areas, but he wanted to be sure that we remained undisturbed.

He backed in and shifted into park before switching the radio from the all rap station to one playing soft tunes and turning down the volume. We both opened our doors and climbed into the backseat, sitting close. I grabbed his hand in mine and tilted my head to rest on his shoulder.

"Are you cold?" he asked.

"No, I'm okay." We gazed out the front window in silence, watching the falling snow. It was so peaceful. "It's pretty, isn't it?"

"Yeah, until you have to drive in the crap." I chuckled and snuggled against his side. He draped his arm around me to pull me closer to him. "I was hoping you were cold."

I lifted my head. "Oh yeah? Why's that?"

"So, I had an excuse to put my hands on you…to help you warm up, obviously."

"An excuse, huh? You know you don't need an excuse."

I leaned in and caught his mouth with mine. Our lips lingered before restraint broke and he increased the demand of the kiss. Our breaths ratcheted up to pants and gasps as the heat between us flared, the intensity of which always caught me by surprise. His fingers fisted in my hair as he angled my head and deepened the kiss. Our tongues tangled before I retreated, catching his lower lip between my teeth with a gentle nip, loving the way he moaned.

Empowered by his response, I shifted, straddling his lap, and recaptured his mouth as his hands squeezed my behind before grabbing my hips when I rocked against him, pulses of pleasure rippling out from my core. My fingers scraped through his short hair, and when I sat back, I noticed the air in the car had become heavy, fogging the windows to envelope us in our own little safe and warm cocoon.

Growing more confident every time I was with him, I trailed my lips along his neck, wanting to taste him everywhere, and loving his stifled groans whenever my mouth landed on his skin, making me wonder what other reactions I could pull from him. I unzipped his hooded gray sweatshirt under his black puffy jacket, pushing both away to reveal a white tank. Energized by the fact he hadn't stopped me, which was his usual, claiming he didn't want to rush me despite my protests that I was more than ready, I ran my hands down his hard chest, following with light nips when I spotted the ink on his shoulder. Curiosity piqued, I studied the design, trying to figure out what it was, when I recognized it was an old English-styled "D" with a padlock. I outlined the lines of the lock with my fingertips as he watched.

"What's this?"

"A tattoo."

I swatted his arm as I laughed, and he smiled. "I know that. What I mean is, why did you get this?"

"It's a reminder."

My eyes met his and my brows puckered, unable to understand his meaning. "Reminder of what?"

"That I need to look out for myself. That nobody else will."

I sat back on his thighs, putting space between us. "Does this apply to me?"

"No." He wrapped his arms around me to pull me back. "You're the only real thing in my life."

"Who then?"

He sighed and shifted. "Let it go, G."

"Does it have to do with your parents?"

I regretted the question as soon as it fell past my lips, understanding I'd crossed the invisible line when his body stiffened underneath mine and his arms fell away.

"Drop it."

I was suddenly very tired of him always hiding things from me. He never talked about his past or his parents, and changed the subject whenever I asked. I was sick of our relationship being one-sided, where he refused to tell me anything while I bared all. Even though his home life was less than ideal, I didn't understand why he refused to talk about it. It wouldn't change my feelings for him.

My face tightened, and I shoved away to sit back on the seat next to him, crossing my arms.

"What?" he said, his irritation clear.

"Why won't you tell me anything?"

"Because there's nothing to tell!"

"Yes, there is! I know nothing about your parents. I've never met your dad, and I've never even seen where you live."

"Trust me, G. You don't want to know, and you definitely don't want to meet my father. He's an asshole." He scowled at me. "Besides, it has nothing to do with you and me."

"Yes, it does! It's part of you, who you are."

He ripped up the zipper of his sweatshirt in frustration, and, leaning forward with his elbows on his knees, scratched his fingers through his hair as he took a deep breath.

"My mom left when I was a baby. She said she couldn't handle it and took off. My dad, well, he reminds me every day how I ruined his life and what a worthless piece of shit I am."

I reached out a hand to touch his arm, but he brushed it away.

"Stop. I don't want you feeling sorry for me, and I don't want your goddamn pity."

"Danny—"

"I'm telling you because you demanded to know, and I'm tired of you always asking and getting pissy when I refuse to say anything." His eyes were cold and hard. "I'm laying it all out here so you can do whatever you want with it. This tattoo—" he pointed at his shoulder, "—is a reminder of how someone can take your heart out and stomp the shit out of it. My mom; she left, she didn't care, and she still doesn't. My dad, he hates me. End of story."

"He doesn't hate you...," I murmured, not believing that could be true.

He gave a quick snort. "Oh, Jesus, G. Yes, he does, I have no doubt about that. He's a lazy drunk. He won a disability suit somehow, and now he waits for his checks to come in the mail so he can restock his booze and score weed. That's all he does. That, and tell me every day what a waste I am. He screws a different whore every night, and each one of them hopes he'll take a liking to them so they can live off his crooked money and get high. If the broom is outside the door, I need to crash someplace else."

My eyes widened with shock, not able to comprehend what he was telling me. I would never treat an animal so poorly, let alone my child. "Where do you go?"

He shrugged. "Sometimes I sleep in the car. Sometimes at Big T's. His mom's cool, but I try not to overstay my welcome. There's an apartment over the garage, and I crash there when I can."

"Do you want to find your mom?"

He thought for a moment before shaking his head. "No. She left, and she hasn't tried to find me, so it's obvious she doesn't care. I mean, if I had a kid, I would go to the ends of the earth for him. Nothing would stop me. I don't understand how anyone could turn their back on their kid like that. So, no, I don't want to meet her."

I scooted over, putting my arms around his neck, but he pulled away again. "Stop pushing me away!"

"I said I don't want your fucking sympathy."

I understood he was trying to protect himself, no doubt feeling exposed and vulnerable from what he'd shared, but I refused to let him turn me away. "Well, too bad! I love you and you're going to get it. I'm sorry you have to go through this, but I don't feel sorry for you."

"What's the difference?"

"I love you, Danny, and that means when you hurt, I hurt, but I'm not disappointed in you or think any less of you." He eyed me before he relaxed against the back of the seat, allowing me to nestle against him. "I'm sorry. It isn't fair."

"Yeah, well, life isn't fucking fair."

I shook him. "Come on, Danny. Stop putting your wall up with me. This doesn't change anything."

A few minutes passed before his arms wrapped around me and everything was right again. "I'm not used to anyone caring."

"I care…a lot."

"I'm starting to believe it."

"It's about time."

"It's hard for me to believe." His eyes were still full of wariness, but behind the guardedness was a small glimmer of hope. And trust.

"And now I understand why."

He leaned in for a soft kiss. "You're too good for me, G."

"Then let me be good for you. Stop putting up the walls between us. Stop trying to protect me."

"It's for your own good, believe me. You're better off not knowing this, how fucked up everything is."

"Let me be the judge." I paused for a moment, gauging his mood. He was still edgy, but since he'd opened up about his parents, perhaps he would about other things. "Can I ask you a question?"

"Anything."

"And you'll tell me the truth?"

He hesitated, but then nodded.

"A while back, I was talking to Kat, and she warned me about you."

He smirked. "Did she?"

"She said you'd gotten messed up with some people and you never knew when they would try to get paybacks, as she called it. What was she talking about?"

He hissed a breath through his nose before clearing his throat. "It's just the way it is around here, G. You get in the middle of something and piss the wrong person off…you never know how they will react. Have I pissed people off? Hell yeah. Am I going to stop living my life because of it? Hell no."

"And?"

"And—" he shrugged, "—just like Kat said. You never know when they might try to get paybacks, if that's what they want."

"And that's why you carry a gun?"

"One reason. You can never let your guard down in this hood, G. That's what I keep trying to tell you. It may seem quiet, but there's a lot going on you can't see."

I stared out the front windshield, filled with cracks and chinks, and now covered by a light dusting of snow. I didn't understand how everyone walked around every day acting as if nothing was amiss if, at the same time, needing to look over their shoulders and tote guns. To act carefree and unconcerned wasn't logical to me.

"How are you not stressed out about this?"

He actually smiled. "Used to it." His eyes passed over my face. "Hey, what are you thinking?"

"I don't…" I stopped as I shook my head. Trying to make sense of everything made my mind go numb and unable to process the information. "I don't know what to think."

"Are you scared?"

"Well, yeah. Aren't you?"

He shifted toward me, taking my hands in his, his sharp blue eyes intense. "You have nothing to be scared about. I won't let anything happen to you."

"I'm worried for you, not me," I told him, which was the truth. He was in the middle of whatever, not me.

Danny took a deep breath. "Listen, you need to decide. This is the way my life is. I told you it would be better if you stayed away from me, and I'm giving you the choice again. Walk away now, or this is the way it will be until we can get out of here."

"But—"

"No buts. Choose now, G. This is how it is, and I can't change any of it."

The first flutters of panic flickered at his words, an irrational reaction which I tried to fight, but didn't succeed. "But I don't understand. I'm worried about you, so now I have to choose whether to be with you or not? Why do you keep putting this on me? It's like you want me to break up with you or something."

"You're finding out stuff about my life I didn't want to expose you to. Now that you've heard it, you're free to go. I'd fucking run, if I were you." Danny shifted, opening the distance between us, which felt expansive even in the small confines of his backseat, cold air blasting me from the space he vacated.

I frowned, angered by his retreat, and reached out, but he backed away. I moved again, and this time he gripped my wrists. "I'm serious, G." His eyes held a stony intensity to them. "You better think hard about this."

I jerked my arms, struggling to free my hands from his grasp, but he clutched them tight. "Stop it!"

Danny tugged me toward him and my chest landed against his. I straddled half his lap, one leg draped over his thighs, and his mouth hesitated inches from mine, so close but still out of reach. "What's it gonna be?" he whispered.

I shuddered from his pull on me, which only seemed to build the more he threatened to keep the walls up around him. Resistance on his part was becoming futile since, whenever he tried to shield himself, I was learning how to dodge and ignore. I leaned in to take his mouth with mine and he inched back, staying out of my reach. A frustrated moan escaped me, and I shifted, sitting in his lap, managing to trap his head in the corner between the car door and the headrest. Determined to crumble his wall, I captured his mouth with mine, and he gave in on a groan, but he kept my hands manacled at my waist. He finally relented, releasing them and pulling on my hair, exposing my neck to him. His lips left to feast a path across my collarbone as I grazed my fingers through his hair.

Without warning, Danny lifted me to shift positions, laying me out on the seat. He stretched over me, his blue eyes glowing with an intensity in the dim light, as he unzipped my jacket. The sound of heavy, ragged breathing filled the backseat, and both of our hands shook as we struggled to remove the extra layers of clothing between us.

I shed him of his sweatshirt again as my short fingernails bit into his shoulders. He hiked up my sweater and palmed one breast over my simple white cotton bra. His mouth found mine again with renewed eagerness and he shifted, allowing access to unbutton my jeans and lower the zipper. I gasped at the touch of his exploring fingers, this being the furthest we'd gone yet.

"I want to make you come," he said.

Insecurity flooded me at his words and I hesitated, uncertain what my next move should be. I had done nothing like this before, and I wanted to, but was clueless as to what to do and embarrassed by my inexperience.

Danny caressed me with slow, consistent strokes, and soon a warmth seeped throughout my body, causing my limbs to loosen and relax. I closed my eyes, starting to enjoy his ministrations as my hips moved in time with his finger. My breathing quickened until he slid one finger inside of me and I tensed.

"Fuck, you're tight," he moaned in my ear. When I remained rigid, he propped up on an elbow. "Relax, G. Just go with it."

I let out the breath I'd been holding and tried to relax as I had before. Closing my eyes, I worked to calm my mind. Soon a flush covered me, and everything tingled.

His warm lips pressed against my neck. "That's it," he grumbled in the back of his throat. "Fuck, you're hot."

I squeezed my eyes shut tighter and concentrated, all my muscles tightening and quivering. He brushed his thumb over my most sensitive spot, and I almost shot off the bench.

He continued to make small circles while his finger stroked, and a light sheen of sweat beaded on my skin. Everything in me coiled before spiraling out, a warm wave of release rushing out from my center, my hips grinding hard against his hand.

I gasped, and he swallowed it with his mouth, his tongue seeking mine. He moaned and moved with me, but didn't stop.

~ *Danny* ~

I was a fucking idiot. I shouldn't have taken things this far, knowing as soon as I laid her underneath me, feeling her come on my finger, walking away would be impossible.

I lifted, needing the space to gather the strength to tell myself no, that I could take it no further, but when I spotted the passion shining in her eyes, the color now a stormy green, my need amped up even more.

"Jesus, you drive me insane. I want you so bad," I murmured before taking her mouth once again.

She adjusted, freeing her arm and her fingers trailed over to undo my pants. Since I wore them low, it wasn't difficult to loosen them more. When her hand brushed my dick outside my boxers, I moaned and shifted out of her reach, unable to handle her touch without going out of my mind. She tried to push my jeans down further and I grimaced, recognizing it was time to take her home before I lost my head. This was not how our first time together would be.

"No, don't do that, baby."

"Why not? I want to. I want you." She gripped me.

I clenched my eyes and took a deep breath, resisting the urge to take, even as painful as it was. I put my hand on hers, stilling it. "I want you too, more than anything, but not like this. Your first time is not going to be in the back of an old Buick beater."

Gabrielle draped one leg over my hip and pressed herself closer, the heat of her reaching me through our clothes, and everything in me tightened and my dick throbbed. "We don't have many options, Danny."

I shook my head, adamant with my decision, as I unhooked her leg, struggling to keep a fragile hold on my control. "No, no. I'll find a way. Trust me, I'll make it special."

"It will be special because it's with you!"

I kissed her hard before pulling back, even though doing so almost killed me. "Not in the car, G. That's it."

Deep hurt flashed on her face before she shuttered it and turned her head to the side. "Fine."

"Hey." I cupped her chin to turn her face toward me, but she fought against my hand. "Hey, look at me. Gabrielle, look at me." I waited until she lifted big, glassy green eyes. "Baby, come on. Don't do that."

"It's okay. I understand."

"No, you don't. You think it's because I don't want you or something ridiculous like that. Girl, you can feel how much I want you—so much it hurts—but, baby, I want your first time to be special. Please give me the chance to make it that and not a cheap time in the backseat of a car." I lifted her chin so her eyes met mine again. "Okay?"

She nodded and attempted to smile, but her lips wobbled.

"I love you. You know that. Never doubt that. We have all the time in the world to be together. There's no need to rush it in this piece of crap. Okay?"

"Okay."

"Now tell me you love me."

"I love you."

I leaned in and kissed her. "Always."

"Always."

Chapter 14

~ Gabrielle ~
Six Years Earlier

I stepped outside the dance studio to wait for my mom and shoved my arms through the sleeves of my coat. Sticking my hand in one pocket, I hesitated when my fingers brushed against something hard before pulling out the small digital recorder Danny forever carried around with him. I sighed. If he thought he'd lost it, forgetting he'd asked me earlier to hold it for him, he'd pull his hair out searching everywhere.

My mom drove up, and I opened the door to climb in. "We need to swing by Danny's."

"What? Why?"

"He left his mp3 player with me."

"Can't you give it to him tomorrow when you see him?"

"Mom, please. He'll go crazy, thinking he's lost it or something. He uses this thing day and night."

She released a heavy breath, tiredness etched in every line of her body, but she slouched her shoulders in defeat. "Fine. Do you even know where he lives?"

"Go down Parks and turn right on Hunter, which runs into Bonaventure. It will be on the right."

"Okay, but do you know which place is his?"

I nodded. Despite Danny making it clear he would never take me to his home, curiosity had won out. I knew his address—he'd told me that much—and, using local maps of the city at the school, I'd located the trailer park in which he lived. He would be mad when I showed up, but once he understood why, he would be relieved, so I was willing to take the risk.

When we turned into the complex, I couldn't stop slight tremors from rippling through me. The area was dark, many of the streetlights burnt out or missing. Most of the trailers resting in their assigned spots sat in disrepair and showed signs of serious neglect. Trash and junk piles littered the grounds, making everything appear much more ominous. Understanding dawned on why Danny kept this aspect of his life from me, and I belatedly wondered if I should have stayed away. My mother must have been thinking the same thing as she continued to glance my way, uncertainty and apprehension filling her face.

We pulled up to the trailer bearing his address, and she shifted the car into park. "I'll wait here. Hurry up so we can get out of here."

I studied the structure, taking in the expanding rust and broken window covered by cardboard, anxiety growing, but told myself everything would be okay since Danny's car sat parked outside. "Go ahead. I'll get Danny to drive me home."

She frowned. "Are you sure?"

"Yeah, it's fine, Mom." I hoped she didn't hear the quiver in my voice. "I'll be home in a bit."

She didn't look convinced, but agreed. "Okay. Be careful."

I climbed out of the car and up the two cracked concrete steps resting in front of the trailer. Lights filtered through the drapes on the small window panel lining the side of the door, and laughter from within revealed people were home. I rapped on the doorframe. No one answered, and after a few moments, I knocked again, this time harder.

The door jerked open, knocking back a broom leaning against the handle, and his father stood in the doorway scowling at me, his blue eyes dull and flat. He wore nothing but a white tank with unidentifiable stains and black sweat pants riddled with holes. His dirty blond hair hung long and tangled, in desperate need of a wash and a brush, and deep lines creased his face, signs of the hard life he lived. He might have been handsome at some point, but not anymore.

"What the fuck do you want?" he grumbled.

I resisted the urge to shrink under his glare. "Uh, I'm sorry to disturb you, but I have something of Danny's to return."

"Danny?"

"Yes, your son. Danny."

"Who is it, Dan?" a woman's voice said from behind him.

His father continued to eye me before stepping back to look at the full length of me. "Come in."

I wasn't sure I wanted to, or if I should, but I didn't want to be rude. Plus, Danny had to be inside somewhere since his car was here.

I stepped in, cowering away from him when he refused to give me space, and cringed at the surrounding mess. Piles of clutter and trash littered everywhere. A variety of dishes and glasses sat piled high on the kitchen counter, and the sink was MIA under the cluttered heap. The trailer reeked of stale smoke and alcohol, along with curdled milk, and old, tattered sheets covered the furniture, soaking in the acrid scents.

A woman, wearing only a thin, worn T-shirt, so threadbare it did nothing to cover her ruby-colored nipples, lounged on the couch in front of a small television, smoking a cigarette, a steady cloud of smoke billowing over her ratty hair. An open bottle of whiskey sat on the small table next to an overflowing ashtray, filled to the edges with ashes and butts. She eyed me with such intense hatred that I took a step back, smacking into Danny's father standing behind me. I whipped around, almost at eye-level with him, and again questioned my decision to come here.

"I don't want to be a bother," I said, my voice shaky. "If you could let Danny know I'm here, then I can return this to him and be on my way."

When he continued to gape at me with a dazed expression, I tried again, but my throat tightened as worry settled in. "Is Danny here?"

"No, the loser ain't here."

"Oh, well, then I'll be leaving. I'm sorry." I didn't care if I had to walk home. Desperate times called for desperate measures, and I had to get away, even if doing so meant risking the dark streets at night.

I tried to step around him, but he shifted, blocking my exit. He leered at me with bleary eyes and smiled, revealing rotten teeth and a gap where a front tooth should have been.

"What's your hurry? Why don't you join…uh…?" He glanced at the woman, obviously forgetting her name.

"It's Barbara, you asshole."

"Oh, right. Barb and me. Come on, honey." He reached out, attempting to steer me toward the couch.

I jerked back and planted my feet into the ground. Fear coursed through me as my eyes flicked around, searching for anything to use as a weapon. "Uh, no thank you. I should be going. It's a school night and everything."

"A school night." He let out a roar of hacking laughter. Barbara joined in, and they cackled until tears ran down their faces.

"She's a young one, Dan." Barbara now eyed me as if I was candy. "She should be fun."

Danny's father grabbed both my arms and pulled, causing my heart to slam against my ribcage. I was no match for his strength, even as drunk or high as he was, but I still fought against him, determination and survival my fuel.

"Come on, bitch. Don't make me slap you."

"Please. Please, just let me go."

He tugged harder. "We're not going to hurt you."

I twisted and turned, anything to make his hold on me difficult, and stretched to grab whatever was within my reach off the kitchen table. My hand passed over something hard and I picked it up. It was a stone block ashtray, also filled to the rim like the other one. Using all the force I had, I pitched it at his head, but he ducked at the last second when Barbara cried out a warning. It hit the wall behind the couch, causing Barbara to shriek as the ashes poured down on her.

"What the fuck?" His eyes narrowed before he launched himself. He crashed into me, and we fell to the ground with him landing on top, knocking the wind out of me.

My head slammed into the leg of a chair, undoing my bun, and my vision blurred as the pain raged, but I fought to keep consciousness. I tried to scream and struggled to punch his shoulders with my fists, fighting him as he pinned down my arms. He unzipped my jacket, and my energy to fight was plummeting, when a rush of cold air brushed over me.

The space above me went empty as someone lifted him off me and threw him into the nearest wall, which he crashed into and crumbled to the floor. I pushed up, shoving my hair out of my eyes, and scooted back on my butt as far away as I could as Danny gripped his father by the collar and pounded on him. Barbara bounced up and down on the couch, screaming, but I couldn't wrench my eyes from the rage on Danny's face. He was going to kill his father. As much as I wanted his father to pay for what he'd tried to do, I couldn't let him beat him to a pulp.

I shoved to my feet, and when he reached back to drive his fist into his father's broken and bloodied face, I tugged on his arm. "Stop it, Danny!" He yanked against my grasp, unable to hear me past his blind fury, and I pulled harder. "Stop it! You'll kill him."

He finally looked at me with wild eyes. His skin was flushed red. "That's the fucking point."

"No, stop it. Please, Danny. Just stop."

He stared at me, as if just seeing me, before glancing at his father with disgust and tossing him back against the wall. He collapsed further, making odd gurgling sounds as Barbara knelt beside him, crying as she attempted to rouse him.

Running his hands over my hair and down to my shoulders, Danny searched me for obvious injury. "Are you okay? Are you hurt anywhere?"

"I'm okay. I'm fine. I just want to get out of here."

He grabbed my arm and steered me out of the trailer. He opened the passenger door of his car and shoved me in before walking around to the driver's side, getting in and revving the engine. Slamming the car in gear, he peeled out, the tires skidding on the gravel.

We drove in silence as I tried to process what had transpired, but after a few minutes, vicious nausea roiled in my stomach as fear and horror pulsed throughout my body in high quantities without relenting.

Saliva flooded my mouth, and I swallowed hard. "Pull over, please."

Danny stopped just in time as I threw open my door and heaved onto the sidewalk while he rubbed my back.

Emptied, I collapsed in the seat, closing my eyes.

"You okay?" he asked.

I nodded, not trusting myself to speak, and only lifted an eyelid when the car turned and stopped. He walked into a convenience store and returned minutes later with a can of ginger ale. He handed me the drink.

"Here. This will help to settle your stomach."

I studied his profile as he drove. He still burned with rage, struggling to temper his fury, with his blood-streaked hands fisted and his jaw clenched. I wanted to reach out and touch him, to soothe away his tension, but the gesture would be the wrong thing to do right then, only succeeding in setting him off further. So instead, I took a small sip of the soda and rested my head against the headrest, watching the world pass outside the window.

For the first time since meeting Danny, I questioned what kept me with him. Everyone had tried to tell me being with him was dangerous—that *he* was dangerous—to which I'd defended our relationship with all the conviction I had, but I had to concede there might be merit to their concern if his own father could do something like this.

It wasn't his fault—he hadn't chosen this life—but was being with him worth dealing with one threat after another? No matter where I turned, was peril threatening, waiting to launch itself at me?

Imagining my life without him, however, recalling the crushing loneliness, I became empty, desolate, and distraught. I loved him more than was comprehensible, more than any words could convey. It was a feeling I couldn't explain, but it was as if he was the air in my lungs, the life in my soul. I couldn't live—couldn't survive—without him. What we had was a precious gift, one many never experience, and I refused to turn my back on him, no matter what dangers I faced.

It had been my fault, anyway; I shouldn't have gone to his trailer. He'd warned me multiple times, and I ignored him. I'd believed at the time his warnings stemmed from embarrassment and shame, but now realized he'd only wanted to protect me.

I sat up and dropped my chin, studying my hands in my lap. "I'm sorry."

Danny glanced my way, but didn't respond or acknowledge my apology as he turned his attention back to the road. Understanding the anger thundering through him was because of my actions, I remained quiet.

He pulled into the parking lot of the garage where he worked and shut off the engine. He opened the car door without a word, and I hesitated, watching as he strode toward the building, before following. I trudged up the stairs and waited as he unlocked the apartment. Stepping inside, he turned on a lamp perched on a side table.

I glanced around the small room. A chair and table sat arranged in the middle, along with a small worn loveseat, and a twin bed on a wireframe with a nightstand beside it rested next to the far wall. The kitchenette was in the opposite corner, and a door to a bathroom stood open in the back.

"Whose place is this?"

"Nick's, my boss. He lets me stay here every once in a while. He used to live here when he was single and worked late. Now that he's married, it's pretty much empty all the time. I figure I'll be staying here after what happened tonight. I'll have to work out rent or something with him."

I slumped into the chair, covering my face with my hands. I'd made a mess of everything. "I'm sorry."

He sank onto the edge of the table, which creaked under his weight. "What the hell were you doing there?"

"I had your digital player. I wanted to give it back to you because I knew you'd be looking for it."

He stared at me in disbelief before he stood and chuckled without humor, running his hand back and forth over his head. He remained facing away from me before throwing his keys across the room so they slammed against the wall and clattered to the floor. "Goddamnit!"

I cowered, but didn't move or say anything.

He whirled back, his blue eyes piercing, his voice shaking with anger and pain. "Do you have any idea what it was like to see you under my dad like that? Do you have any idea what went through my mind? Do you?"

I shook my head and tried to shrink further away from him.

"It made me see red! I wanted to grab him and tear his fucking head off!" he roared as he waved his arms around, miming such action. "He had his fucking hands on you, Gabrielle! My father! And all because of a stupid fucking music player. Unbelievable." He put his hands on his hips and hung his head. "Un-fucking-believable."

"I said I was sorry. I don't know what else to say!"

He sunk to his knees and grabbed my hands in his, his eyes tortured and filled with anguish. "Tell me you understand now why I didn't want you to go over there. Tell me you understand why I keep you from the things that I do. Tell me you understand it all now, please."

Tears streamed down my face as I nodded. "I do. I'm sorry, Danny, I am.

I understand now."

He wrapped his arms around me, resting his head against my stomach. "I never want to see anything like that again. I can't survive seeing you like that. It kills me, baby."

I hugged him tighter, folding myself over him. The adrenaline had worn off, and I trembled from head to toe in its wake. He gathered me onto the floor with him, holding me in his lap as he rocked me and ran his hands over my hair, trying to soothe me. "I'm sorry, baby. I'm so sorry. It's all over and you're safe now. You're safe with me now."

When my crying ceased, he leaned back and wiped at my tear-streaked cheek. Pain lined his face. "I'm sorry, Gabrielle. It makes me sick to think about it. I'll never forgive myself for this."

"It's not your fault. I shouldn't have gone there. You tried to tell me."

"It is my fault. I should have made it clear why I didn't want you there. You're just so important to me that I didn't want to scare you away."

I shook my head. "You could never do that."

"My life, and everything in it, is a fucked-up mess. That should scare the shit out of you. You should run away from me. I would."

"But you don't. You don't scare me." I fisted my hands in his sweatshirt and yanked him close as panic filled me. "Danny, I can't live without you. Don't make me live without you." The idea had me almost hyperventilating.

Danny paused and fresh fear flashed through me, assuming he was having second thoughts, but then he sighed and shushed me. His hand cupped my cheek.

"Baby, calm down. Come on. Take a deep breath. Take it easy. I'm not going anywhere."

"Don't make me go away."

"I'm not going to make you go anywhere, and I'm not going anywhere. We'll get through this together, I promise." He kissed me. "I love you with everything I have, G, and that's all there is to it. It's not much, but it's all I have to give."

"I never want to be without you."

He finally smiled, and my world was right again. "We'll never be without each other. If there's one thing I can promise you, it's that. You have my word."

Chapter 15

~ Danny ~
Present Day

Over the next few weeks, I made sure to spend at least one day a week with Dani, and the effort was paying off. She was warming up, accepting me much quicker than I would have ever guessed. It amazed me that this cheerful, beautiful little girl was my daughter, bringing a happiness into my life I never thought possible.

Now, I had to work on her mother. Gabrielle remained skittish around me, wary and uncomfortable, and I fucking hated it. I needed her to see me in a different light, see I had grown as a person, so I scheduled a day outing with both of them.

Pulling into the lot a few minutes after the agreed upon time, Gabrielle parked her small compact next to mine, her car dwarfed by my black Hummer with dark tinted windows that prevented anyone from seeing inside. My crew sat in two big SUVs parked in the surrounding spaces, and Big T climbed out of one of the other vehicles and strode over.

"Hi, Teddy," I heard her say with a smile in her voice as she opened the back door, waiting for Dani to climb out.

"Hey, hey, ladies. Looking nice, looking nice." Big T stepped over to my Hummer to open both doors on the passenger side before turning with a grand sweep of his arm. "Your chariot awaits."

Dani giggled as she clamored up and Gabrielle glanced through the front door, spotting me behind the wheel. She jerked in surprise before a small smile curved her lips.

"Hi. Where are you taking her?"

"Not just her. Get in."

Her brows creased. "Where are we going?"

"Just get in, would ya?" I turned in my seat, waiting for her to climb, and smiled at Dani. "Hey, cutie. How are you?"

"I'm good." She leaned back in the booster seat I had purchased for her, allowing Big T to fasten the seat belt across her.

"Good. You ready to go?"

She nodded, and I put the car in gear and pulled out, the caravan of cars following close.

"Where are we going?" Gabrielle repeated.

"Would you just sit back and relax? Let it be a surprise."

"Why would you want to surprise me?" Genuine confusion covered her expression.

"Damn, you're impossible, girl. You never used to be this hard to please."

"Danny—"

"Stop," I pleaded in a low voice. "Please, let me do this."

Stopped short by my tone, she gave me a small smile, which I returned. "You look very nice," I said.

She glanced down at her simple yellow shirt and jean shorts. "Thanks, I guess."

I wanted to tell her she was always beautiful, but I lost the thought when Dani shouted from the backseat.

"Dad!"

Taken by surprise, Gabrielle and I stared at each other, this being the first time Dani had called me Dad. I clenched my jaw tight, a huge rock of emotion clogging my throat, as I fought to compose myself before making eye contact with her through the rearview mirror. I coughed, but my voice still sounded hoarse. "What, baby?"

"Is that a Xbox under the seat?"

I grinned. "Yep, it is. You want to play something?"

She cheered, laughing in excitement as I reached to pull down the small TV from the ceiling at the next stop light. I leaned over to open the glove box in front of Gabrielle, brushing the back of my hand against her bare leg. She tried to act like it was no big deal, but I spotted the goose bumps rising in response. She wasn't fooling me.

While I took my time sorting through the choices, she turned in her seat, trying to be discreet as she angled herself away from me. I noticed, however, and after selecting an age-appropriate game, I slammed the door shut and grazed my hand along her smooth leg again, my eyes never leaving her face, before handing the disc to Dani. Gabrielle flushed and her lips parted as if she wanted to say something, but the light changed, and I turned my attention back to the road; not before I saw what I wanted, though. She still reacted to me, which gave me hope of turning things around with us.

We rode in silence, except for small squeals from the backseat as Dani played the car racing game, but the further we drove, the landscape became all too familiar, and I could tell when Gabrielle figured out our destination.

"Danny, where are we going?" she asked, even though I knew she knew.

"A special place we used to like to go."

She took a deep breath and closed her eyes. "I'm not sure it's a good place to take her."

"Why not? You ashamed of where you're from?"

"No, it's not that. I want her safe and the last time I checked, that area wasn't."

"It was safe enough for you."

"That's different. Look," she interrupted when I opened my mouth to reply, "I'm only looking out for our daughter, that's all."

I stared at her for a second and then shook my head. Leaning an elbow on the door, I covered my mouth with my hand before turning back. "Do you really think I'd take her someplace not safe?"

"Well, no..." she stated, but I heard the uncertainty in her voice.

"You don't sound too certain about that." I tried not to feel offended. This perception of me was my doing, so it was up to me to change. She wasn't upsetting me on purpose, and I understood she was only protecting our daughter, but she needed to learn that Dani was now also *my* top priority. I wasn't a fucking idiot.

"Danny, I don't think you'd intentionally put her in danger, but you know how things go."

"And I'm well prepared for that."

She glanced over her shoulder to make sure Dani was still too engrossed in her game to be listening to us. "Do you have a gun in the car?" she hissed.

I wasn't going to lie, and gave a small nod to the center console sitting between us. At the next light, I leaned close to her and lowered my voice. "It's locked, so you don't need to worry about it, but it's nice to know you think so highly of me that I'd be fucking careless about something like that."

"Danny, stop."

"Well, come on, G. Give me some fucking credit. I wasn't even referring to that. I meant all the people following us, in case you haven't fucking noticed. They're there for a reason, not to inflate my ego."

"Would you quit swearing?" She glanced over her shoulder again.

"She's not listening, she's playing the game. She's fine."

"I know your past, and hopefully it isn't following you around anymore. That's all I'm saying." Gabrielle turned and crossed her arms, staring out the passenger window and putting an end to the conversation.

"That's all you're saying, huh?" I shook my head and looked away. "That's all you're saying."

I didn't push further, but kept an eye on her face as I turned into the park. When she noticed, she sat up in her seat. "Oh my God," she whispered.

One of the first things I did when I made money was identify places in the community in which to give back. Since this park held so much meaning, as Gabrielle and I had spent a lot of our time here when we were dating, this was the first place into which I poured my donations. I gave the city enough to clean up the area and add multiple jungle gyms. The big open spaces became soccer fields, baseball diamonds, and basketball courts.

Kids ran everywhere while families enjoyed picnics or sitting and relaxing next to the water. Numerous streetlamps lined the parking lot, preventing it from being plunged into complete darkness at night, as it had when I had frequented the place. I parked and watched as her eyes bounced around, taking in everything. Her reaction made my heart smile since I'd had her in mind while doing this, but her assumptions still pissed me off.

I leaned my back against the car door and arched a brow. "This safe enough?"

"Oh my God, Danny. How did they do all this? Where did they get…?" She stopped and gaped at me. "You did this, didn't you? You gave them the money to do this."

I gave her a steady gaze before turning and smiling at Dani. "You ready, baby?"

~ *Gabrielle* ~

Danny opened the door and climbed out as my eyes followed him around the front of the car. To look at him, you'd think he hadn't changed. He still wore his standard attire of jeans, riding low, tennis shoes, and a t-shirt, but everything was top quality, new, and clean, rather than worn and ratty. On his wrist sat a big, chunky platinum watch I didn't even want to know the price of, when there'd been nothing before, and more tattoos decorated his muscular forearms. His hair was now a skull cut, still as black as the night, but he looked healthy, fit, and immaculate in his appearance. He still moved with the same slow demeanor, as if he didn't have a care in the world, even though he missed nothing. His mirrored sunglasses hid his eyes from view, but I knew the intensity I would see behind them.

Everything appeared the same, except for he was someone now. He walked the streets, and everyone knew him by name, wanted to talk to him, touch him, and be near him. He was such a private person, the attention most likely drove him crazy, but he would deal with it, understanding it as the price of success—and the money. Unlike others, however, he was putting his earnings to good use, and I was more touched than I wanted to admit.

To survive these visits with him, I needed to believe he was still running with the wrong crowd, making bad decisions, and just an outright jerk now that he was a mega-star, but it wasn't true and would never be. That had been the common misconception about him when we'd dated; everyone warning me to stay away from him, assuming he was bad news and corrupted down to the bone, but he was good with a big heart, even if he didn't always show it, believing the disclosure made him weak.

I climbed out of the car and followed behind the two of them as they made their way to a field, away from everyone else, where Big T waited with a bright red kite. Danny held his daughter's little hand in his as he talked to her and she listened to whatever he was saying before they took off in a sprint, leaving me with Dani's high-pitched giggle on the breeze.

I continued behind at a slow pace, enjoying the warmth from the sun on my skin. Everything was so different, but the park still held its charm and a special place in my heart. I stopped at the edge of the field, the wind blowing my hair around, and watched as they ran, trying to get the big kite to take flight. It took a few tries before catching and soaring high, the colorful face standing proud against the bright blue sky.

They pulled the kite along, Danny positioned behind our daughter, holding onto the spool with her, fighting against the drag and steering it higher and higher, when it veered to the right at a sharp angle. I followed the kite's path until I caught something out of the corner of my eye, causing me to turn and gasp.

I walked to the point of the peninsula, toward the water and the bench, where he'd taken me on our first date and told me he loved me for the first time. But it wasn't the bench, the water, or even the city skyline in the distance catching my interest; instead, it was a beautiful gazebo sitting at the water's edge. I stepped in, letting my fingers run across the smooth, cool wood. The structure was square rather than round, and a single bench sat in the middle, while boxes lined every railing and overflowed with flowers in a bright shock of pinks, whites, reds, and purples. Two kids played inside, but when I approached, they scurried off, leaving me alone.

The temperature was cooler under the cover of the roof and I sat, letting the fresh air pass over me, bringing with it the sweet scent of the surrounding Geraniums and Impatiens. I closed my eyes and tried to control the flow of memories of our first date flooding my mind—the first kiss, the declarations of love. I had truly believed we would last forever. How naïve I'd been.

I felt his presence behind me even though he hadn't made a sound. I turned and smiled. "This is beautiful."

Danny said nothing as he sat beside me, removing his sunglasses, but keeping his gaze over the water.

"Do you still come out here?" I asked, and then chuckled. "That's a stupid question, sorry."

"Why is it stupid?"

"Why?" I nodded toward the picnic area behind us a few hundred feet away, but close enough for people to realize who sat in the gazebo, and they stared.

He shrugged as he studied the ground. "Yeah…well maybe it isn't as easy as it was, but yeah, I still sometimes come out here. At night," he added.

"Oh." I was unsure what more to say as uneasy tension fell between us. I fought against the desire to give in and fall back under his spell, which would be easy to do if I allowed myself to surrender. "Where's Dani?" I asked, changing the subject to safe territory.

"Flying the kite with T. She's fine."

We sat together in silence, before I broke it, uncomfortable with the left-over strain from our argument in the car. "I'm sorry, Danny. I didn't mean to imply you hadn't changed at all. It's just, I'd heard about…well, I can see it isn't true."

He leaned back and grinned. "You're forgiven."

"That easy, huh?"

"That easy because you're right. I haven't changed that much, or at least I hope I haven't. I'm still this punk kid from the streets and I don't ever want to forget that. It's made me who I am. All the other stuff…" He waved his hand and shook his head. "It was stupid, and it wasn't me. I let things get out of control, and even though I had my reasons, it's no excuse."

"What were your reasons?" I wanted to kick myself for asking, but I was curious about the Danny who sat next to me, if I would recognize the old Danny within him.

He studied me for a second, but then shook his head again. "That's for another day, but my point is, I would like to think I can put who I am now to good use and make the right decisions because I have something I never had."

"What's that?"

"Choices. I never had choices, no options, nothing. But now I have loads of them, and I want to give that to Dani. I want her to have the choices and chances I never did."

My heart swelled. "That's sweet."

"I'm not saying it to be sweet, G. I'm saying it because I'm her father and it's my responsibility to do that for her. I want to do it for her. I want to be there for her. I want her in my life more than one day a week."

I swallowed and averted my eyes. "I understand, and you should be."

Danny saw how hard this was for me and didn't press further, for which I was thankful. "We'll figure something out. I need to straighten some shit out first, but once I do, we'll figure out a plan."

I nodded again, but said nothing as I studied my fingernails as if they were the most interesting things ever. I tried not to get upset, telling myself I knew this conversation would happen one day, but despite attempting to prepare myself, I wasn't ready.

Also, the gut-clenching hurt knowing he didn't want me as part of his life was humiliating, and I told myself to stop, mad I would be stupid enough to think it. I needed to be happy for Dani, who now could have a relationship with her father, and I needed to keep my personal feelings out of it.

"You know," Danny said, breaking into my thoughts. "I designed this myself."

"You did? Wow." I peered around again. "It's gorgeous, and this is the perfect spot for it."

He gave me a crooked smile. "Do you remember the one time we came out here, and I carved into the bench?"

I laughed as I remembered how horrified I'd been as he defaced the wood by carving our names into it before surrounding them with a heart, so certain the police would come and arrest us for destruction of property. I glanced over my shoulder to the bench sitting outside the gazebo. "Did they replace it?"

"No." He slid over, revealing the heart and our names, clear as day, if only faded with time.

My fingers traced the engraving as my heart warmed with an emotion I hadn't experienced in so, so long. "Oh…"

"I asked them to move the bench in here. This is what I wanted to capture with the gazebo." His fingers reached out and trailed behind mine.

I glanced up and found his sharp blue eyes looking at me with their usual intensity. My breath caught in my throat and I trembled as I always did whenever trapped in his powerful gaze.

Jerking to my feet, I gave him a wobbly smile and stepped away, needing space. "That was nice of them. I'm sure they'll want to keep all mementos of the hometown star. I should get back to Dani," I prattled.

He walked over, stopping me with a hand on my arm. "Wait. I want to ask you something." I took a small step back from him and waited. "What did Dani mean when she said you didn't dance?"

I swallowed. I didn't want to go into the full, sordid details. "She doesn't know I used to dance."

"What? Why not?"

"It was easier that way."

"Why aren't you dancing, Gabrielle?"

~ *Danny* ~

Her eyes flicked up to mine, and something flashed in them before she buried it away again. "Choices. Just like you said, Danny. I had to make a choice, and I made it."

She brushed past me to head back toward the field and I didn't stop her. I sighed before I grabbed my sunglasses and shoved them on, swallowing against the guilt surging through me. Yet again, something else to add to the list of how I'd fucked up Gabrielle's life. I wondered if there would ever be an end to that list, or if it was my destiny to screw things up for her forever. I leaned on the railing, trying to figure out how I could fix things—if they could even *be* fixed—before pushing off from the wood beam.

I attempted to ignore the people standing around watching and overlook the fact some of them were taking pictures with their cell phones. This was my life, whether I liked my celebrity status or not, and I couldn't change it. One thing I didn't have to accept, however, was not having Gabrielle in my life anymore.

The more I was around her and Dani, the more I realized this was what I'd been missing and what I'd been searching for, but looking in all the wrong places. I wanted the love of my life back, my soul mate, and I wanted my family. I may not have known about Dani, but once I'd found out, my focus and priorities shifted, and it was all I wanted now. That, and Gabrielle. I wanted her more than anything I could remember. Time hadn't changed my feelings for her, instead only strengthening them, and I'd been stupid to believe I could have ever lived without her and still be happy. I was getting my shit together and getting her back was now my number one priority. This was what mattered, what everybody wanted in life; the stuff money couldn't buy, and I wasn't going to let it slip away.

I glanced once more at our bench and made a vow to get her back. I would have my family and my girl, no matter what it took. We only had to get through the ugliness of what I did before we could have forever, as I always promised we would.

But first, I had to deal with Dollar. Just like before, he wasn't on the same page as me when it came to Gabrielle, and now Dani, but unlike before, this time I didn't give a fuck what he thought. I was only doing what I wanted, and he could go fuck himself if he didn't like it.

Chapter 16

~ Danny ~
Six Years Earlier

The music cut, and I pulled off my headphones. I took a deep breath before grabbing the bottle of water sitting on the counter. We'd been working for four hours straight and my throat was raw, but I needed to keep going to make up for time otherwise spent with Gabrielle rather than recording. I glanced at where she sat on the other side of the room, her schoolbooks spread out on the table in front of her, but she ignored her studies as she watched me. She caught my eye and broke into a big grin, which I returned.

"That wasn't it, man." Dollar rewound the tape, prepared to start over. "You need to do it again."

I slumped in the chair behind me. "Come on, man. Give me a break."

"No breaks, dawg. We've got a lot to do."

I closed my eyes and hissed a breath through my nose. Exhaustion pulled at me, but I had to finish this. If I didn't, Dollar would never get off my back and I might never cut a decent demo if he bailed.

I stood and grabbed my jacket. "All right, but let me take G home so she doesn't have to sit here all night."

I ignored the narrow look Dollar gave me at the mention of her. He had practically fallen out of his chair when we walked in earlier, but one glance at me and he'd kept his opinions to himself. I didn't understand what his issue was, and I didn't care. I was going to be with her, regardless of what anyone else thought, but why one of my supposed best friends was an outright dick to her, didn't make sense. She and Big T got along, which didn't surprise me since Big T loved everyone and everyone loved him, but Dollar hadn't even tried, which bugged the hell out of me. So far, I had mentioned nothing, resorting to keeping him and Gabrielle apart or ignoring the snide remarks from him, but my breaking point was hovering and ready to crack. The tension hadn't escaped her either, and she'd asked if she was coming between Dollar and me. I couldn't keep denying it when the strain was fucking obvious.

"Come on, baby. Let's get you home." I approached where she sat and gathered her books.

She gave me a playful pout. "But I don't want to go. I want to stay here. I love watching you."

"I know, I know, but we're going to be here late." I peered over my shoulder at Dollar, who busied himself with the equipment, muttering, and dropped my voice. "Besides, it's about to get real in here."

"I told you he hated me," she said under her breath.

"He's pissed at me, not you. Come on, let's go."

She shrugged into her jacket before grabbing her bag. She smiled at Big T, who sat minding his own business. "Bye, Teddy. I'll see you later."

"See ya, Gabrielle. It was nice seeing you."

She glanced toward Dollar as we strode by. "Bye, Dollar."

"Yeah, we'll see you around, girl." His lips twitched into a grimace. "Take it easy."

I shot him a cold glare behind her back as I steered her out of the room and to the street. After loading her in the car, we rode in strained silence before she sighed.

"I'm sorry to cause problems between you and your friend."

"It's not you, baby." I reached over to grab her hand in mine, trying my best to reassure her. She had no reason to feel guilty because Dollar was being an ass. "He thinks I should record every second, and so he doesn't like how you take up some of my time."

"Well, maybe he's right. Maybe you should be recording all the time. Maybe I keep you from it."

"No, it's cool. I have a lot of stuff already down, and now we're only putting on the finishing touches. I don't need to be there as much as he thinks I do, and besides, I'd rather spend the time with you."

She returned my smile, but then ducked her head. "Good, because I don't want to lose any time with you."

"I don't either."

I pulled up in front of her apartment building and put the car in park before sliding across the seat to tuck her against my side. "I love you, baby. Dream about me tonight."

"I always do," she promised before my lips settled on hers. The kiss started sweet before heating and deepening, until we were panting, but refusing to break apart.

When we drew away, she rested her head on my shoulder. "I can't wait for the day when I don't have to leave you."

"That's what I'm working for. I'm doing this for you."

"No, you're doing it for you. I'm just along for the ride."

"You'll be by my side the whole way."

"I can't wait." She gave me another kiss. Pulling away, she reached for the door handle. "I better let you go before Dollar gets even madder at me."

"He can kiss my ass."

Gabrielle smiled and climbed out. "I love you."

"I love you too, and don't you forget it. I'll see you later, all right?"

After she disappeared inside her building, I yanked the car into gear and drove away. I wasn't sure how to handle the situation with Dollar, but I had to do something. I couldn't turn my back on my friend because he had a beef with my girl, and I refused to end things with her.

There had never been issues with any of the girls I'd tangled with in the past, but Dollar had known I hadn't been serious about any of them. My relationship with Gabrielle was very serious and my feelings very real. Maybe that truth scared Dollar—worried I would suddenly have new goals; ones which included an office job, along with the house in the suburbs complete with the white picket fence, and two and a half kids. That wasn't going to happen. I still wanted success as a rapper, and if I could get the house and kids because of it, so be it, but there would not be any white-collar jobs in my future. I would never forget who I was; reaching my dreams would not change me, and neither would Gabrielle. She accepted me for who I was, and didn't ask or want me to be anything else. She was proud of me and what I strove to become. Why Dollar couldn't see the positive influences she had on my life, I didn't get, but I was going to get to the bottom of it.

Arriving back at the studio, I studied the sorry excuse of the surrounding neighborhood, everything tired and beaten down, and hoped one day to help rebuild the city. The area could be a destination for people to visit or live, without worrying about safety. I wanted to bring my kids back here and point out where I grew up with pride, and honor my roots, an integral part of me and my music; the roughness and rawness providing the hard edge in my lyrics, which would forever define me.

I stepped into the room, interrupting Big T and Dollar wrapped in a heated discussion. They fell silent when they spotted me.

I quirked a brow at them. "What's going on?"

Big T shook his head at Dollar. "Don't do it, man."

"No, it has to be said." Dollar turned to face me. "She's got to go, man."

"Aw, shit." Big T dropped his large frame into a chair, which groaned in protest.

"And why's that?" I kept my stance loose, but my shoulders tightened and my fists balled, and Dollar took note.

He raised his hands, trying to calm me down. "Now, before you get yourself worked up, since I know you're going to, hear me out. You always get worked into a fit if anyone says a thing about your girl so that no one can talk to you."

"I didn't realize anyone wanted to say anything about her."

"Man, she's messing with this." He waved his arms around the room. "We here all hours of the night, trying to get this shit together because you too busy running with her all the damn time. You ain't serious about this anymore."

"I'm here, aren't I? You know, Dollar, I think you're jealous of her or something."

"Jealous? That don't even make sense."

"Then what is it? You haven't liked her since day one, and I don't understand what she did to you. She's been nothing but nice to you."

"That's just it, man. She *nice*. She all uppity and better than all of us. No one's that nice who's real."

I took a step toward him, but then stopped myself, clenching and unclenching my hands at my side, trying to keep in control. "She's never acted like that. Ever. She's not like that and you know it. She's more real than anyone I've ever met."

"She don't, man," Big T agreed. "What?" he said when Dollar narrowed his eyes at him. "She ain't like that at all."

"You think anyone will take you seriously with Mrs. Goody Two-shoes by your side?" he said, attempting a different angle. "Come on, man. Think about it. You'll be laughed at with a rep like that."

"My music is about me, not her. Two separate things."

He gave a dark chuckle. "Right. You think it will stay that way? Just wait, dawg. They'll bring her up, and it ain't going to be pretty."

"Then I'll deal with it." I closed my eyes and took a deep breath, trying to calm myself down before I went at my friend. When I had control back, I stared hard at him. "You're going to have to figure out a way to deal with this because I'm telling you, she isn't going anywhere. One of us would have to die for us to be apart."

He nodded as he studied me, considering. "Well, I'm sorry to hear that."

"What is with you?" I launched myself toward him, only to stop short with mere inches separating us. I heaved in shallow breaths. "Why can't I be happy, you motherfucker?"

"Oh, D, my boy. You *can* be happy. You can have it all, the whole mother-fucking world," he drawled, unfazed by my outburst. "But you choosing not to. You choosing her over everything." He straightened and stared down his nose at me. "I need time to think this over."

I stepped back and frowned, not expecting him to relent so easy, and his retreat, not his usual behavior, confused me. But I would let him take all the time he wanted. I wasn't stupid; I needed Dollar and I would give him whatever he needed, if it meant an agreement.

"Sure, man. Take the time you need."

He nodded at me and tipped his head in Big T's direction before saunter-ing out of the room.

When it was just Big T and me, I dropped into a chair and covered my face with my hands. If I couldn't get Dollar to work with me on this, I was fucked. There was no question about it, I was in a lose-lose situation. If I wanted success, I needed Dollar. If I wanted happiness, I needed Gabrielle. And, for some reason, I couldn't have both.

Chapter 17

~ Gabrielle ~
Present Day

"I'm sorry, Dani. You can't go to ballet today." I grabbed the hair falling into my face in frustration, brushed it back, and tied it into a ponytail, ignoring the daggers shooting out of her eyes.

"Why not?" she whined.

"Because, like I explained to you before, until I get a full-time job, I can't afford to pay for your classes. We paid only up to this month. So, you'll have to be patient. I'm sorry, honey, I really am."

She glared at me again, before stomping down the hallway and slamming the door to our shared bedroom. I slumped back on the couch, letting out a blustery breath, and closed my eyes. We'd been at Kat's for a few weeks, and so far, I hadn't been able to find a job close to Dani's school, or allowing flexibility in my schedule so I could drop off and pick her up when the school year started.

I took another deep breath and tried to muster the energy to go through the websites again, but my motivation waned. I had no idea what I was going to do. I needed more than the part-time transcription job I'd been doing, but finding a company that would take someone with only a GED and a lackluster work history was proving to be difficult, especially one with the pay I needed so I could afford my own place along with benefits, but I had to do something quick. Kat would never say anything, but I wanted to get an apartment soon before we overstayed our welcome.

I lifted my head when the bedroom door opened and Dani came walking back into the room. "Can I call Daddy?"

I frowned, but sat up as I patted the papers scattered over the coffee table, looking for my cell phone. "Uh, sure. I'm not sure if he'll be available, but you can try."

I scrolled through my contact list and selected Danny's number, before placing the phone in her waiting hand. She listened for him to answer, her eyes brightening when he did.

"Hi, Daddy!" I couldn't hear what he was saying, and Dani turned back into the bedroom, her giggles trailing behind her.

I closed my eyes and let out a heavy sigh. I was so happy she had her father in her life, but it was still a knife to my heart to be in contact with him again. It took everything I had to keep things on a neutral level, even though a part of me burned to scream at him, demanding to know what had changed, and then cry for all we'd missed from the years apart. But since he'd made it clear he'd moved on, never mentioning anything about our past, I followed suit.

Soon, everything would be different, after we came to a custody agreement and I wouldn't have to see him as much. Dani would spend a few weekends with him, and I needn't be there. Once that happened, my life could go back to the way it was before Danny had re-entered it—out of sight, somewhat out of mind.

"Mommy." Dani returned and handed me the phone. "Daddy wants to talk to you."

I took a calming breath. "Hello?"

"What the hell is going on? Why are you at Kat's?" he said, dismissing the preliminaries.

"Uh…what?"

"What the hell is going on, G? Why is Dani calling me, asking me to pay for her ballet classes and telling me you're now living at Kat's?"

"She what?" I stared in shock at her smug expression before narrowing my eyes. "Oh my God. I'm sorry, Danny. I had no idea that was why she wanted to call you."

"I don't care about that, just tell me where to mail the fucking check, but I want to know why you're at Kat's, and why she's saying you can't afford her classes."

My face flushed in embarrassment. "Uh, things are a little tight, that's all. It will work itself out."

"Stop beating around the fucking bush, G. I'll be right there," he yelled to someone in the background before coming back on the line. "I'm in the middle of recording right now."

"Oh, I'm sorry. I won't keep you any longer." I was more than anxious to get off the phone with him.

"Fuck them, they can wait. What's going on? Where's Brad?" His voice tightened at Brad's name.

"I, uh...I left him."

"You left him, huh?" He sounded happy at the news. "So now you're at Kat's?"

"Yes, but only until I can find a job and get us a place to live..." I trailed off. When he said nothing for a few seconds, I thought I'd lost him. "Hello?"

"I'm still here." He paused and then cleared his throat. "Look, this is BS. You're not going to stay with Kat. You and Dani, pack up your things and go to my place."

"What?" There was no way I could live in the same house as him. "We can't do that, Danny. That's ridiculous."

"What's ridiculous about it? My house is big enough, plus it will give me more time to spend with Dani. That's what we want, right?"

"Well, I guess..."

"It's only for a while, right? Until you find something. Believe me, I have more than enough room for you two. This way, you guys have your own space to do what you want, I can spend more time with Dani, and we'll see what we can do about these ballet classes she wants to go to."

"I don't know, Danny..."

The last thing I could do was live with him. What was he trying to do, torture me? But what he said was true. This arrangement would give him more time with Dani, and I wouldn't have to lose any. In addition, I wouldn't feel pressured to find a job as soon as possible in order to get out of Kat's small apartment.

I squeezed my eyes shut and took a deep breath. I couldn't believe I was considering it. "I guess it could work—"

"I'll text you my address after I hang up. I won't be back until late tonight, but I'll send T there to meet you guys. See you."

I stared at the phone in my hand after he hung up, wondering what in the hell I agreed to.

* * *

I pulled up to a heavy black gate and gaped in disbelief. The address on the gray stone column at the end of the driveway matched the one he'd given me, so I had the right place, but a gate? He lived behind a gate?

I opened my window and hit the square red button on a silver box that stood next to a column, housing a speaker and a camera. I waited a few seconds before it squawked.

"Hey, girl! You made it," Teddy's voice boomed out of the box. "I'll open the gate for you. Pull up the front drive by the main door."

I waited as the large gate swung around before driving up the long, curvy driveway. When I came over a small crest, the house came into view and I slammed on the brakes as my mouth fell open. I knew he was successful, but for some reason, I never pictured him in a mansion. Standing before me was the most beautiful house I'd ever seen, and I couldn't believe this is where Danny now lived. He'd come a long way from his trailer home.

It was a huge colonial, layered in bricks, in all different shades of deep red. The center stood tall, at least three stories, and off each side, wings spread out and wound around. A high arch of curved block glass framed the beveled glass door with long frosted windows lining the sides, emitting a soft glow from the lights within.

The driveway continued straight and disappeared around the side of one wing, while another leg cut left to create a circle drive. The grounds, landscaped with beautiful, overflowing flowerbeds, lined the front of the house and followed along each wing and out of sight. Acres of grass flowed in all directions as far as the eye could see, making me wonder how much land he owned.

I tried to take everything in, but found it was almost too much to believe. I glanced at Dani; her eyes were big and round, and her mouth formed a small circle as she stared at everything. The door swung open and Big T walked out, waving us up. I took a deep breath and removed my foot from the brake.

Stepping out of the car, I shook my head. "Oh my God, Teddy."

He chuckled as he reached in to grab our bags out of the trunk. "The boy's done good. He's done real good. Come on. Let's go in."

We followed him in and I didn't know where to look first. The tile floors gleamed under the bright lights; everything neat and clean, with nothing out of place, and all the furniture appeared to be brand new and unused. Canvases of art hung on walls, displaying Danny's eclectic tastes as everything ranged from conservative to racy. Each room I passed showed a different side of him; the living room sleek and sophisticated in blacks and whites, while the dining room was dark and seductive with its large mahogany table and deep red walls.

Big T took us into an expansive kitchen, which had shiny, stainless steel appliances between white marble counters under white washed cabinets. "Help yourself to whatever you want. We can go this way up the back stairs," he said to us as we trailed behind him.

"The back stairs?" I asked. A large winding staircase had sat by the front door.

"Yeah, your rooms are closer to this one, but you can use the other one, if you want."

"I can't believe there are two," I muttered, but he heard me and chuckled.

We went up the narrow stairwell and emerged on the second floor at the end of a long hallway. Big T nodded toward the opposite end, which turned the corner and held only one door. "That's D's room, but both of you are down here." He stopped outside a closed door and smiled down at Dani. "You ready to see your room, little D?"

She grinned and giggled, as she always did at the moniker. Dani followed him into the room, and her eyes popped and her jaw dropped. I stepped in and almost did the same.

A light ballet pink colored the walls, and soft white drapes billowed above the windows. A double bed sat in the corner, dressed in different shades of pink with a sheer white netting hanging down from the canopy. One wall was all mirrors, and a freestanding ballet barre stood nearby.

I glanced through a door into the huge walk-in closet already housing tutus and dress-up costumes. A private bathroom connected to that. Danny had had his daughter in mind when he decorated this room. "When did he do this?"

"He started as soon as he found out about her. She was wearing pink ballet stuff the day he met her."

"Oh my…" I clamped my mouth shut, afraid I would break down.

"I love it!" Dani exclaimed, and she raced around, trying to take in everything. She touched every stuffed animal and ran her fingers over the ballet art hanging on the walls. She even did a couple pliés at the barre in front of the mirror.

"I'll never get her to leave." I followed Big T out to another room a short distance down the hall, but that much closer to Danny's. I tried to ignore how near it was and reminded myself I could do this for our daughter.

It was nice, but a standard guest room. It didn't matter, however, just as long as I was near Dani and had my own space, which I did. We wouldn't be here long, anyway.

I stayed in my room after Big T left, unpacking my things into the dresser, and hung others in the closet. I stepped into the bathroom to splash cool water on my face before returning to Dani's room to help her. Deciding we were hungry, we retraced our steps and went into the kitchen.

I sat her on one of the bar stools lining the front of the island, and scrounged through the large sub-zero fridge for something to eat. Having expected it to be full of beer and liquor, I was surprised to find the shelves stocked with food, including fruits and vegetables, as well as many options of juices. I was digging through its contents when a door opened from around the corner and a group emerged, all talking and laughing at once as they strolled by the kitchen.

They stopped when they spotted Dani at the counter and then their eyes met mine where I stood with my hand on the fridge door, watching them. It was a mixed group, all of whom I had never seen before. The men eyed me with interest while the women narrowed their eyes.

"Who are you?" one of them asked.

"Uh, I'm Gabrielle and this is Dani."

A woman wearing heavy makeup with her blonde hair in a high ponytail and her body squeezed into a tight red spandex dress, stared at Dani and gasped. "Is she…?"

"Yes, she's Danny's…I mean, D's…I mean, DOA's daughter." I had no idea what to call him anymore.

One of her friends cackled. "Oh my, Cassie! Looks like you've got competition now."

The rest of the group laughed, but Cassie didn't join in. Instead, she straightened and glared at me. "Are you her mama?"

"Uh…" I started to answer, but Danny interrupted me when he rushed in from some other door out of view.

"Hey, you made it. Good. I was able to get out of there earlier than I thought. Hey, baby, how are you?" He lifted Dani into his arms and gave her a tight squeeze.

"D, what is going on?" Cassie stood with her hand on her hip and an expectant expression on her caked face.

"Oh, hey, Cass. How's it going?" He glanced at her without interest before walking over to the fridge next to me with Dani. "Everything all right? You find everything okay?"

"Yeah, everything's fine. Great." I gave him a weak smile, trying to ignore the glare boring into me from across the room. "I was just looking for something for us to eat."

"I told them to stock up. What do you want, baby? I'm sure we've got it."

"Chicken nuggets," she said.

"Nuggets, huh? Yeah, we've got that." He opened the freezer and dug through its contents.

I reached over to pull Dani out of his arms and lowered her to the floor, but kept her by my side. "It's okay, Danny. Maybe we should get out of your way, so you can be with your company."

He stopped and frowned. "My company?" I rolled my eyes toward the group still standing there watching us with frank curiosity, and his frowned deepened. "They're not my company. What are you all doing?" He hitched his head toward the back door. "Go on, get out of here."

"Danny!" I said, embarrassed by his rudeness.

"D!" Cassie exclaimed, shocked he would be so crass to her.

"What?" He ignored Cassie. "I'm telling you, they're here all the time. They're Dollar's crew, not mine."

He moved over to direct them out. "Go home. Get out of here. Go."

Cassie pushed herself away from the group and stomped over to him. "Can I talk to you privately, please?"

Danny sighed and walked out of the kitchen with her rushing behind him. I couldn't hear what they were saying, but didn't miss when their voices rose. I glanced down at Dani, her eyes wide with alarm, and was about to take us both back upstairs when Cassie stormed through the kitchen and slammed out the door. Danny returned, rubbing his hands together with a big smile on his face.

"Okay, where were we? Chicken nuggets, right?" He opened the freezer again.

I frowned. "Danny?"

He continued to rummage through the shelves. "What?"

"I hope we didn't cause any problems by being here."

"No. No problems. Everything's cool."

"Are you sure? Because we can go back to Kat's if we're—"

He shot upright and grabbed my arms. "No!" He took a deep breath. "No," he repeated. "I don't want you guys to go. Everything's fine. Trust me."

I studied his face before nodding. "Okay, if you're sure."

He smiled and pulled Dani over to him. "Now, we've got to find nuggets for my girl…"

I watched them laughing with each other as he played "find the chicken nugget" until they located some. I didn't know what was going on or what the story was with Cassie, but I hoped his house wasn't a constant party like the ones we'd gone to in the past. Those had been nothing but trouble, and filled with danger, and I wouldn't subject Dani to that.

Watching the two of them together, father and daughter, however, I forgot all the ugly memories and my heart broke a bit realizing this family scene wasn't reality, and how much I wanted it. Too bad it wasn't meant to be.

Chapter 18

~ Gabrielle ~
Six Years Earlier

I stepped inside the studio after Danny drove away, and sat next to Kat, who was tying up her toe shoes.

"Boys night out tonight?" she asked. At my confused expression, she nodded toward the now empty spot where Danny's car had been. "I overheard you and D talking outside."

"Oh, yeah. He said he needed to record with them since he hasn't been spending as much time with them because of me. No girls allowed," I added with a small laugh.

"What are you doing?"

"Me?" I shook my head. "Nothing."

"Come out with me and my girls. Girls' night out."

Even though Kat and I had become friendly through dance, I didn't believe her friends would want me hanging around. "Oh, I don't want to intrude."

"You're not intruding, silly. Come on, it will be fun."

I mulled over the invitation, admitting it sounded like a good time, never having a girls' night out before, and spending my nights alone when I wasn't with Danny was getting old. "Okay."

After practice, I rushed home to get ready as fast as I could. Monica let me borrow her clothes again, elated I was getting out of the house without Danny, and I took the time to do my hair and makeup.

When the doorbell rang later, I opened the door to Kat and her two friends.

"Hey, Gabby. This is Lisa and DeAnna." Kat waved to the girls standing behind her. "You ready?"

I smiled at their blatant shock, and tried to forget about their snide comments since people were more accepting of me now because of Danny and Kat. "Yep."

I followed them out into the hallway and down the stairs. When they came to DeAnna's car, I piled into the back with Kat. "You look amazing, girl," Kat said. "No wonder D can never take his eyes off you."

My cheeks heated at the compliment. "Thank you."

Lisa turned around from the front seat. "No shit, girl. It's like night and day from what you look like at school."

"Lisa!" DeAnna scolded.

"What? You've seen her."

"It's okay," I said. "That's what I'm comfortable in, not this."

Kat shook her head. "Well, you should be. You gorgeous."

"So, what's the scoop with you and D?" DeAnna asked, as she eyed me through the rearview mirror.

"We're dating, I guess you could say."

"Girl, you more than dating," Kat said. "I see how you are. You two are in *looooovvvve.*"

The girls giggled around me, and I smiled, but said nothing.

"Has he?" Lisa asked.

"Has he what?"

"Has he told you he loved you?"

"Yes." I was unsure if I should share our intimate details, but it felt good to have girlfriends to gossip with and share in my excitement.

The two girls shot a peek at Kat, and I remembered what Danny had told me about them casually dating in the past. "Oh, I'm sorry. I didn't mean to diminish what you and—"

She flicked her wrist with a dismissive wave. "Girl, don't worry. What you two have is different from what we had. It's like the real thing, and I'm happy for you guys. Really, I am."

When we pulled up to the curb in front of a house, I peeked out the window. "Where are we going?"

"To a party. Come on." Kat opened the door and stepped out.

My anxiety skyrocketed, but I refused to give into my nervousness. I'd always wanted to attend the parties Monica told me about, and I would not chicken out now. I wished Danny was here so I'd feel safe and at ease, but I needed to be independent. He couldn't be by my side day and night to make things more comfortable for me. I needed to build my confidence.

As we neared the non-descript small bungalow, which resembled every other house on the block, loud music boomed out the open windows. Groups huddled outside, smoking what I guessed were cigarettes, even though the scent wasn't familiar, and eyed us as we approached.

One of them broke away and leered at me, his eyes red and bloodshot. "Hey, baby. I haven't seen a fine thing like you around here…"

"Back off, Lenny." Kat shoved his shoulder and kept on walking.

I ducked my head, starting to second-guess my decision not to stay home. But once inside, where the music pulsed and people gathered, drinking and talking, while others ground against each other to the heavy beat, curiosity and fascination surpassed my skittishness, and I steeled myself, determined to see the night through. There was no backing out now.

Trailing behind Kat, my eyes were wide as I tried to take in everything and not become overwhelmed by the commotion and noise. I glanced over my shoulder, expecting to find Lisa and DeAnna trailing, but they remained by the front door, laughing and flirting with two guys. Kat stopped when we reached the kitchen and turned back.

"What are you drinking?" she yelled.

I shrugged.

She shook her head before handing me a bottle of pink liquid. "Here's a wine cooler. We'll start you slow."

A fizzy strawberry scent filled my nose when I took a quick sniff. With Kat watching, an amused look on her face, I raised the bottle for a hesitant sip and then grimaced at the sweet and sour flavor.

Kat let out one of her loud, bawdy laughs. "Girl, you a virgin in so many ways, aren't you?" She laughed harder when I blushed. "Hang with me, and I'll take care of you."

She selected a glass of light brown liquid for herself, and took my hand, guiding me toward a group of people dancing near a table, on which sat speakers, a CD player, and a mixer. A guy moved around behind the set, wearing big block earphones as he kept the music spinning.

Kat pulled me into the middle of the crowd and lifted her glass as she whooped and moved to the beat. I stood frozen, unsure of what to do. I danced, but not to music like this. I didn't know how and would look like an idiot if I tried. My body refused to move that way.

She noticed my hesitation and nudged my hip with hers. "Come on, Gabby. Move. You can move."

"Not like this."

"Sure, you can. You just need to loosen up." She danced around, her hips circling and her shoulders swaying to the music. "Do what I do."

I watched in awe, wishing I could dance the same way, unguarded and carefree. But I'd be stiff and awkward, and I didn't want to embarrass myself. I laughed and shook my head. "I'll leave the dancing to you, and that way I won't scare anyone away."

Kat gave another laugh of hers, and the next thing I knew, Danny was standing in front of me. Pleasant surprise lit within me and I beamed, but then I noticed his deep scowl and the bottle of liquor he held, and my smile fell.

"What are you doing here?" he asked.

"I came with Kat and her friends. What are you doing here? I thought you were recording."

"Baby, this isn't a place for you," he said, ignoring my question.

I frowned. "If you can be here, why can't I?"

"It isn't safe. Come on, baby, I'll take you home."

I planted my feet and resisted his tug. "Danny, I don't understand why I can't be here. If it isn't safe for me, then it isn't for you either."

"Yeah, D. Leave her alone." Kat clamped her mouth shut when he shot her a menacing glare.

"Don't be mean to Kat. She's done nothing wrong."

He took hold of my arm and pulled me away from our audience, taking me outside. When we were out of earshot, he spun back. "You shouldn't be here."

"Why? I didn't mean to intrude on your night out with your friends. I didn't know you'd be here since you told me you would be recording." I raised an eyebrow at him, wondering why he would lie to me.

"No, baby, that's not it." He gave a quick shake of his head. "It isn't safe here. The crowd here isn't one you should be around."

"But it's okay for you to be here?"

"This is my crowd!"

I took a step back. "Are you ashamed of me? Do I embarrass you?"

His eyes widened and then he gave a sharp shake of his head. "What? No, baby. God, no. It's nothing like that."

"Then what is it?"

"Just like I said, it's not safe here for you. Shit always goes down at these parties."

"Like what?"

"I don't know...shit." He scrubbed his hands over his face. "It doesn't take much for people to start beating on each other, or for guns to be pulled."

"Oh," I said, catching on. I was quiet again, studying him. He looked... odd. "What's wrong with your eyes, Danny? Why are they so red?"

He averted them and waved his hand. "It's okay. There's nothing to worry about."

"Are you on something? Are you doing drugs?"

He sighed. "It's only pot. It's nothing."

I stumbled in surprise, for some reason believing he stayed away from drugs. I thought he understood what was best for him, and would do whatever to keep his reputation clean if he wanted to make it big in the music industry; which was ridiculous, given the environment in which he lived, but I'd held onto that confidence in him.

Now, to have my belief shattered in my face, left me uncertain. Danny was a good person at heart, but sometimes made the wrong decisions. I would never tell him how to live his life, but perhaps I could steer him in the right direction.

"You shouldn't—"

"I don't need a fucking lecture, G." He pinned me with a sharp glare. "It's just weed, that's all."

My chin came up at his tone. "It may be nothing to you, but it's something to me. I don't want to be around you when you're on it."

I turned, and his hand shot out and grabbed me, pulling me back in front of him.

"Don't do that. Don't walk away."

"Then don't get snippy with me. I'm only worried about you."

"I know, and I appreciate it, but it's not a big deal."

"Then you won't mind not doing it, if it isn't a big deal," I pressed, holding my ground.

He paused before shaking his head, a slight curve playing at his lips. "Fine. I won't do it, if it means that much to you."

Surprise filled me at his quick concession. "Really?"

"Yeah." He put his arms around my waist and pulled me closer. "You're way more important than that stuff."

A warm glow radiated within me at his words. "That's nice to hear. Thank you."

"It's the truth." He moved in, his mouth mere inches from mine, making my heart trip in my chest from anticipation. "You're my girl, G, and I'd do anything for you. Anything."

My arms circled around his neck as his lips settled on mine. The malt, almost gasoline-like flavor of his drink filled my mouth, but I didn't mind, However, when Danny jerked away, I tensed. "What?"

He grimaced. "You taste like Kool-Aid, girl. It's awful."

I smacked my lips against his. "You don't taste too hot yourself."

He smiled before pulling me back to him. His mouth caused me to melt under his touch, as I always did when he kissed me this way, his tongue sliding against mine. Our breathing hardened as we deepened the kiss and tightened our hold on each other before a purposeful cough interrupted us.

Danny broke away, but kept me tight against him, and spotted Big T standing on the small porch watching us.

"You comin' back in, D?"

"Yeah, we're coming. One sec." When Big T remained where he was with a grin, Danny raised his brow. "You mind?"

"Oh, sorry, my man." He winked at me before he walked back through the door.

I giggled and ducked my head as my face flamed in embarrassment.

Danny smiled. "I love the way you blush."

I scowled, still humiliated at being caught making out. "I hate it. I blush at everything."

"That's what I love about you. My little innocent GE."

"I can't keep up with all the names you call me."

"I go with what I feel and right then, you were my light again."

I shook my head, but continued grinning. "You're crazy."

"About you." He leaned down and kissed me again. "Come on, let's go back."

I followed him into the house and to the corner where he and his friends were hanging out.

"Hey, girl," they murmured as I waved.

Danny moved across the room toward the couch and sat, pulling me onto his lap, causing Dollar to raise a brow, but neither said anything. I worried I was coming between them, but he had assured me they worked out whatever disagreement they had. Noticing the disgust on Dollar's face, however, I wasn't so sure.

The guy manning the DJ station stepped into the room. "How about giving us a little something, D?"

"Nah, man. Not tonight."

"Come on, D. You need to do this, get your name out there," Dollar encouraged.

"Yeah, I want to see you do your thing," I added.

Everyone around, overhearing this exchange, joined in, pushing and urging, and he sighed in concession. "Okay! All right, all right. Calm the fuck down." He took me with him into the front room and, letting go of my hand, grabbed a microphone.

"Hit me with bass, Kev."

He was amazing, freestyling and throwing out words in what seemed like impossible rhymes. He spit them without hesitation, and I marveled at the speed in which he relayed them, bending the verses to fit the beat, lyric and music becoming one, and the clarity in which he whipped through them. Back and forth, he moved with confidence, in sync with the heavy bass as he laid it all down, and the crowd cheered and swayed with him.

I had never seen him perform in front of others, and it was natural for him; nothing forced or uncomfortable. He pulled the audience into the song with him, even though they didn't know the words, but it didn't matter. This was what he was destined to do.

His language was colorful—more than usual—using slanderous terms that made me flinch, but I understood it was part of the hip-hop culture. I tried not to let the sexual innuendoes bother me, but my cheeks flamed, exposing my discomfort. They were not words I would ever utter, but I couldn't fault him. In his music as he told a story was one thing; toward me was another, which he would never do.

When he finished, he kept his face neutral despite the loud cheers as he pushed his way through the crowd. I beamed and clapped my hands as he crossed the room, people patting his back as he passed.

I threw my arms around his neck. "You were unbelievable!"

He broke into a crooked grin and kissed me. "I'm glad you liked it."

"Liked it? Danny, you were amazing!"

We returned to where Big T and Dollar waited for us, but then Danny turned and gave me a quick kiss. "I'll be right back. I'm going to get a drink." He looked toward Dollar and Big T, hitching his chin in my direction, and they both nodded.

My gaze followed him as he crossed the room, disappearing into the kitchen, before catching Dollar observing me, mistrust clear in his eyes.

"Is there a problem?" I asked.

He continued to eye me before shaking his head and smiling, but the smile was anything but friendly. "I'm wondering what a girl like you sees in a guy like him."

Despite my unease, his insinuation irked me. "And what exactly is a 'girl like me'?"

"Nice and sweet. Refined. You refined. He ain't."

"Refined? You make it sound like I'm stuck up."

He raised a brow, but he didn't expand.

"Like I told Danny, I'll tell you. It's dangerous to make assumptions about people because of how they look. Would you like me to do the same with you?"

Big T laughed and shook his head. "She got you there, Dollar."

He continued to eye me, but then his gaze sharpened at something over my shoulder. A hand gave my behind a friendly slap, and I jerked.

"There's my girl. I've been looking all over for you."

I turned and gazed up into the leering smile of Terrell.

Chapter 19

~ Gabrielle ~
Six Years Earlier

I jumped back and bumped into the wall, the breath in my lungs clogging. My heart rate skyrocketed, and shivers of fear slithered through me when the immediate room quieted, everyone focused on Terrell and me. The way he eyed me, a lion ready to pounce on its prey, triggered chills to course through me, commanding me to turn away, but I remained fixated; a deer in headlights, frozen and unable to escape.

His gaze took its time traveling over the full length of me before he broke into a wicked grin and licked his lips. "Girl, you can clean up. I can't wait to taste you all over."

Dollar stepped up with Big T, creating a human barrier in front of me.

"Hey now, Terrell, that ain't cool, man," Dollar said in a placid tone.

"No, what ain't cool is you interrupting us." Two of Terrell's crew flanked him. The group eyed each other, waiting for someone to make the next move.

I cowered behind Big T, thankful his size kept me out of view, but still longing to disappear. The tension oozed throughout the house and everyone stopped to witness the exchange. Kat stood across the room, the color drained from her face and her eyes bright with fear, and I tried to figure out a way to get to her side without being noticed, but then turned back when Terrell spoke again, his tone indicating he was losing patience.

"Why don't you two move the fuck out and let me talk to the lady."

"The lady's not interested." Big T refused to budge.

"Not interested?" Terrell repeated with a snicker. "Why don't you let her speak for herself?" He peered over the meaty shoulder of Big T to leer at me, and I shrunk away.

Danny's voice entered the mix. "Back off, Terrell."

A new fear, this time for his safety, had my skin flushing hot then cold. "Danny, don't!" I reached out to stop him, forgetting my wish to stay out of Terrell's field of vision, because all I cared about now was keeping Danny out of the situation. But Dollar grabbed my arm and pulled me back, his eyes warning me to keep silent.

Terrell spotted Danny and clapped his hands. "My good friend, D. I was wondering where your white ass was."

Danny situated himself in front of Big T and Dollar, eyeing Terrell and ignoring the two thugs behind him. "This is between you and me. Keep her out of this."

"Out of this?" He stepped closer, reducing the gap between them. "She right smack in the middle of this shit."

Danny didn't back down. "Stay away from her."

"Says who?"

"Says me."

"I think she should decide for herself." Terrell flicked his head in a signal, and hands yanked me out from behind Big T, who reached for me at the same time. I gasped as they stretched my arms like a scarecrow.

Danny grabbed my waist and pulled me away from everyone, wrapping his arms around me. His head whipped around as his gaze bounced from face to face in the small house until he spotted Kat. He hitched his head, and she hesitated, debating, before pushing her way through the crowd. When she was close, he shoved me at her. "Get her the fuck out of here!"

"Wait!" I attempted to wrench out of Kat's tight grasp. "No, Danny—"

"Go!" he shouted at me before he turned back to Terrell, stopping him in mid-pursuit after me by grabbing him by the collar, which prompted Terrell's crew to jump on Danny. Big T and Dollar entered the fray, and fists flew while bodies slammed together as people parted, giving them room to brawl.

Just as Kat shoved me out the front door, a gunshot rang out. We both screamed and flinched at the sound before scampering out of the way of the stampede.

"Oh my God!" Stone cold terror flowed through me as I imagined Danny sprawled on the floor in a pool of blood with a bullet lodged in him. "I've got to go back in there!" I tried to push through the swarm, but got nowhere.

Kat pulled on me. "No, Gabby! No!"

"I have to make sure Danny's okay," I wailed, jerking out of her hold.

She yelled at me to come back, but I pushed forward, my blind efforts fruitless as the emerging wave of people crashed against me, preventing any forward progress. Frustrated, scared out of my mind, and exhausted, I refused to give up, convinced Danny was in trouble and needed me.

The wail of police sirens caught my attention as two squad cars pulled up on the street. They shone their spotlights on everyone milling in front, and everybody ran. One officer emerged from his cruiser and trotted toward the house as he yelled into the radio on his shoulder, but his presence didn't stop my determination to find Danny first.

The surrounding crowd dissipated, allowing me room to move, but a hand grabbed my upper arm and forced me in the opposite direction.

"Let's go." Danny led us through the bushes separating the house from its neighbor, and over to the next street.

Relief washed through me. "Danny! Are you all right?"

"Just move, G."

We got into his car parked down the block, and he pulled away from the curb. I studied his profile as he drove, and apart from a bloody cut above his eye and another on his chin, he didn't appear to have any life-threatening wounds. It was then I remembered the pistol he carried.

"Was that you who fired the gun?" I was uncertain if I wanted the answer.

He glanced at me, but didn't respond and kept driving, the streetlights passing his face in and out of darkness. We rode in silence until he pulled into the park we frequented and turned off the car. He slouched in his seat and exhaled deep before turning in my direction.

"Are you okay?"

"Me?" My voice was thin and rose with the fear tremoring throughout my body. "I'm not the one who got jumped!"

He shrugged as he fingered the cut on his head and peered at the blood left on his fingers. "That wasn't anything."

I gaped at him. "That wasn't anything? Danny, you could have been killed!"

He said nothing and continued to probe around his face, taking inventory of his wounds. I grabbed his hand, stopping him, and forced him to look at me. "Did you fire the gun, Danny?"

"And if I did?"

"Someone could have been hurt. You could have been hurt, or worse."

"I didn't aim at anyone. It was the only way to stop everything. It was the only way, G," he repeated, seeing my skepticism.

Danny, lying on the floor, surrounded by blood, with a gunshot wound to his head flashed in my mind and I rested against the headrest with my eyes closed. I shuddered at the terror of the mental image, horrified how close it had become to being real. "I thought you were dead."

"Hey." He reached out and pulled me into his arms. "I'm not dead. I'm right here, baby."

"I'm not built for this. I was scared out of my mind."

"That's what I keep trying to tell you. That's why I didn't want you at the party. Shit like this always breaks out." He leaned back and forced me to make eye contact. "This is the way things are around here. It's the way things are with me. I keep trying to tell you that."

"I don't know how you handle it—"

"It doesn't matter about me. What matters is you, and if you want to stick around or not. It's not going to change."

The back of my throat burned and my heart ached at the notion of not seeing Danny anymore, not being with him. Even with the tiny voice of reason insisting I remove myself from the situation, arguing everything would only get worse from here, I rebuffed any suggestion to being without him.

"I'm not going anywhere." Frustration etched his face and panic flooded me. "Do you want me to go away?"

"What? No," he claimed, and I heard the truth in his voice. "The last thing I want is to not be with you, but it worries me having you around this. What if I'm not around to protect you, you know?"

"I don't understand why I would need protection. Why would anyone care about me? I'm nobody. Unless..." I paused and eyed him. "Is there a reason Terrell keeps bugging me?"

A curtain dropped over his eyes and he hesitated, as if weighing what to say. He gave me a smile, which failed at genuineness. "Because you're hot as shit, baby. He's jealous he can't have you all to himself."

"Danny, I'm serious. What's going on?"

"Don't worry about it. There's nothing going on."

"Danny..."

"I'm serious." He dropped a quick peck on my nose. "He's just an ass who needs to be reminded of that. He'll leave you alone now."

I attempted to read between the lines, but couldn't decipher any meaning from what he let me see. I trusted him with my life and believed he would do anything in his power to protect me; so, if the situation with Terrell were critical, he wouldn't hide it from me.

I sagged against him, exhaustion replacing my dropping stress level. "I'm glad you're okay, and I'm glad you were there."

~ *Danny* ~

I closed my eyes and leaned my head back on the headrest, grateful she wasn't pushing things further. My heart raced, and fear mixed with hot adrenaline pounded through me, making something basic like breathing difficult. I was thankful I'd been there too because I didn't want to think about what Terrell would have done to her if I hadn't been. I didn't want to know what Terrell was planning to do to her, now that he knew she was with me.

I should do the right thing, and the right thing would be telling her the truth about Terrell and getting her away from me. Tell her that her safety was in jeopardy because of me and walk away without a backward glance. But I couldn't. If she knew the truth, knew that I'd once considered joining Terrell's gang, had once hung among them, she would fear me as she did Terrell. She would think less of me, pity me that the only family I could have had—might have secretly wanted—was a gang, and I couldn't have that or go back to life without her.

Things between us had intensified, and we could never be without each other. To do so would be a slow, painful existence. She was my heart, my blood, the air in my lungs, the light of my life, and any other fucking cheesy thing I'd ever heard. I'd never believed people felt that strongly about another, but I did now. Soul mates and all that, and now, after finding mine, I refused to turn away, even if doing so was the best thing for her.

So, I'd keep quiet and do whatever possible to keep her safe until we got out of there. I'd keep my ear to the ground to head off anything before it started. She had to remain untouched, even if it meant me dying. Her safety and her happiness were all what mattered. Nothing more, nothing less.

Chapter 20

~ Gabrielle ~
Present Day

I walked through the back door after dropping off Dani at a dance camp her father had paid for, and dumped my purse on the kitchen island, relieved to find the room empty. I never knew what I would encounter in Danny's house. There always seemed to be an endless party going on—big groups of people hanging around doing a lot of nothing, at all times of the day.

Danny's troubles with drugs and alcohol were no secret, both contributing to his "bad boy" image the critics used to prove why he was such a horrible influence, along with his controversial lyrics. I was sure some of the reports were true; I'd witnessed him drinking and smoking pot when we were dating, but he had never appeared to be out of control. Perhaps with the new lifestyle came harder drugs, ones more difficult to shake.

His recovery was supposedly successful. I hadn't seen any evidence of him being under any influence of anything, but maybe after Dani and I turned in for the night, he partied. I'd never seen him hanging out, but truth be told, I knew little of what he did throughout the day. For the most part, he disappeared, and then reappeared out of the blue to spend time with Dani.

I hated whenever his friends were around. The girls glared at me, making snide remarks under their breath, and one girl even accused me of falsifying Dani's paternity to get at Danny's money, which was amusing, since anyone who wasn't blind could see he was her father. Put him in pigtails and they were almost twins.

Whoever they were and for whatever reason they hung out all the time, their constant presence gave me pause when I thought about letting Dani stay the night at her father's house once we moved out. I wouldn't expose her to that behavior, especially if I wasn't around to shelter her from it; even if he was her father.

Opening the fridge, I scanned the contents for something to eat for breakfast before plopping in front of the computer to continue my daily job search, since I had time to kill before meeting my mother and sister, who were both in town, for lunch. I cringed when someone trudged into the kitchen, afraid the group had wandered in from some other part of the house, despite the early hour, and I regretted my plan. When I closed the door and turned, however, it was only Danny.

All assumptions about him partying during the night appeared to be true as I took in his appearance. He looked worse for the wear with his short hair flattened against his head, and his eyes red and bloodshot. He hadn't shaved, and the stubble only accentuated the gray pallor to his face. The way he squinted at me, I guessed he had a monstrous headache.

"Hey," he said, his voice barely above a whisper. "She get off okay?"

"Yes. You all right?"

He shrugged, but said nothing as he opened the cupboard and pulled down a mug before walking over to the coffeemaker.

I remained silent, watching as he doctored his coffee with sugar and cream before taking a hesitant sip. He winced, but followed with another drink, as if trying to inject the caffeine into his system as fast as possible.

"Danny?"

"What?" He slouched down at the kitchen island and rubbed at his temples.

I stood right next to him, and up close, his coloring was worse. "What are you on?"

He scowled. "What do you mean, what am I on?"

"Danny, I'm going to ask one more time. What are you on?"

His eyes narrowed. "I'm not on fucking anything."

"Oh, really? Is this the way you look every morning?"

"You trying to say I look like shit or something?" His lips quivered as he wavered between trying not to smile and grimacing in pain.

"I'm serious. I will not have Dani here while you're doing whatever drugs you're doing. I heard about all that."

He took a sharp breath through his nose. "And you believe everything you hear?"

"Come on, I'm sure some of it was true."

"Well, then you would have also heard I went to rehab."

I shrugged my shoulders. "Yeah, but that doesn't mean you didn't go right back."

"I'm glad you have so much confidence in me." He turned away, and guilt swept through me. I was just as bad as everyone else, jumping to conclusions when it came to him. My voice stopped him when he reached the threshold of the room.

"Well, tell me what's going on then."

He turned. "You'll believe me?"

"I'll hear what you have to say."

He shook his head and studied the floor. When he glanced up, there was a brief flash of hurt in his eyes before the curtain fell. "You used to believe in me."

I sighed. I wanted to trust him, but I had, and look where that got me—six years of heartbreak and loneliness, all my dreams crushed. "I want to, Danny. Believe me I want to, but this isn't about me. This is about our daughter."

He walked back into the room and stopped in front of me. The color was returning to his face. "I guess it's a start. For now."

I hesitated, unsure what he meant, and tried to read his steely gaze; but like always, he was good at hiding what he was thinking and feeling. "What's going on?"

"I can't sleep, and when I can't sleep, I record. I was up all night, recording."

"Recording?" I frowned. "Where? At some studio?"

"In the basement."

My brows shot up to my hairline. "You have a studio in your basement?"

"Yeah, just a little one. I can't always be going somewhere to record, especially when inspiration hits in the middle of the night."

"So, you can't sleep and you go record, and that's why you look like…" I waved a hand at him.

He smiled. "We can't all be beautiful all the time like you, G."

"Danny..." I rolled my eyes.

"Well, when you don't sleep for fucking, I don't know how many days, yeah, you're going to look like shit, eventually. When you're a recovering addict, they won't give you anything to help you sleep anymore." He rubbed his hair with his hand and took another sip of his coffee.

I studied him, trying to decide if I believed him. When I said nothing, he scowled. "What?"

"What about all the people always hanging around? You're telling me you're not partying with them?"

He snorted. "Fuck no. I told you, those aren't my people."

"Then why are they always here?"

"I don't know. They're friends of friends or something. They come here to hang."

I shook my head, struggling to make sense of everything. "So, you're telling me—" I ticked my fingers, "—you're not doing any drugs, you don't sleep at all, you disappear into a recording studio in the basement, and the people who are always here hanging out, as you say, are not your friends and you don't know why they're here. Did I get everything right?"

"Yeah, that sounds about right."

I threw up my arms. "Why would you want random people here all the time?"

He shrugged. "Why not? They're somebody's friends. The house is big enough. You have a problem with it?"

"Well, yeah; not that it's any of my business, but I have a problem with it. Dani doesn't need to be around that. Some of them seem to be... inappropriate."

"Okay. They're gone."

"Wait, Danny." I put my hands up, attempting to keep up with him. "This isn't my house, and this isn't for me to decide. I'm simply telling you I don't want Dani around it. If they can find another time to hang out or whatever—"

"No. You're right. They don't need to be here. I've got a family now, and that's what this house will be used for."

I frowned and tried to understand what he was getting at, which became clearer when he placed his mug on the counter and cleared his throat.

"I wanted to talk to you..."

My heart flipped into panic mode and I stepped back. He could only want to discuss two things—a custody agreement for Dani, or give me some lame excuse about the horrible night when he ripped me apart in front of the world, and by his expression, it was the latter.

"I've got to go." I reached around him to grab my purse. "I'll be back later," I called out over my shoulder before rushing out the door.

I sat in my car with my hands gripping the steering wheel, and took a deep breath. There was no way I was ready to have that conversation with him, and I probably never would. As much as I wanted answers, it would kill me to relive that night, and hear whatever weak justification he might try to give me.

It was time I got out of there.

* * *

I walked into the restaurant and glanced around. When I spotted my sister and mother in the back corner, I smiled with a wave and weaved my way through the tables before pulling them both into big hugs. Now that they both lived elsewhere, I didn't see them a lot, and I missed them. We tried to get together at least once a month to catch up, or whenever Monica came into town, but the time was always too short. This visit, they'd miss Dani, much to everyone's dismay, since she was attending the dance camp.

"How are things in Chicago?" I asked Monica.

"They're good." She glanced between our mother and me. "Michael and I are moving in together."

"Oh wow! That's great," I said as Mom reached over to hug her.

"I'm so happy both of my girls have found such nice men."

"Yeah." I shifted in my chair and dropped my eyes. Then the waiter arrived to take our orders, saving me.

Monica waited until the server left before turning back. "Spill it."

I smiled. "Never could hide anything from you."

"What's going on, Gabby?" Mom asked, her faced etched with concern. "There isn't trouble with you and Brad, is there?"

"Uh." I cleared my throat. So much had changed that I had no idea how I would dump everything on them. "Yes, actually, there is. I left him, and I've moved out."

"What?" my mom said in alarm. "Where are you living?"

"Ah, yeah. That's the funny part." I chuckled and scratched my head. "I'm living with Danny."

"Danny who?" Mom asked, not catching on.

"Oh no," Monica groaned. "What the hell are you doing, Gabby? How did you even get back in touch with him?"

My mother caught up and gasped. "No! Don't tell me you are back with that horrible man!"

I scowled. "He's not a horrible man, and I'm not back with him. It's a long story how our paths crossed again, but he was kind enough to offer us a place to stay while I figured things out, so he could spend time with his daughter."

"You told him about her?" Monica asked.

"Of course, I did. She's his daughter. He has a right to know her."

"Well, he didn't want to when you were pregnant."

"According to him, he never saw our texts or anything."

"Oh, baloney," Mom huffed and took a drink of her water.

"I believe him," I told them, ignoring their twin scowls of disbelief. "You didn't see his face when he found out. He was shocked."

"Of course, you're going to believe him," Monica said. "He can do no wrong in your eyes. Did you forget what he did to you?"

"No, I didn't forget." I was tired of defending my decisions and him. "I understand how you guys feel about him and why, but I've decided I want Dani to have her father in her life, and since he wants to be, I will do all I can to help their relationship grow. What happened between me and him is in the past, where it will stay."

"Gabby, honey, he isn't safe," my mom pleaded. "You hear all the time about the horrible things he says in his songs. Plus, all his issues with drugs and stuff. He's no good."

"Mom," I said in exasperation. "I've told you this before; that's his music. It's an act, an alter ego, if you will, based on things he's witnessed. He doesn't believe those things. It's part of the hip-hop culture. Both of you conveniently forget how you once invited him into our home, treated him like family, and were curious about him and his music. You weren't worried about safety then."

"What about the drugs?" Monica asked with a raised brow.

"He finished rehab and cleaned himself up."

"And that's it? Everything's good?"

"No, everything isn't good, but he works hard every day, and he will continue to. He wants to do what's right for Dani, and he knows if he screws up again, I won't let him be around her." I saw the doubt on their faces and sighed. "Give him a chance. That's all I ask, and all I'm doing. He deserves that, if nothing else. You don't see him with her. He loves her like crazy, and she's nuts about him. He would do anything for her."

They sat in silence for a moment before Monica asked, "What about you?"

"What about me?"

"How are you handling being around him again?"

"I'm fine," I lied. "It isn't about me anyways; it's about Dani."

"You're okay with seeing him every day and not knowing why he did what he did?"

I swallowed past the tight lump in my throat. "It doesn't matter, Monica. It was so many years ago."

"But you're still not over him," she stated.

I met her gaze. "It doesn't matter. Dani is what matters."

"So, you'll suffer in silence for her?" She reached out to squeeze my hand.

"Yes," I said, and squeezed back. "It's all I can do."

Chapter 21

~ Danny ~
Six Years Earlier

Big T and I walked into the opulent theater, an old and famous landmark deep in the city, ignoring the curious glances tossed our way due to the stark differences in our cheap clothes to the suits and dresses of everyone else. The performance of *The Nutcracker* wasn't the usual draw for the likes of us, but since my girl was the star of the show, there was no way I was going to miss it. Big T had begged to come along, wanting to support Gabrielle, and I was grateful for the silent backing.

We walked down the main aisle to our row, spotting Monica and Mrs. Wells already sitting in their seats. They stood when we came up to them.

"Hi, Danny." Mrs. Wells gave me a hug. "I'm so glad you could make it."

I hesitated, uncomfortable with the display of affection, but made myself relax, thankful for the acceptance, even though I hadn't realized I cared about receiving approval. "I wouldn't have missed it for the world, Mrs. W. Hey," I said to Monica as she waved. I gestured over my shoulder. "This is Big T. T, this is G's mom and her sister, Monica."

"It's so nice to meet you. I'm sure Gabrielle is thrilled to have you here." Her mom gave him a big smile as she shook the meaty hand he extended to her.

"I'm excited to see her do her thing." Big T looked around, taking in the old theater still standing proud in the heart of the city amongst the empty shells of its neighbors. "This place is awesome."

Gabrielle's mom stared down at the small bouquet I held in my hand with an odd expression, and I felt foolish for the gesture. "I thought she might like them…" I scratched my head and shrugged.

Her eyes flew up to mine and she smiled, but it seemed forced. "She'll love them. It's sweet of you."

As we took our seats, waiting for the house lights to fall announcing the start of the performance, Big T leaned over and whispered, "Your girl's on the big stage before you, dawg."

"She deserves it. I don't…yet."

"Do you guys know the story of *The Nutcracker*?" Mrs. Wells asked.

"Not really."

"Gabrielle is the lead, Clara, so you'll see her a lot through the show, but I think she's danced almost every part." She glanced back at Monica for confirmation. "She did an amazing job when she was the Sugar Plum Fairy, which was her best performance to date."

A strange look passed between her and Monica, but I didn't have a chance to ask about it when music swelled out of the orchestra pit and the lights dimmed, drawing my attention to the stage. The heavy velvet, dark burgundy curtains rose, revealing a party scene in a large mansion. People of all ages danced around a huge Christmas tree, and then Gabrielle stepped into view and my breath caught in my throat. She wore a simple white dress with matching tights and toe shoes. Her hair, pinned away from her face, was loose in back, curling in big waves down past her shoulders, and the light caught all the different shades of blonde.

Even from a distance, she was stunning, a beautiful vision glowing under the bright lights. She smiled and started her performance, and I lost my breath. She was a remarkable sight as she danced around the stage, in one fluid motion after the next, dictating the flow as if the music came from her movements.

I had no idea what the story was about, other than what her mother had relayed, but I didn't care and I didn't want the show to end, wanting to watch her forever. If anyone else was on stage, I didn't see them, only having eyes for her, and my heart filled with pride when the performance ended and the audience gave her a standing ovation as she lowered into a graceful bow at center stage. I clapped along with them and smiled when her mom hugged me again, wiping away tears on her face.

When we emerged into the lobby, Mrs. Wells grabbed my hand and directed me to a hallway running the length of the auditorium toward the back. "Come with us. She'll come out this way when she's finished."

I followed her around the corner and into the mix, where others were already waiting for the performers to exit. The door would open to a scattering of applause and the dancer would smile, and perhaps give a slight bow, before moving off toward their friends and family. I leaned against the wall and waited for what seemed like an eternity, when the door opened and she emerged.

The group erupted into loud claps at her appearance, and even from my distance, I caught her blush, but I stayed where I was, letting her soak in the attention. Gabrielle beamed and bowed her head, but kept walking toward us as the applause trailed in her wake. She hurried over and her mother pulled her into her arms.

"You were wonderful, honey. Absolutely beautiful."

"Thanks, Mom!" She stepped back and hugged her sister before Big T. "Thanks for coming, Teddy. Did you like it?"

"I really did. You were amazing, girl!"

She turned to me, her eyes bright with excitement. I grinned as she walked into my embrace. "You were incredible," I whispered in her ear.

She pressed a light kiss to the side of my neck. "I'm so glad you came."

"Wouldn't have missed it." I pulled back and handed her the bouquet. "Here. These are for you."

A shadow darkened her features before she pushed it aside. She shoved the mixed arrangement under her nose and made a production out of inhaling the sweet fragrance. "Thank you. They're beautiful."

I grabbed her hand, about to ask what was wrong, when her mother interrupted. "Well. Shall we go get a sundae?"

A weird, uncomfortable air settled over the three women, something unreadable passing between them, before Gabrielle took a shaky breath. "Okay."

"It's a tradition," Mrs. Wells told me. "After every one of Gabby's shows, we would get a sundae. She was so nervous to eat beforehand and always wanted ice cream afterward. I hope you two will join us." She glanced between Big T and me.

"Uh," I said, not wanting to intrude on their tradition, but when I caught Gabrielle's eager expression, clearly hoping I would, I nodded. "Sure."

Gabrielle tried to keep up a happy demeanor the whole time, but it fell short. After everyone finished their sundaes, she excused herself, retreating to the restroom at the restaurant, and my gaze followed her, narrowing in concern at her hunched shoulders and bowed head. I considered following, but when her mom sighed, I looked her way and she gave me a wistful smile.

"This is the first show she's done without her father. This was his tradition; to take her to get ice cream afterward." She nodded at the bouquet left on the table. "He was also the one who presented her with flowers. His little ballet princess, he always said to her."

A lump grew in my throat and I sagged in my chair, feeling like a complete ass. "I'm sorry. I didn't know…" I stammered.

"You couldn't have." She squeezed my hand. "You did good, Danny. She loved having you there and getting flowers from you. It's just a little sad for her, that's all."

I appreciated what she said, but I still regretted the fucking stupid bouquet. "Maybe I should try to talk to her…"

She gave me a grateful smile and stood. "That's a good idea. She'll want to be alone with you."

"Uh…" I glanced at Big T, but Gabrielle's mom was already motioning for him to join her.

"Of course, I can take him home." She put her arms around me. "Thank you, Danny. Thank you for being there for my baby."

They left the restaurant, and Gabrielle emerged a few minutes later, stopping right next to the table. "Where did everyone go?"

I helped her into her jacket. "They left. I wanted to be alone with you."

"Oh, okay. Where are we going?"

"I've got this."

I drove to our park and, sticking to routine, we climbed into the backseat. Putting my arm around her, I pulled her close and she snuggled against my side, resting her head on my shoulder.

"You okay, baby?"

"Yeah. I'm just drained. Did you really like it?"

"Like it? Girl, I loved it. You were amazing. I couldn't keep my eyes off you, so I have no idea if everybody else was crap or not."

She chuckled. "They were all good."

"Not as good as you."

"You're biased."

"Damn right, I am." I lifted her chin and seeing the glassy sheen of her eyes tore at my heart. "Come on, baby. Talk to me. Your mom told me about your dad."

She took a shaky breath, struggling with the emotions churning within her, before her face crumpled and the tears spilled out. I said nothing, only pulling her tighter into my arms and holding her as she cried.

"I'm sorry. I didn't mean to upset you with the flowers."

Gabrielle shook her head and peered up at me through bleary eyes. "No, they were beautiful. I loved them. It was just sad, you know."

I nodded as I wiped the dampness from her cheeks, but couldn't stop my scowl, not liking the deep ache building in my chest from seeing and hearing her pain. I hadn't believed I would ever care for anyone like this, but she dragged it out of me and made me feel things I never thought possible. I wanted to do anything I could to erase her hurt or, at the very least, take her distress on as my own burden, but I couldn't. All I could do was be there, listen, and hold her.

"It isn't fair," she was saying. "Not having him here. Why did he have to kill himself? Why did he have to leave us?"

"I don't know, baby." I brushed her hair away from her face, wanting more than anything to have the answers she wanted and needed. "I wish I did."

"I missed him being there. I miss him being here."

Her head dropped as the sobs racked through her, and I gathered her onto my lap, rocking her until her tears slowed and her breathing calmed.

Leaning my head back, I peered down at her. "You better?"

Gabrielle smiled weakly and sniffled. "Yeah. Sorry."

"Don't be sorry. Don't ever be sorry, baby. But don't hide it from me either. I'm here for you, Gabrielle."

She touched her lips to mine. "I'm so lucky to have you."

"Not as lucky as I am to have you."

She smiled again, this time the brightness reaching her eyes, and the ache inside me eased. I hated to see her upset for whatever reason.

"I should get you home."

"I don't want to go."

"Where do you want to go then?"

She caught her bottom lip in her teeth before twisting herself in my lap and wrapping her arms around my neck. "I want to go to your place."

My hands gripped her hips and my dick took notice, even though I needed to back off, telling myself she was in no position to take such a big step after draining herself. "Oh, baby. Come on. Let's not get into that now."

"Fine, we'll stay here. I don't care," she said, before she crushed her mouth down on mine.

~ *Gabrielle* ~

Edgy and impulsive, I needed to reaffirm I was alive. I needed heat and intensity, and Danny kept both locked within him. But I was determined to unleash everything tonight. I was desperate to feel how much he wanted me, how much he loved me.

Shoving his jacket down his shoulders, I caught him off guard and trapped his arms at his side. Something flashed in his expression, but he dampened it. My mouth found his again and my fingers scraped and twisted through his hair.

"Come on, Danny. Stop holding back."

I worked the top button of his jeans as he struggled out of his jacket sleeves once he understood my intent. Before he could stop me, my fingers snaked in and took a hold of his firm length outside his boxers, and he hissed in a breath.

Hands free, he grabbed at mine, attempting to pry me away. "Slow down, baby. There's no rush—" My mouth cut off his words.

When I tugged him down, pulling him on top of me in the backseat, he resisted, but I still got him over me, even though he locked his arms on either side of my head and kept himself upright. He closed his eyes with a sharp inhale before opening them again, the blue of them dark with desire. "You've got to stop, Gabrielle. You don't know what you're asking for."

His slip on his tight control was right there, I could see it, almost within my reach, and I wasn't going to give in. I gave him a sly smile, bold and brazen. "I know what I'm asking for and I want it." I stroked him again.

It was as if his eyes went black. In one second, he went from restraint to blindness. I didn't have time to question my decision before he was on me.

He was all over, suffocating and grabbing at everything, as his full weight pressed down on me. I smiled; this ravishment, this possession, this was what I needed, feeling more alive than I could remember.

His hands threaded into my hair to yank down, grazing his teeth against my exposed neck. He pulled hard, causing me to wince before jerking my mouth to his. He kissed me and kissed me, biting kisses before soothing with his tongue, until I was sure my lungs would burst. Arching my back, I rubbed against him to relieve the pressure building, but it wasn't enough, and I wrapped one leg around his waist, pinning him closer. He rolled his hips, a glorious sensation building from the movement.

He moved down, pulling my jeans with him. Yanking off a shoe, he removed my jeans, one leg at a time, and leaned forward, placing a hot, open-mouthed kiss where my underwear covered me. I jerked upright, mortified to have him so close.

He clamped a hand on my shoulder and pushed me down. "Just relax. Jesus, you smell amazing. I can't wait to taste you."

"But—"

He shushed me and hooked his fingers into my panties, discarding them. I closed my eyes and swallowed, covering my face.

When his tongue made a swipe across me, I almost jumped off the bench. I fought against the urge to move away from his mouth, and told myself to enjoy it, but my mind was going a mile a minute, detailing all the things to be embarrassed about. He continued to make soft, unhurried passes, back and forth, and I relaxed, my brain slowing from its turmoil.

When he set focus to one spot and sucked gently before rolling his tongue, the pressure within me skyrocketed and I squirmed with a gasp, needing to move and needing his mouth to continue whatever it was doing. He remained where he was, continuing his concentration, and I broke, splintering into a thousand pieces as I cried out and gripped his hair, holding him in place while I writhed and ground against him.

Collapsing back down, my limbs were loose and languid, and a pleasant warmth filled me from head to toe. Danny rose over me, unbuttoning his jeans. He pulled them down, but when his eyes caught mine, he stopped, and his whole body stiffened.

"Fuck," he muttered and shifted, sitting up. "What the fuck am I doing?"

He ran his fingers through his hair and let out a deep breath. Glancing over, he tugged at my clothes, a disheveled, tangled mess around me. "Put yourself back together."

"Danny—"

"I'm serious, Gabrielle. Just don't." His tone left no room for argument.

I frowned and scooted up, trying to right myself, and kept my eyes on him as I buttoned my shirt and tugged my jeans and underwear back on, but he gazed out the side window, refusing eye contact with me.

I shuddered in a breath. "Please don't ignore me. Please don't be mad at me."

He exhaled on a hiss as he shook his head. "I don't fucking get it. Why do you keep pushing it?"

"Why don't you want me? Why do you always push me away?"

His eyes widened in disbelief. "You think because I won't have sex with you in the car that I don't want you? I tell you all the time how much I love you and how I can't live without you."

I swallowed, and I dropped my voice to a whisper. "You won't leave me if you sleep with me..."

His head whipped around. "What?"

"You won't leave..."

Danny stared at me, his face full of shock before he turned toward me. "You think, if I don't sleep with you, that I will leave you? Why the fuck would you think that?"

"I don't know! I can't bear the thought of losing you, so I want to do all I can to keep you happy."

"Baby, it's me holding off, not you."

"I know, but I don't understand why you would with other girls, and not me. Maybe there's a reason you don't want me—"

"Stop right there." He grabbed my shoulders. "There is no other reason than the fact I love you more than anything, and I want it to be special for you. That's it."

"But it's not happening. What are you waiting for?"

"This is the most bizarre fucking conversation I've ever had," he muttered before looking back at me. "I have it all planned out, baby. Trust me, I do."

"You do?"

"Yeah, I do. Girl, believe me I'm as eager for this as you are, but I want it to be dope, all right? You're better than a quick fuck in a car. I keep telling you that."

I launched myself and threw my arms around him. "I'm sorry."

"It's going to happen, believe me. I want to more than you can know." He pulled back and grimaced when he noticed a red mark on my neck where he had nipped me too hard. "Christ, I hurt you."

"It's okay. I liked it… needed it…" My face warmed.

He frowned. "Needed it?"

"I needed to feel alive. I needed to feel what you feel for me."

"Jesus, G. I could have hurt you."

I pulled myself onto his lap. "You didn't, though. You could never hurt me. I need all of you, Danny."

He closed his eyes. "You don't need the ugly."

"Yes, I do." I smiled and nudged him so his eyes would open. "I love all of you—the good and the ugly."

"I don't like being out of control around you, baby. It scares me. I don't want to hurt you."

"You don't scare me."

"Yet."

I shook him again. "Stop it. I'm telling you, Danny. Nothing you ever do or say will scare me. Nothing will make me not want to be with you. Ever." I waited until his gaze caught mine again before lowering my mouth to kiss him. "You own my heart and my soul, Danny. My life is in your hands."

"You can't leave me," he told me.

"You can't leave me."

"Never."

"Never," I agreed.

Chapter 22

~ Danny ~
Six Years Earlier

On Christmas Day, I ate a homemade dinner with Gabrielle's family. On the small kitchen table sat a tiny spread, only what her mother could afford. Even though they kept insisting the meal wasn't much—a ham with mashed potatoes and green beans—it was more than I'd ever had, making me wonder what Christmas had been like for them in their previous life. Something I'd never seen before, that's for sure, but wanted to offer Gabrielle again in the future.

"So how do you go about writing your songs, Danny?" Gabrielle's mother asked. She went out of her way to make me feel comfortable and included, which I appreciated.

I shrugged and took a sip of water. I hated these questions. I never knew how to explain something that happened naturally for me. "Random words or phrases just come to my head that I try to work into beats later."

"He has all these papers so he can write everything down. You should see them. I don't think there's an empty space on any of the pages," Gabrielle said.

"I like to jot it down as soon as it comes to me, so I don't forget."

"And then how do you put it together?" Monica asked. She was quiet around me for the most part, but she'd been warming up, which I was sure was for her sister's sake.

"I have an idea of the mix in my head, so I know what I'm looking for." At her blank expression, I added, "It's hard to explain." I shifted in my chair, uncomfortable with the attention.

"It can't be as easy as you make it sound," she insisted. "I mean, I wouldn't know where to start."

"Of course not," Gabrielle said. "You have to have talent for it, like Danny does. Not just anyone can do what he does. He's amazing."

Eager to get the focus off me, I smiled at her. "Not everyone can dance on their toes and make it look effortless."

Her mother nodded in agreement. "She is wonderful."

"Well, let's hope Juilliard agrees." Gabrielle sighed and turned her attention back to her plate, moving beans around with her fork.

Mrs. Wells gave her a hopeful grin. "They will, and they'll give you a big fat scholarship."

Everyone knew without it, she had no chance of going.

After dinner, I grabbed Gabrielle's hand and pulled her out of earshot. "Do you think we can get out of here?"

"Sure. Let me tell my mom."

She moved over to the small fake, sad-looking tree in the corner, wrapped in one string of white lights and a few ornaments, and gathered two gifts. "Mom, Danny and I are going to head out for a while."

"Okay, honey. Be safe."

"Thanks for the awesome dinner, Mrs. W.," I said.

"Oh, you're welcome, Danny. Anytime. Merry Christmas."

* * *

I drove to the apartment over the garage, my temporary home after the fiasco with my father. I shut off the engine and turned to Gabrielle. "Wait here a second, okay?"

She nodded and waited as I raced up the stairs, disappearing inside, getting everything ready and making a few adjustments. I had it all planned and was excited for our first Christmas together. I hoped she liked what I did.

When she stepped over the threshold, she gasped in surprise, and my insides warmed. Strings of multi-colored lights hung around the doorframes, and there was a small tree with a gold star glowing on the top. Multiple tea lights glowed from every corner of the room.

"Danny, this is beautiful."

I lifted one shoulder, but I loved that she loved it. "It isn't much, but I wanted to do something for our first Christmas."

She smiled as she walked over to the bed, dumping her jacket into the chair. She patted the space next to her. "Come here." I removed the sweatshirt I wore over a plain white T-shirt as I made my way across the room, and once I sat, she handed me a gift. "Here."

"You didn't have to get me anything, baby."

"Of course, I did. Open it." I studied the silver wrapping and red ribbon, overcome by the gesture, and made no move to open it. "Danny, is this your first Christmas present?"

"From anyone who cares about me," I murmured.

She paused, but then she smiled. "It won't be the last. Now open it."

I ripped off the paper covering a book with a leather cover, stamped with the letter "D" in the bottom corner. I fanned through the pages, all of which were blank.

"It's a journal. I figured you could write in this instead of carrying around loose papers. When you fill it up, you can replace the inside with new paper." When I remained silent, staring at the book in my hands, she cleared her throat. "It isn't much, I know, but—"

I cut her off with my mouth. When I pulled away, my voice was rough. "It's perfect." My fingertips trailed over the embossed 'D'. "Thank you."

She smiled, relief and happiness filling her face, and reached behind her. "Well, that's not all."

I shook my head. "No, this is enough."

"Let me spoil you." She took the journal out of my hand and replaced it with the other gift. "Open it."

I sighed before unwrapping a new digital music player, a newer and better model than the one I had before. "You didn't."

"It was my fault your other one broke."

"Gabrielle, it's too much. Take it back."

"Nope. I'm going to do it. Get used to it."

I captured her mouth with mine again, before resting my forehead against hers. "Thank you. I love you."

"I love you too, and you're worth everything. I only wish I could get you more."

"I have you. That's all I need."

She pressed her lips against mine. "You have me."

I sat back to place the gifts on the nightstand next to the bed. Opening the drawer, I retrieved a small box wrapped in red paper and handed it to her.

"Danny, you shouldn't have."

"You can't tell me you can buy me things, but I can't."

"But—"

"No buts, open the damn thing."

She eyed me with one brow lifted before removing the foil paper from the package. When she spotted the logo of a jewelry store, she shook her head and tried to give the box back. "No, Danny. Whatever it is, it's too expensive. Take it back."

"Just open the effing box before I toss you in the snow for being a pain the ass." She grinned, but hesitated and I smiled at her. "Come on. Open it."

She lifted the lid and her mouth dropped open on a silent gasp. Nestled in soft padding was a fragile gold chain necklace with a pendant made of gold lines weaving and winding around each other to form a small circle on which sat sporadically placed chips of rubies and aquamarines.

"It's beautiful."

"It represents our lives. The intertwined lines are our lifelines. The rubies and the aquamarines represent us. They're our birthstones."

"Danny, it's gorgeous. I can't believe you did this. It must have cost a fortune."

I ignored her and pulled the thin gold chain out, fastening it around her neck. "It looks good on you."

"Thank you. I love it."

The candles and Christmas lights draped the room in a hazy hue, and she'd never looked so stunning. "You're so beautiful."

Her breath stuttered as she cupped my cheek, leaning in to touch her lips to mine. I lingered before tilting my head to deepen the kiss. Her arms circled my neck, and I tugged her closer, pressing her chest against me. I reclined, my hands making slow trails down her sides, and with our mouths never parting, I switched our positions, rising above her.

I propped up on one elbow and brushed her hair away from her face. "Are you sure you want to do this?"

Gabrielle nodded, even though her throat moved as she swallowed hard.

My mouth descended on hers again, but this time with more intensity. She pulled my shirt over my head, her eyes feasting on my bare chest. Her fingers lingered over my other tattoos, before moving to the ridges of my rib cage and over my stomach, causing my skin to tighten and raise in goose bumps, and my dick to twitch. My hand traveled up her sweater and she raised her torso so I could remove it, followed by her bra.

She kept her eyes on mine. "I know I'm not big…"

My gaze flew up to hers, and I cupped her in my hand with reverence. "You're perfect," I said before my mouth was on hers.

She let me take her where I wanted to go, willing to follow wherever, and I started slow, but soon we were panting for air, our hands roaming over each other, never hesitating in one spot for long.

I unzipped her jeans and dragged them down her legs. Clothed only in her pink bikini underwear, my eyes skimmed over the length of her, fully laid out instead of crammed into the backseat, and I palmed her strong calves. "I love your legs. They're a fucking mile long."

She reached for my belt, unbuckling it, and once undone, along with the button and zipper of my jeans, she pushed down my pants. I pulled them off the rest of the way before throwing them onto the floor, where our clothes lay in a pile. I extended behind her and drew down the blankets so we could get underneath, before tugging off her panties and my boxers. My fingers brushed over her stomach before touching her, testing her readiness, and when I encountered wet, slick heat, I closed my eyes on a moan as everything in me flamed. I yanked open the drawer to the nightstand, desperate to be inside her, and grabbed a condom, rolling it on as she watched, her eyes wide.

"Are you nervous?"

"No," she said, but her voice was thin.

"Scared?"

"No."

"It might hurt a little."

She nodded, but said nothing more, positioning her legs wider in silent invitation. I situated myself between them, and intertwined our fingers before placing our connected hands over where my heart thudded in a quick rhythm. "I love you, Gabrielle."

"I love you—" She cut off with a gasp when I eased into her, and squeezed her eyes shut. Waiting for her body to adjust around me, she sucked in a breath, and I held still, fighting the urge to move, and trying to ignore how fucking hot and tight she was, sweat breaking out on my skin from the effort.

After what seemed like an eternity, she smiled, pulling me closer for a kiss, and I moved within her.

"It will always be you, no matter what," she said.

"Always," I promised before we lost ourselves in each other.

Chapter 23

~ Danny ~
Present Day

Gabrielle padded down the back stairway, dressed in a snug yellow t-shirt and boxer shorts. She hadn't seen me yet, so I stayed in the dark corner of the kitchen, watching her stroll over to the fridge.

True to my word, the crew had found another place to hang once I told them to move on, and I hoped she realized I was serious when I said this house was for a family—our family. I would do whatever I needed to, whatever she wanted me to, for that to happen. But my attempts at trying to mend things between us were not going as planned, as she had to be avoiding me. It was like she'd memorized my schedule and made herself scarce at the exact moments I was around. She would never be comfortable with me again if we didn't work this shit out, and that would never happen if she continued to evade me.

A few times, we'd ended up alone in the same room, and as soon as I even addressed her, we were interrupted, or she provided a lame excuse why she had to fly out of my presence. Beyond frustrated, I told myself the next time I was alone with her, she wasn't getting away. We would have it out once and for all.

She bent over at the waist, scrounging around in the fridge, and I swallowed hard, taking in her long, golden bare legs, remembering what it had felt like to run my hands up and down them, or have them wrapped around me. I was desperate to touch her, to hold her, but I couldn't make any move until we talked about what had happened between us. Even though she tried to hide the hurt, I saw the pain in her eyes when she thought I wasn't looking. I felt the same way, but hid it better than she did.

It was now or never, and I was going in. It was time we battled it out, and I would ignite the bomb and see where the pieces landed.

Stepping out of the corner, I stood behind her and cleared my throat. She jerked upright in surprise and spun around, almost crashing into my chest.

"Oh, I'm sorry." She attempted to back away from me, but could not move any further because of the refrigerator. "I didn't mean to get in your way."

She sidestepped me, but I stopped her progress by stepping in front of her again. "You're not in my way. I just wanted a bottle of water." I reached over her shoulder and grabbed one off the top shelf, my eyes never leaving her face. She kept her gaze down, refusing to meet mine, so I retreated as I took a drink. "Grab what you want. Don't let me stop you."

"No, it's okay. I'll get out of your way and head up to my room."

I slammed the bottle on the counter behind me and water spewed over the rim. "Why do you always do that?"

Her eyes dropped to the puddle. "Do what?"

"Take off whenever I walk in the room."

"I don't want to be in your way."

"Jesus, G. You're not a guest here. This is your home as much as it's my home. You can come and go as you please. Do whatever you want. Redecorate the fucking place, rip out walls, I don't fucking care."

"This isn't *my* home, Danny."

Not yet, but it will be. I leaned against the counter, studying her. She was fighting not to squirm under my intense study, but was losing the battle as her hands fidgeted. "I want to talk to you."

She nodded, feigning indifference. "Sure. I hope there hasn't been a problem with Dani or me—"

"Stop it. Stop acting like you and Dani are a problem of mine."

She crossed her arms over her chest, her attempt at a protective shield, and looked everywhere but at me. "Fine. What would you like to discuss?"

"You and me."

"You and me? What do you mean? Like custody or something?"

"No." I shook my head and moved closer, pointing back and forth between us. "You and me, what went down."

She paled, and her fingers trembled before she clenched her fists, stopping them. She took a deep breath and stepped away, distancing herself from me, in preparation to flee, as she recited what sounded like a prepared speech. "There's nothing to talk about, Danny. It's the past, where it should stay. We've all moved on and it has no bearing on anything today. So, if that's all, I'll be going up…"

She wasn't escaping again. I planted myself in front of her, blocking the doorway, and she stopped short. "Danny, please move."

"No." I clutched her arms with my hands, noting her skin was cold to the touch. "We've got to do this, G. For Dani, and for us."

She whipped her head back and forth, continuing to stare at the ground, but said nothing.

"Yes," I said.

Spinning away, she jerked from my grasp and sprinted across the kitchen, trying to find escape up the back stairway, but I was quicker and snagged her around the waist, stopping her again. I pulled her tight against my chest and she strained to fight me off.

"Please, let me go, Danny."

I held her as her body trembled, and rested my forehead on her shoulder blade, cursing myself for doing this to her, but there was no way to avoid this part, no matter how painful or bloody. "No, baby, I can't. I'm sorry. We have to do this."

"No, please. I just want to forget it. Please."

She needed to get this out of her system, and I needed to be done with it. We both needed to hash this out so we could move on and start over.

When she stopped fighting against me, I gentled my hold and turned her. I wasn't sure what I'd expected to see on her face, but not the hot, burning fury glowing in her eyes; something I'd never seen from her before. This is what I'd asked for though, so I couldn't back off now. I'd forced her to go back to the past, to relive all the horror. Now I had to deal with whatever the outcome ended up being, with whatever words she threw at me, with whatever she blamed me for. I straightened and prepared myself for the onslaught.

"Let it out, G. Tell me what you're thinking."

Chapter 24

~ Gabrielle ~
Six Years Earlier

Tugging on my jacket, I turned when my ballet instructor said my name. "Gabrielle, honey, your mother called. She's going to be a few minutes late," Mrs. Greiger said.

"Oh." I swallowed the disappointment that I'd have to wait despite being tired and wanting to get home to a warm shower. "Okay, thanks."

I sat in a metal folding chair in the small waiting area, watching the cars as they passed on the street in front of the building. It was dark and cold outside, and I was thankful I didn't have to stand out in it. But Ms. Greiger would be eager to lock up after everyone had cleared out, so I hoped my mother showed up sooner rather than later. I peered out the windows, willing my mom's car to pull up to the curb.

Ten minutes passed, and she still hadn't arrived while the last of my classmates left. Ms. Greiger walked around the studio, turning off the lights, and came to a stop next to me.

"Not here yet, huh?"

"No." I glanced at her. "I can wait outside so you can leave. I'm sure she'll be here soon."

"Oh, no, honey. It's fine. We'll wait," she said, but the tired lines on her face were unmistakable.

I stood and walked to the door. "Really, it's fine. I'm sure you want to get out of here after a long day, and I don't want to keep you any longer. I'll be okay."

She hesitated, but the desire to get home must have won out. Following me outside, she locked up behind us before eyeing me. "Are you sure, honey?"

"Yes. Please go home, Ms. Greiger. I'll be fine." I smiled. "My mom is probably coming now."

She still didn't look at ease, but continued to move toward the parking lot around the back of the building. "Okay. You stay safe and I'll see you tomorrow."

"I will. See you tomorrow."

She rushed down the dark sidewalk, tugging her jacket closed to block the frigid air, and turned the corner out of sight, leaving me alone and exposed. An icy breeze blowing across my face and neck, mixed with fresh panic of vulnerability, made me shiver. I huddled further into my coat and shoved my hands in my pocket, staring up the street with longing.

I bounced from foot to foot, trying to keep warm, and moved closer to the building, hoping to find shelter from the brisk wind. A constant stream of cars buzzed past, but not one slowed with my mom at the wheel. A few minutes later, I noticed noises behind me, and glancing over, my stomach took a violent pitch.

The temperature of the surrounding air plunged as a bone-deep chill of terror raced through me. Eerie silence surrounded me when a sudden break in traffic had the streets empty, without a soul in sight. Paralyzed with fear, I stood frozen, unable to move as the group approached.

"Well, well." Terrell stepped up with a wide grin. "If it isn't the woman I been looking my whole life for."

He stopped in front of me while four others formed a circle, placing me in the center. My gaze jumped from one leering face to another before coming back to Terrell's pleasant-looking expression. It was almost easy to believe he meant me no harm and wanted to be my friend, but I knew that wasn't the case.

My breaths came in short pants as my lungs clamped up, refusing to allow even a puff of air to pass.

"What do you want?" Fright clogged my throat and turned my voice into a breathless squeak.

"It's all you, babe. You hot as shit."

The gleam of maleficent want in his eyes was unmistakable, and I took a hesitant step back, but stopped when I banged into the solid wall of a chest behind me. "Please, leave me alone."

"Now, why would I do that?"

"Please." Tears rolled down my cheeks. "Please."

He stepped forward and leered over me as he fingered the track of moisture on my cheek. "Now, come on, baby. There ain't nothing to cry about."

I tried to turn away from his contact, but the move only pushed me into another body. Even in the cold air, I smelled their mixed odor of sweat, alcohol, and something else; a sweet aroma I couldn't identify. The scents collided and weighed on me, making me want to gag, but I forced myself to breathe through my mouth and ignore the bile rising in my throat. My heart threatened to burst out of my chest, but I recognized I had to fight or else I would never make it out of this mess alive. Somewhere in the back of my head, in the midst of the terror, I wondered where the hell my mother was.

Terrell tugged on my bun, causing my hair to fall around my face, and ran a few strands through his fingers as if they were threads of gold. "Beautiful."

At that moment, the adrenaline of flight rushed through me, giving me a strength I didn't know I had. I ducked and shoved my shoulder into the stomach of the body standing behind me. When he stumbled with a whoosh in surprise, his hand clutching his gut, I attempted to rush past Terrell and the others as they paused in shock. There were too many of them, however, all of them reaching, clawing, and grabbing, to pull me into the alley between the buildings.

I screamed as I hit the sidewalk, but the noise of traffic passing by, out of sight from the alleyway, drowned it out. My head bounced off the hard cement, and bright, colorful stars exploded behind my eyelids. I staggered, dazed by the pain, before resuming my fight against them, thrashing against the hands clutching at me, twisting and contorting, but I was tiring and blackness hovered at the edges.

They surrounded me and one of them pounced on my knee, wrenching it to the side and sending a jagged sting up my leg. Someone else snatched and twisted my ankle, turning my foot further than it ever meant to go, and nausea lurched in my stomach from the fiery pain. With my eyes closed, I couldn't see who came over me, but a heaviness settled on top of me and he ground against me, his foul breath assaulting my face.

When I screamed again, knuckles caught my right eye and a gruff voice told me to, "Shut the fuck up." Someone grabbed my head, holding me in place as I struggled to release myself from his grasp.

"Hold her still," he grunted as the weight shifted and a hand grappled to find the zipper to my pants. A hot, acrid breath panted next to my ear. "If you say anything, your boy Danny is a dead man."

I somehow freed one of my hands and punched out, connecting with the face above me.

"Fuck!"

A fist slammed into my jaw, turning my world black.

~ *Danny* ~

Full of energy after the Christmas I'd spent with Gabrielle, I was happier than I could ever remember being in my whole life, motivating me to complete my demos and send them out, so that she and I could start our lives together.

Dollar and I were working in the back room, experimenting with beats, when I heard what I thought was Big T yelling my name.

I held out my hand. "Hold up, hold up. Turn it off."

We listened and sure enough, Big T's booming voice was calling for me.

He sounded out of breath and frantic, and we frowned at each other. Dollar stuck his head through the doorway.

"What up, T? Where's the food?"

"Where's D?" Big T asked.

I stepped in front of Dollar. "Right here. What's your issue?"

"Come on, man. We've got to go." He put his hands on his knees as he struggled to catch his breath.

I stepped into the hallway. "What the fuck is going on? Why are you out of breath and sweating?"

Big T squinted up at me, his chest still heaving. "It's G, man. Let's go."

I stopped dead in my tracks and went rigid as a sharp, hard edge settled within me. "What about G?"

"What you talkin' about, dawg?" Dollar asked.

"There isn't time to explain." He stood and took a couple steps in the opposite direction. "The ambulance headed that way—"

I flew past him, shoving him aside, and racing out the front door. I drove with tunnel vision toward the ballet studio. The one night I hadn't picked Gabrielle up, something had happened. Where the fuck was her mother? I didn't know what I would discover when I pulled up, but if I didn't find my girl standing with a smile on her face, someone would pay.

Flashing lights surrounded the building in the distance. I counted three police cars, a fire truck, and an ambulance. A growing crowd gathered around the alleyway, gawking at the scene, and I elbowed my way through the mass of people.

I'd left my sweatshirt back at the makeshift studio, but I didn't feel the cold through my thin t-shirt. In fact, I felt nothing, steeling myself for whatever greeted me on the other side of the police tape. I pushed through, and when an officer spotted me, he held out his hand.

"You can't go any further, sir."

I stopped, but stepped from side to side, trying to get a clear view behind the cop, hoping, praying Big T was wrong and it wasn't Gabrielle on the ground. But once my gaze settled on the white tennis shoes and the long legs attached to them, I didn't need to see the rest to know who lay there.

Rage and fear coursed through me, and I broke out in a clammy sweat that flashed hot. I wanted to strike out at anything standing between us, while at the same time wanting nothing more than to sink down next to her and cry my heart out.

Rage won.

I pushed against the chest of the cop in my way. "That's my girl there!"

"Sir, please. Calm down." The officer placed his hands on my shoulders to restrain me.

"Fuck that! Get the fuck out of my way."

The commotion caused others to notice, and somehow over the deafening sound of the fury screaming through my head, I heard my name.

I scanned across the crowd and spotted Gabrielle's mother. Pulling away from the cop, I rammed through the mob toward her, and when I reached her side, she threw herself against me.

"Oh, Danny! I pulled up and she was like this. We don't know what happened to her." She fisted her hands into my shirt. "She won't open her eyes, Danny! She won't open her eyes!"

I didn't offer her any comfort as she sobbed against my chest, her tears soaking the thin fabric. My focus stayed glued on Gabrielle's body as the paramedics worked on her. They were strapping something around her neck and hooking up tubes to her as they arranged her on the gurney. One of the EMTs stepped aside, giving me a clear view.

Dark bruises and blood covered most of her face, in stark contrast to the ghastly pallor of her skin. Her hair fell loose, its healthy hue harsh compared to everything else, and off to the side, her jacket lay shredded to pieces. She looked so fragile and brittle, as if she would break if a feather landed on her. The swelling of her right knee and left ankle was obvious to the naked eye.

Her mother was saying something, but I couldn't hear her. Somewhere in the back of my head, I registered Dollar and Big T yelling my name, but I didn't acknowledge them either. I stood rooted to the ground, deaf to the world as chaos moved around me. The center of my earth lay shattered in front of me, and I felt sick. But more than sick, I felt absolute terror. The rock in my gut told me who did this. This was a message. A message in bright, neon letters, and a message directed right at me.

Worse than that, I'd been wrong; I couldn't protect her. In fact, I'd failed.

Chapter 25

~ Gabrielle ~
Six Years Earlier

I cracked an eyelid and winced at the pain from the bright light. My head throbbed, and my body ached as if I'd survived a hit and run. I swallowed against the cottonmouth sensation and attempted to open my eyes again.

A cool hand touched my arm. "Gabby, baby? I'm here, honey. Mommy's here, baby."

I squinted before opening them further, letting my gaze wander the room before settling on my mom, who sat propped up in her chair, looking at me with anticipation. I tried to turn my head, but something constricted me, not allowing the movement.

"It's okay, honey. Don't move. The brace is there to help your neck." She stood, perching on the edge of the bed so she was in my line of vision, and attempted a smile as she smoothed my hair, but it didn't hide her worry and concern. "What do you need? Do you want water?"

"Yes, please," I croaked, my voice only a whisper.

I sipped out of the straw my mom held for me and closed my eyes at the pleasant sensation of the cool water sliding down my throat. When I reopened them, she was studying me.

"Do you know where you are?"

I tried to nod, but winced from the pain as soon as I moved. "Yes."

"Do you remember what happened?"

At the complete distress on my mother's face, I wished I could keep this from her, but I could not hide the fear and terror that rippled through me as the events replayed in my mind. "Yes."

"Do you know who did this to you? The police will be back to ask you questions."

The threat echoed in my head, Terrell's sinister voice warning me to keep my mouth shut or else he would harm Danny, and a shiver passed through me before I could stop it. I would do whatever needed to protect Danny, even if that meant lying.

"No. It was a group of guys. I've never seen them before."

My mom's face scrunched as her eyes filled with tears. "Oh my, baby. I'm so sorry. If only I hadn't been running late, and then I had a flat tire…" She finished on a sob.

"It's okay, Mom." I reached out to grab her hand. "It's not your fault."

She squeezed my hand tight and shook her head. "Yes, it is. All of this is. Moving here, exposing you to this, being late…everything. All of it is my fault. All of it…I'm so sorry…"

Tears slid down my face. "You were doing what you had to do."

We wept together and left everything else unspoken. Since we couldn't change what my father had done, there was no use in going back. Even after the tears had subsided, we sat in silence before I cleared my throat in preparation for hearing the complete story.

"So, what's broken?"

My mother blew her nose into a tissue and wiped at her eyes. "Well, you most likely have a concussion, along with mild whiplash, and your right knee has a strained ligament since it was hyper-extended. Your left ankle is twisted. Thank God Mrs. Greiger came back when she did, so nothing further happened." She stopped, as if contemplating how much more to tell me before reaching over to the small table beside the bed and grabbing a mirror.

I gasped at my reflection. The stranger looking back at me had an eye surrounded by a riot of colors in vibrant purples, yellows, and greens. Another dark smudge of purple lined my jaw, and several deep red scratches scored the rest of my face. Fresh tears filled my eyes as I studied myself.

"Everything will heal, honey." My mom rubbed my arm, trying to comfort me.

"I know." I leaned back and my eyelids drooped, exhaustion making my whole body heavy. "It's everything. This." I pointed at my face. "My audition for Juilliard. There's no way my knee and ankle will heal in time. The bills for this. How are you going to pay for it?"

"Oh, honey. Everything will be okay. You'll be able to try out another time."

"Mom—"

"Let's focus on getting you out of here first and getting better, and then we'll figure out what we need to do for Juilliard. Okay, baby? One thing at a time. And don't you worry about the bills for this. I'll figure something out. You have nothing to worry about, except getting better."

Overwhelmed, my head swam and everything throbbed even more. The door opened, and a doctor walked in, putting an end to the conversation.

~ *Danny* ~

So much guilt and hatred of myself flowed through me at seeing her lying in the bed, battered and bruised, knowing she was here because of me. But I couldn't stay away either. It was torture to be here, to see her like this, but I had to do it as punishment for my failure.

I watched her until the day turned to night. All the scrapes and scratches that she'd had to endure, the braces that she had to wear on her neck, knee, and ankle seared themselves into my memory. After a while, she opened her eyes. She didn't notice me at first, but then, sensing my presence, she squinted toward the corner where I stood.

"Danny?"

I stepped out from the shadows, but stopped, rigid and tense, almost afraid to approach her, since I had no words of comfort, and could do nothing to take away her pain.

She tried to smile, which made it worse, and held out a hand. "I know I look scary, but come here." When I still didn't move, her bottom lip quivered. "Please, don't do this, Danny. I need you."

She crumbled in front of me, and the weight of her emotions pulled me down. I was fucking useless.

"I don't know what to do," I whispered.

"You don't need to do anything. Just be here with me."

"No! I can't sit here and do nothing! I can't sit here while you suffer."

"What are you saying? Are you saying you can't be around me?"

"No." I ran my hands over my hair before clenching my fists in frustration. "No," I said again, and paced around the room before turning back. "Seeing you laying there makes me want to put my fist through the wall." I took a step closer. "It makes me want to track down the bastards who did this to you and take them out. Gabby, baby." My shoulders dropped, and I returned to the side of her bed, grabbing her hand, the only part of her not black and blue. "You have no idea what it was like to see you on the ground, knowing there was nothing I could do for you; that I'd failed you. I can't forget that. I won't forget that. This is something I can do."

"No. Don't do anything. I know you know who did this, but please, I'm begging you, don't take it into your own hands. I already told the police I didn't know who did this. We just need to get past this, and then we can get out of here, just like you always promised."

"Please don't ask me to sit back and do nothing. Please, don't."

"I couldn't stand it if something happened to you."

My eyes widened. "But I'm supposed to stand this? I'm supposed to handle this happening to you?"

She pulled on my hand, bringing me nearer. "I can handle this more than I can handle something happening to you. Please, don't do anything. I couldn't bear it. Please."

A war raged within me—the need to find release for my anger and the desire to do as she wished, simply because she asked it of me. "This is fucked up," I said as I hung my head. "This isn't right. You shouldn't have lied to the cops."

"I know, I know. Please, Danny, please. Just stay here with me."

I sighed and pressed my lips to her forehead. "I'm not going anywhere, baby. I'll be here until they kick me out, and then I'll be back."

"Hold me, please?"

I sat on the edge of the bed and waited as she adjusted herself before putting my arms around her, being cautious of everything connected to her, careful not to hurt her. I rested my head on the pillow above hers and let out a deep breath.

"Danny? Is there a reason they keep coming after me?"

A rock lodged itself in my throat. *Yes*, I wanted to tell her, *because of me. Paybacks*, I wanted to say, *had made you the perfect target*, but the words wouldn't come out, continuing the lie, even though it was destroying me.

I hated myself. I'd promised never to keep anything from her, but the lie had taken on a life of its own, and it was now out of my hands. I'd lost control of everything, and I had no idea what to do anymore.

"I don't know, baby. I wish I did, but I don't."

* * *

"So, how's your girl?" Dollar asked when he saw me next.

I blew out a breath as I sat in a chair, exhaustion dragging me down. We had planned to meet at the studio to catch up on recording since I'd been spending all my time at the hospital. Big T had yet to arrive.

"She's okay. She's home, but she's still pretty banged up."

"Was it Terrell and his crew?"

I nodded. A look passed between us before I dropped my head in my hands. "I know what you're going to say."

Dollar sank into the seat next to me, the equipment sitting around us forgotten for the time being. "It ain't gonna stop, D."

I leaned back and threw my hands up. "So, what am I supposed to do?"

"You know what you need to do."

I stood and paced. "No. I can't. I *won't*."

"D, it's you they're after. They're using her to get to you, and it's working."

"What do you mean, 'it's working'?"

"They want you to come back at them. Give them an opening, start the war, and you sitting here trying to figure out what you gonna do."

"I can't let them get away with this. They put her in the fucking hospital!"

"That's what I'm saying." He stood in front of me. "They have you exactly where they want you. Terrell still pissed you snubbed him and his boys, and you took away his chance at serious dough; now he's trying to make sure you don't get it either. You do what you thinking about doing...then he wins. Look man, you gotta put space between you two; if nothing else, for her safety."

I blew out a breath and leaned against the low counter. "I can't." The thought made me ill. "I can't."

"D...dawg...you've got to. If you don't, next time, she won't be as lucky. You know that, and I know that."

I continued to shake my head. "Anything but that—"

"Danny." He dropped the nickname, which he rarely did. "This is what you gotta do. You on the brink of making it big, nothing can interfere with that. If you stay with her, things with Terrell is gonna get ugly, and then what? You end up in jail? No, dawg. You bigger than that. You meant for bigger things."

"She's supposed to go with me." I hated the weakness in my voice as I pleaded with him to understand.

"D, if you stick with her, she ain't gonna be around to go."

I stared at him as his words hung in the air between us. Dollar was right, but the thought of her not in my life left a hole the size of a crater in my chest. I couldn't live without Gabrielle, but that may be what happens if I stay with her. Eventually, I might be able to deal with her not in my life, but a world without G's bright smile was unacceptable. Dollar was right; I had to get away from her, for her own sake.

I took a shaky breath. "This will kill me, but you're right. I've got to do something."

He nodded and squeezed my shoulder. "You doing the right thing. It don't feel like it, but you are."

I wiped at the moisture in my eyes with a trembling hand, hoping it had gone unnoticed. "What do I do?"

"You make a clean cut and you get out of town. It's the only way."

"It's not going to be that easy. She isn't going to just let me walk away." I dropped my head into my hands and rubbed at my temples. The very thought of leaving Gabrielle made my head throb.

"Then you gotta make it clear and give her no choice. You're gonna hurt her, no doubt."

The last thing I ever wanted to do was hurt her, but it was my only choice.

"It's better than her being dead."

"Exactly, my man. Exactly."

Chapter 26

~ Gabrielle ~
Present Day

I needed no further invitation. I'd suppressed my hurt and anger for six long years, and now that Danny forced the issue, everything rushed up and simmered below the surface, waiting for the volcanic explosion. Locking in on those intense blue eyes that read me so well and touched me in places no one else could ever reach, I erupted.

I put my hands on his chest and shoved him hard. "I hate you!"

Caught off guard by my explosive outburst, he stumbled, but recovered. "I know."

"No, you don't! You can't possibly know how I feel. If you did, you never would have done what you did. How could you?" Tears were streaming, but I wasn't sad. I was pissed.

"I had to."

I stopped and stared at him, his simple answer throwing off my anger. "You had to?"

He took a deep breath and scraped his fingers through his short hair. "Look, those details are not important. What's important is—"

He glanced up in time to see the glass I'd grabbed off the counter come flying at his head, and ducked. It exploded from the contact against the fridge behind him.

Whirling back, he was hot. "Don't fucking do that again!"

I got in his face. "Don't placate me, Danny. Tell me the truth!"

He held his arms out to the side. "I'm fucking trying, but you're throwing shit at me!"

"No, you're not. You were going to tell me to forget about it." I jabbed his chest with my finger. "That you did what was best for me. I don't want to hear that BS!"

"I *did* do what was best for you," he ground out in a low, strained voice, attempting to rein his temper back in.

"Stop saying that! You can't know what's best for me." I pounded my chest with my finger as I screamed at him. "Only *I* know what's best for me. Not you, not anyone else. Me!"

"Is everything okay in here?" Big T asked as he walked in, having heard the glass explosion. Spotting us in each other's faces, both hot with anger, he stopped, uncertain what he was interrupting.

Danny gave him a quick nod, telling him to get out of there, and he backed out of the kitchen.

Alone again, Danny took a deep breath and wiped his mouth with the back of his hand. "You're right. You're right, I'm sorry."

"No." I shoved him again, my anger rebuilding. "No, you're not allowed to give in and apologize, damn you."

He didn't fight against my shoves, even though I couldn't move him, as he stood strong and solid.

"Look at me!" I yelled. "You gave me your word, damn it! You promised me we'd never be apart. You deserted me, just like my father!"

He flinched, but when he lifted his head, his expression was blank. Closing himself off, like always, and wiping the slate clean, which only pissed me off more. I needed him to show emotion, show me he felt something, that he cared about anything. I raised my hand to slap him, despising myself, but he caught my wrist and walked me back until we hit the corner. "Don't even think about it." His face, mere inches from mine, was red and full of rage. "This is not us. Stop."

I jerked against his hold, but I heard him. "Get off me!"

He pushed his lower body against mine, pinning me in. "No, you're going to stay right here, just like this, and hear me out, damn it." When I didn't fight against him anymore, he lowered his voice. "I did what I had to do because they were going to kill you. Don't you fucking get it?"

"Who?"

"Who do you fucking think? Terrell and his crew."

I stilled and stared at him. "Wha…why would they kill me?"

"To get back at me, G. I had to get you away from me. Paybacks, remember?"

"But you told me you didn't know why they were bothering with me!"

"I lied, okay? I was afraid if I told you about my history with him, you'd pity me. Feel sorry for me because I was so desperate to belong, to have a family, that I'd once considered joining his crew, knowing that was better than anything with my father. I was embarrassed and ashamed."

"What…why…you could have just told me!"

"And what? You would have let me go? Walk away and never look back?" When I remained silent, he gave me a knowing smile. "Exactly. That's why I did what I did. I had to get you to hate me, so you'd let me walk away."

I closed my eyes against the humiliation. He was right. Even if he had explained everything, I never would have agreed to a separation. I would have followed him to the ends of the earth, and he knew it.

"How do you know it would have come to that?"

"Because, G, that time in front of the studio was a message to me. As bad as it was, that was mild for them. The next time would…" His voice trailed off, unable to complete the thought.

"Why was Terrell so fixated on you?"

He hissed in a breath and glanced away before fixing his gaze back on me. "I refused to kill someone."

My eyes widened. "What? Why did he want you to kill someone?"

"He wanted me to join his crew. It's like an initiation thing. I refused, and that pissed him off since I didn't want to be in his 'family,' especially since he'd given me money to buy recording equipment. He wanted to ride my coattails and cash in on me. He said he would wait and kill the one thing that was most important to me, and you became the perfect target."

I pieced everything together. "So…so, you didn't want to end things with me?"

His expression softened. "God, baby, no. That was the last thing I wanted. It nearly killed me."

The remaining anger in me deflated, and I was empty. I'd spent all my emotions, leaving me wrung out dry. The hard feelings toward him, dragging on me like a ball and chain, evaporated, alleviating the persistent heaviness surrounding me. I had my answers, but was clueless what to do with them, and I didn't know where that left things between us. Danny's feelings for me had been real, as I'd believed before doubt took over, and the separation had been just as hard on him, if not harder, but resentment settled in behind the relief. We'd lost a future because he hadn't trusted me enough to tell me everything, to believe I wouldn't have thought less of him. He'd made decisions without discussing them with me and kept things from me; something he'd promised never to do, especially considering the history with my father.

My mind reeled, trying to digest everything, when a new fear took over.

"Wait a minute, what about Dani?"

"What do you mean? What about her?"

"Is it safe now? I mean, Terrell didn't succeed with me, but who's to say he won't go after her." I breathed hard as panic flashed through me, threatening to push me over the edge to hysterical. "She can't be in the middle of this, Danny. It's one thing if it's me, but not her. Nothing can happen to her."

"Hey, hey." He cupped my face in his hands, trying to soothe me. "Breathe, baby. Breathe." When I calmed down, he ran his hand over my hair. "Everything's all right. Terrell's in jail, and his little gang broke apart after that. There's nothing left of them. I checked that out when I found out about Dani. There's nothing to worry about. But if there was any threat, which there isn't, I won't let anything happen to you or Dani. I'll get you both your own security team. Whatever it takes. Okay?"

I gazed into his eyes, so earnest and sincere, and believed him, feeling the same reassurance I did years ago; that, no matter what, he would always keep me safe. I might not like his methods of doing so, but at least he'd kept his word when it came to that.

"Okay."

I glanced down at his hard body still pressed against mine. "You can back off. I won't try to hit you again."

My embarrassed smile fell as soon as I caught the heat in his eyes. Deep hunger shone in them as his strong hands molded themselves to my sides. I shook my head and my breathing hitched, not believing what I was seeing, but there was no mistaking the intense, familiar passion blazing up between us.

"You don't know how much I've missed you, baby," he said, his voice rough and deep. "I've been empty for so long without you." His gaze met mine, and I jerked in surprise at the depth of need and loneliness within his eyes.

My heart rate sped up and my breathing shallowed. "Danny…"

He shifted, lifting me onto the counter. Stepping between my legs, he grasped my head with his hands, forcing my eyes to his. "Tell me to stop now, Gabrielle. If that's what you want, tell me to stop."

The way my name rolled off his tongue in a low rumble sent hot ripples of need through me. Hearing him say it never failed to make me quiver, and still did, all this time later. My body heat surged in temperature and a light sheen of perspiration broke out over my skin from anticipation. I needed to feel him, and I needed him to touch me, or else I was sure I would die. I didn't have to think twice about what I wanted. I would worry about the consequences later.

I locked my legs at his waist and threw my arms around his neck, closing the last inches between us, and crashed my mouth onto his. Our tongues sought the other as we pressed ourselves against each other, his hands moving up and down, and all over, trying to touch me everywhere at once before ripping my shirt up to feast on my breasts.

Grabbing his t-shirt in my fists, I yanked it over his head, a renting sound filling the air. His chest was hard and cut, bulk replacing his slim, wiry frame of his youth, and his abs chiseled. More tattoos decorated his skin, dark ink wrapping the knot of muscles and the ridges of his ribcage, around to his back. They begged me to study them, learn the story behind each one, but I couldn't take the time now with my need spiraling near out of control.

He placed my feet on the counter, holding my knees out, spreading me to him, and his mouth trailed a scorching path from my knee up one thigh before covering me outside of my shorts. I gasped and mewled at the caress of his hot breath through the thin cotton, wishing there was nothing between his lips and me. His tongue gave a hard lick over the fabric before he shoved the material out of the way.

My hands fisted in his hair and I squeezed my eyes shut. "Oh my God, Danny."

He hummed his approval and took another deep swipe.

I pushed into the cabinet, letting my head fall back with a thud. My release hovered just out of reach, and I emitted a frustrated sigh, which he recognized and slid a finger inside while he continued to feast. A wave of warm pleasure crested and then exploded, flooding over me from head to toe. I didn't realize I'd made a sound until his other hand covered my mouth as he rode me out, not breaking contact until I sagged against the cupboard, depleted.

Kissing another path up and over my stomach, stopping to flick at one nipple with his tongue before standing upright, his mouth found mine, and he lifted me into his arms. He headed over to the back staircase, never halting from the ravenous kisses.

We crashed into the wall at the base of the stairs, but didn't break apart. Our lips remained molded together as our hands rubbed, grabbed, and squeezed. He regained his balance and started up, but missed a step when I reached into his shorts and wrapped a tight hand around his erection jutting between us, giving his hot, velvet skin a firm stroke. We fell to the floor, but he turned so he took the brunt of the fall.

"Oh!" I exclaimed. "I'm sorry. You okay?"

"Yeah." He sat up and took my mouth again, plastering me against the stairwell before moving his lips to nip at my neck. "But maybe hold off on doing that for when I'm not trying to carry you up the stairs." His kiss silenced my giggles, and he pulled me back into his arms. He carried me up the remaining steps and down the hallway, pausing to press me to the wall as we ground hard against each other, both of us breathing heavy and sweating.

I cracked one eye and glanced at the closed door to Dani's room. The last thing I wanted was for her to emerge and find her parents going at it right outside.

"Danny," I breathed against his lips. "Danny."

"What?" he panted as his mouth continued to move over mine.

"Dani's...door...move..."

He understood what I was trying to say as he stepped back and strode into his bedroom, slamming the door shut with his foot. Carrying me over to a large four-poster bed in the middle of a room as big as most apartments, he dumped me onto the comforter and laid over me.

He jerked my shirt off and traveled down my body with his hands and his mouth before returning to my lips.

"I need to be in you, baby," he said, his voice quiet and urgent. "I can't wait any longer. I'm out of my fucking head."

In one quick movement, my boxers and panties were gone before he yanked off his shorts, along with his blue boxer briefs. He shifted and, with shaky hands, rolled on a condom he'd grabbed from the nightstand drawer. Settling back over me, he plunged into me without hesitation, and put his hand over my mouth to muffle my shout as he gritted his teeth on a low moan.

Stars burst in front of my eyes, and only a few powerful thrusts from him sent me over the edge again, right before he stilled, pinning me to him as he groaned his release. We lay in each other's arms, slick with sweat and out of breath, neither moving as our heart rates evened out.

He lifted his head from my shoulder and grinned. "God damn, I've missed you."

"I've missed you too."

Raising up on one elbow, he brushed the hair away from my face. His eyes tracked a lazy trail over me, seeming to take me all in. "I never thought I'd see you again. It's been hell without you, Gabrielle. I've been so lost." His voice broke at the end.

I held his face in my hands. "I've been lost without you too."

"I hated myself," he said, all emotions on display for once. "I have never forgiven myself for everything." I nodded as tears slid out of the corner of my eyes, and he brushed them away with his fingers. "I hope you can find it in your heart one day to forgive me, G. Now that you know why I said the things I did."

He rolled away and stared at the ceiling. "I know you think my life's been one big party of success and money since then, but it hasn't." He turned his head, the blue of his eyes softer than I'd ever seen. "I've been miserable. I thought about you every day and couldn't ever get you out of my head. There's something about you in all my songs. You're always there, in one way or another." He closed his eyes and took a deep breath. "That's why I started doing shit and getting fucked up all the time. I was trying to forget the pain, dull it somehow, but it never worked."

"Danny, don't..." I touched his arm, not wanting him to relive the suffering.

"But I could never forget you, G," he continued as he opened his eyes again. "I'll always love you, G. Forever. That's it. Even when we weren't together, there was no one else for me."

My heart soared at his words, but my brain screamed at me to take a step back. How could I trust him after what I'd learned? What if he kept things from me again, and made decisions that not only affected me, but Dani as well? I couldn't go through that again, but I also couldn't ignore how I felt about him.

"I love you, too. There is no one else for me either. There never was."

He wrapped me in his arms and held me tight. "I promise to make it all up to you. I'll make it better, baby, I promise."

"You already have," I told him with a wobbly smile.

"No," he said. "It will be better. We're just getting started. Again."

"If we're starting again, you have to promise me one thing, though."

One of his brows creased. "What's that?"

"Don't keep things from me. Please don't keep secrets from me again."

"I won't. I promise."

Danny pressed his mouth to mine, kissing me long and hard. He rolled back on top and gazed at me.

"I've been meaning to thank you."

"For what?"

"For having Dani. For naming her after me."

"She's the reason I'm alive."

A dark expression passed over his face. "Don't tell me stuff like that, baby. It rips my heart out."

I put my hand on his cheek. "You've told me your secrets and you need to hear mine."

He rested his forehead against mine and squeezed his eyes shut. "I know, but it kills me, especially since it's my fault. Another way I fucked up your life."

"New beginning, right?" I smiled when he glanced up and nodded in response. "Then we have all the time in the world to talk about it."

"All the time in the world." He twined his fingers with mine above my head. "Tell me you love me again."

"I love you."

"Always."

"Always."

And this time, I knew it was true.

Chapter 27

~ Gabrielle ~
Six Years Earlier

I trudged up the stairs to Danny's apartment. I didn't have to wear a brace on my knee anymore, which had forced me to gimp from side-to-side, but I still required one for my ankle, making me limp because of the stupid, thick boot. It was frustrating, but I was getting better. I also no longer resembled a survivor of a nasty car accident, the scrapes and bruises on my face having faded. But even though I was healing physically; emotionally, I was a wreck.

Ever since my release from the hospital, Danny had been around less and less. He blamed his lack of availability on recording and needing to make the final edits on his demos so he could send them out to record labels. I understood and supported him, but I didn't like the negative impact the absence drew on our relationship. Even during the rare times I managed to snag with him, he was quiet, withdrawn even, and I couldn't remember the last time he kissed me or extended a simple gesture, such as holding my hand. Anytime I tried to initiate anything, he rebuffed me, drawing back with a look of pain. And again tonight, he was pushing me away.

Rather than spending time with me, he was going to The Sanctuary with Dollar to free verse against other aspiring rappers. Danny often did these battles to build up his name and reputation, but he never allowed me to go to the ones held in this basement club, insisting the place was too rough for me. I begged and pleaded, but he refused, claiming having me there would be more of a distraction to him, worrying about me among the rowdy crowd. I soon learned, however, Kat and her friends attended the battles and, in fact, were going tonight, forcing me to take matters into my own hands.

He wasn't going to be happy to see me, and that sad knowledge made me take a deep, calming breath before I knocked. I heard as he strode across the room and willed the nerves in my stomach to still.

The door flew open and Danny stared at me. Surprise warmed his eyes followed by a flash of pain before he covered it with a cold, hard gaze. "What are you doing here?"

I smiled, struggling to ignore the impatience on his face and praying I wouldn't break down. "I wanted to see you, so I took the bus. Can I come in?"

He hesitated before moving aside to let me pass. "I've got to go in a few."

"I know. I was hoping we could have some time together, since we don't get to see each other much anymore."

"I told you I've been busy with the demo."

"I know. I'm not complaining. I'm just trying to make an effort."

He stayed with the door at his back, eyeing me as I took off my jacket and draped it over a chair. I clomped over to him with a forced smile on my face and put my arms around his neck. He stood his ground with a steely gaze, his hands shoved deep into his jeans pockets, but when I leaned in to kiss him, he jerked his head to the side and stepped out of my hold.

His rejection broke my resolve to stay strong. "What is going on, Danny?"

He wouldn't face me and only gave me his back. "Nothing. Nothing's going on."

"Stop lying. Please stop lying and tell me what's going on. Is there someone else?"

His jaw tensed. "No, there's no one else, G."

I trudged over to stand in front of him, making him look at me. "Then what's going on? Why won't you even touch me? Is it because of what happened?"

He scowled. "What do you mean?"

"Are you disgusted by me now because of what happened with Terrell?"

"Jesus Christ. No, I'm not disgusted by you."

"Then what is it? I'm at a loss here, Danny." Exasperation replaced the hurt in my tone.

"It's not all about you, G. You ever fucking think of that?"

"I didn't say it was all about me!"

"Then maybe you should just back off!"

"Back off? Back off! Danny, I haven't seen you in four days! We haven't been with each other since I was out of the hospital six weeks ago. I think I *have* backed off! You, on the other hand, seem to want to forget I even exist."

His eyes narrowed as he bumped his chest into mine, causing me to back-track. "Is that what this is about? You horny, baby? You want some?" He leered at me and tugged at my shirt.

I batted at his hands and tried to push him away. "Stop it! Stop it, you asshole!"

He pinned me against the wall and nipped at my neck. "I love it when little Miss Goody Two-shoes swears. It makes me hot."

I shoved his shoulders hard, making him step back. Both of our chests heaved as we stared at one another, and I wondered how we had arrived at this crossroad. How had two people, who loved each other more than anything, get to the point where we acted as if we hated each other, and called each other names? Why were we even here? I wanted to cry, I wanted to scream, and I wanted to beg. I wanted everything to go back to the way it was, which, unfortunately, wasn't an option. We had turned a corner some-where, I didn't know when or why, but I was desperate for another route. I didn't like the way my blood surged throughout my body, screaming for a dark release. I'd never considered myself an antagonistic person before, but the intensity of my feelings for him demanded it, for better or worse.

A sense of fragile control settled over me, until I caught his expression, which stopped me cold. He didn't seem mad or upset, but rather amused, even smug, as if my pain and anger humored him, which enraged me more.

A click reverberated in my head, and before I realized what I was doing, I grabbed a glass from the table next to me and launched it at him, the only way I knew how to make him feel the depth of my suffering. He ducked just in time, and the glass hit the wall behind him, exploding into a waterfall of shards. When he turned back, a dangerous glint shone in his eye.

"I wouldn't do that again, if I were you."

My fingers flew up to my mouth, and I gasped, shocked at what I had done. I didn't even know myself anymore, didn't like who I had become. The last thing I wanted was to hurt Danny; I needed him to talk, to tell me what was happening, because I was lost.

I slunk to my knees and dropped my head into my hands, my shoulders shaking as I cried. I was alone in my grief for a few minutes until I heard him sigh. His hands touched my back, and I jumped in surprise, having expected him to leave me where I was. Looking up into his face, I spotted the Danny I loved and who loved me, his blues eyes filled with concern and warmth.

"Don't do that," he said as he rubbed my shoulders.

He sat on the floor next to me, pulling me into his side. I rested my head on his shoulder and relished the comfort he was providing.

"I don't understand," I whispered with a sniffle.

"I don't either," he murmured.

He was slipping away from me. I didn't know why or what I had done, but I was desperate to latch onto the thin threads that remained and pull, using everything with my power to keep him by my side.

Ducking my head, my lips found his, but he jerked.

"Don't start that, please."

I ignored him, and did it again, this time with more insistence. He tried to move away, but I followed, keeping my mouth pressed against his.

His hands gripped my shoulders, and I waited for him to push me away, but they held, and then pulled me closer. He opened to me, and I fell into the kiss. It was sweet and tender, and with a hint of sadness, but it was my life preserver to keep me afloat.

I stretched back, and he came over me, our lips never parting. Shifting my hips up, I pressed against his hardness and he groaned.

"Gabrielle," he whispered.

"I'm here."

His hands squeezed my breasts outside of my sweater and our kiss picked up in urgency. We were rushing toward the end that I didn't want to come, but was clueless how to stop it or turn us in a different direction.

He tugged my zipper, and I lifted, so he could pull my pants down, but he only got half way, hampered by the heavy boot. He leaned back and with one hand, undid his, and yanked them down just as far, and then slid right into me.

We both gasped in pleasure, and I wrapped my arms around his shoulders as he took his time, drawing out each stroke. I moved with him, awkward and clumsy because of the brace on my ankle, but it wasn't long before a warm glow filled me.

Holding himself on one elbow, he kissed me, his tongue twisting and coiling with mine, and I kept pace, rolling my hips against his before he pulled back and hissed in a breath.

"Fuck, you're going to make me come," he moaned.

His words pushed me over the edge and I cried out, writhing underneath him as everything within me expanded and contracted in soft, dreamy pulses, and he stilled, pressing hard into me as he gritted out his release on a groan.

A few seconds passed before Danny swore and rolled onto his back, yanking up his pants. The cold, barren distance opened between us again and slapped me in the face. Nothing had changed.

I eyed him through lowered lids as I righted my clothes, uncertain where we stood.

He leaned down to help me up. "I'm sorry."

"Why are you sorry?" I folded my arms across my chest.

He glanced up, and the curtain was back. "Because that shouldn't have happened." His gaze went past me to the clock on the wall. "Shit. I've got to go."

"We're not done here, Danny."

His eyes flitted over me as he shoved his arms through the sleeves of his jacket. "Yeah, we are."

He walked out the door and shut it behind him without another word, the silence trailing in his wake speaking volumes, but it was nothing I wanted to hear.

* * *

"Move up so he can see you, girl." Kat pushed me forward.

"No, I'm fine here." I tried to shrink into the shadows to avoid standing out like a sore thumb. Not because I was the only white face around—there were many scattered throughout the crowd—but I was the only tall blonde with a big boot on her foot. Thankfully, I had Kat at my side, telling any interested party where to stick it when they came on too strong.

"What do you mean? He'll want to see you." She pulled me to stand next to her, right under one of the few working lights hanging from the ceiling.

I glanced around at the dark, dank green club, which resembled an unfinished basement. Exposed pipes and heater ducts wound and crisscrossed above, and the flooring was nothing but a cement slab. A small raised platform flanked the front of the room, and large speakers loomed in opposite corners, facing outward, with towers lining the back wall. In the middle, sat a table and a DJ, who provided the mixes.

Kat and her friends had arrived late to pick me up, so we'd missed Danny's first two rounds. We'd pushed our way through, ignoring the complaints and glares from those already there. He wasn't going to be happy I was there, if he even saw me, so I didn't want to draw too much attention to myself. However, once he stepped onto the stage, a black ball cap worn low on his head, attempting to hide proved to be fruitless. All he had to do was turn my way, and I stood out like a glowing Christmas tree.

When the MC finished going through the rules, he tossed a quarter in the air and instructed Danny to call. When he called heads, he glanced out at the crowd and his eyes locked on mine. Winning the coin toss, the MC asked if he wanted to go first or second, but he didn't respond, his hard stare staying on me for what seemed like an eternity. People craned their necks my way, wondering what had caught his eye.

~ *Danny* ~

As I stared at the love of my life, absolute hatred of myself coursed through my veins, followed by waves of nausea. The desire to be someone else, along with resentment of the circumstances that had brought me to this point, had never been stronger than at that moment. I knew what I had to do, and now how to do it, but it was the last thing I wanted to do. I was going to humiliate and embarrass her, and she would never forgive me, nor would I ever forgive myself, but I had to cut the final tie. I'd fucked up earlier today, unable to resist her, and that would continue to happen until I broke away. I couldn't string us along anymore; it wasn't fair to her and it was excruciating for me.

Maybe one day she would understand why, but never would she show me forgiveness, not that I deserved any. This was the only way to keep her safe, which was all I ever wanted, and that meant getting her away from me and removing the target from her back.

I took a deep breath and caught Dollar's eye, who had also spotted her. He gave a small nod of approval, understanding what I was about to do. Our wait for the perfect moment to present itself was now over.

"I'll go second."

I stepped to the side as the MC handed the mic to Pac and listened as he called me out in lyrical form. He hit on the color of my skin and my poor status, which I expected, but it surprised me when Pac brought up my prudish girl. That, I hadn't anticipated, but I didn't react and didn't let Pac know he'd struck a nerve. In fact, I was going to have the last laugh when everyone heard what I had to say.

~ *Gabrielle* ~

My color rose at the insults and I tried to step back, but Kat grabbed my hand and held tight. "It's okay. It's what they do. Danny will stand up for you. You've got to have thick skin for this, girl."

I wanted to tell her Danny wasn't going to stand up for me, but I couldn't find the words. Something in his gaze spoke of finality, conveying we had reached our end, even if I didn't understand why.

When Pac finished, the crowd roared its approval. He had successfully slammed Danny, in their opinion, which is what counted, and they now waited for his response.

Danny took the mic from the MC and walked to the edge of the stage. The beat started, and he strode back and forth, readying himself and organizing his thoughts, before he stopped in front of Pac.

He reiterated what Pac had hit on, calling himself out as poor white trash, but then he brought up me, telling everyone the only reason he dated me was because I reminded him of the night spend with Pac's mom under the sheets. He lamented, however, I wouldn't get the hint, following him around and crying about how much I loved him. Turning, he pointed, and countless pairs of eyes landed on me.

"So, tell me, Big Pac, I need you to help me,
How do I get the girl to get the hint?

Tell her, please, tell her that she needs to go back to the sticks.
I can't take it no more, I'm done with this bitch,
You can have her, consider this a thank you gift."

The crowd whooped and hollered, roaring its approval. Tears streaked down my cheeks, and I remained frozen in place with my soul ripped open and exposed to everyone. He didn't even look my way to see if the killing blow succeeded, but rather only turned and sat on a speaker, his head bowed as he waited for the verdict.

Through my daze, someone grabbed my hand and pulled, making my feet move. "Let's go, Gabby. Let's get you out of here and away from that motherfucking asshole. I can't believe that fucker did that. Out of our way, please!" Kat pushed people aside.

I moved like I was in a dream, everything progressing in slow motion. His words replayed over and over in my head, filling me with shock and horror, humiliation and dejection. I didn't even know why, and I wondered if I ever would.

~ Danny ~

After being selected the winner, as judged by the volume of the cheers, I jumped off the speaker and ran backstage without stopping.

"D!" Dollar yelled as he and Big T rushed after me. "D, wait."

I sprinted around a corner, making it into the corroded bathroom stall before everything I had eaten that day reappeared. I spit a few times, trying to rid my mouth of the horrid taste before I flushed, and slammed the door open. Big T and Dollar were standing on the other side.

"What the fuck was that?" Big T asked.

"Just something he had to do," Dollar told him. "Don't worry about it."

"Don't worry about it? He demolished her in front of everyone!"

I shoved past them and moved over to the faucet to rinse out my mouth. "Don't remind me. We don't talk about her from here on out."

"What the hell, D?" Big T was incredulous, not understanding what had just happened.

I caught his eye in the scratched-up mirror hanging over the single rusty sink dripping only cold water. "I had to, T. I had to, or else Terrell is going to fuck her up even more than last time."

"This is crazy!" Big T threw his arms up, appalled on Gabrielle's half. "She don't deserve that, D."

I whirled and grabbed Big T's collar, anger giving me the strength to shove him against the bathroom wall despite our size difference. "No, she didn't! She didn't fucking deserve any of that. But if I didn't, he'll kill her. You know that, and I know that!"

Big T nodded as I backed away, my chest heaving. "Okay, dawg. Okay, I get it. You had to do what you had to do." He tugged down his jacket. "What now?"

Dollar stepped up and rubbed his hands together as he smiled. "Our connection came through and there's a scout out there. Now we go to LA and make our man a superstar with a new tag."

I raised a brow. "A new tag?"

"DOA."

"DOA?"

"Dead on Arrival, which is what the competition will be once we get on the scene."

I sighed. "That's all we can hope for." I stood straight and squared my shoulders, ready to put this behind me and move on, if that was even possible. "Let's go."

Chapter 28

I winced at the daylight pouring through my bedroom window. I wanted to get up and close the blinds Monica intentionally left open before taking off for school, but getting out of bed and moving made me feel depleted and nauseous. Three months had passed since the fateful night at The Sanctuary, and as far as I was concerned, my life ended in that dank club.

I'd lost everything, leaving me no purpose to continue. It didn't matter if I woke up every day—even though I did—because there was no longer any reason to do so.

My mom, Kat, and Monica tried to break me out of my funk, but regardless of what they did or said, I ignored them. They made me get up to at least shower and eat, and I appeased them once in a while, but most of the time, I brushed them off, only wanting to stay adrift in my dark world. My life was empty and meaningless, and nothing would change that.

Not long after Danny's destruction of me in front of what seemed like the entire universe, I'd kept going, determined to move past the heartache and avoid the precarious edge I was toeing, but the following week, the final shove arrived in the form of a simple white envelope. A simple white envelope containing only a few slaying words. An integral part of the application process at Juilliard, the letter informed me, was the audition. If I couldn't perform, then I couldn't apply, and if I couldn't apply, then I couldn't request financial aid. They welcomed me to re-apply later on, allowing sufficient time for my injuries to heal, but perhaps next year. Next year. Not next week, next month, or as soon as you can. Next year…what a joke. I wouldn't be around next year, if I had anything to say about it.

I'd lost the two loves of my life in two short weeks, for reasons unknown. I'd even lied about Terrell and his group assaulting me, hoping to preserve a future for Danny and me. But that had all been for naught. I had nothing… no hope, no dreams, no wants, and therefore, nothing to live for.

I now understood what my father must have felt in those final days before deciding to take his own life. The despair, the anguish, the hopelessness. The darkness…the utter complete darkness. There was no light in anything anymore, no reason to face the day. Nothing to put a smile on my face, a song in my heart, or a spring in my step. There was…nothing.

Rolling over to my back, I gazed through bleary eyes at the ceiling. My head pounded from lack of food and water, but I didn't care and tried to ignore the growing headache. The throbbing became unyielding, however, demanding attention, and I pushed up and plodded into the bathroom. My body ached from head to toe, and I refused to look at my reflection in the mirror, knowing what would face me—unwashed, tangled hair falling over red, splotchy skin surrounding sunken and dull eyes too big for my long, thin face.

I opened the medicine cabinet in search of painkillers, and finding none, moved to the drawers, opening all of them. As I searched through each one, I pulled items out, tossing them on the sink, desperate to find relief from the incessant pounding and allowing me to retreat into my dark, silent world. Grabbing a tampon, I stared at the pretty, purple satin wrapper as my brain struggled to push a coherent thought past the pain. When it registered, I jerked upright. I counted back in my head, trying to remember my last cycle. Unable to recall even the last time I'd eaten, I turned and stumbled, before heading into the kitchen where a calendar hung on the wall.

I yanked it off the nail, not caring when it ripped, and sat at the table staring at the small squares outlining the days of the week. When I recollected nothing, I went back a month and then another. Nothing came, and I leaned back in the chair, puzzling it out. Perhaps I'd screwed up my cycle because I wasn't taking care of myself. I'd heard losing too much weight caused irregularity or stoppage altogether. Or, maybe it was…

The answer hit me in a flash. Like a burst of lightning, I remembered the day in Danny's apartment, our last time together without protection, and words of regret afterward.

"Omigod."

Jumping up from my chair, my body protesting the rapid movements, I rushed into the shower. After drying off, I threw on whatever clothes I found lying about, unconcerned if they were clean or not, and pulled my wet hair into a ponytail. I grabbed my purse and hurried to the drug store down the street, ignoring my aching legs.

I returned and ran into the bathroom with the two purchased pregnancy tests. I followed the directions and then sat on the tiled floor, leaning against the bathtub with the test in my hand, waiting for the results. Either way, my life was going to change. If positive, I was going to have a baby; negative, I was succeeding in destroying myself.

Opening my eyes, I took a deep breath and turned over the plastic stick. The word "pregnant" glowed at me, bright and blue. I stared, unsure of how to react, before breaking into a wide smile. I laughed and then cried.

I could envision it; a life with Danny's child, giving me love and happiness, and keeping his spirit in my life. Having the baby would remind me of the love we'd shared, and not the ugly way we'd ended. We'd had something beautiful, and from that, created a new life.

Even though he'd destroyed my life, without knowing it, he'd given me a reason to live.

* * *

"I can't believe you're up and out of bed, and even showered," Kat commented as she walked into the apartment. "When you called, asking me to come over, I wasn't sure what I would find."

I bounced on my feet, unable to contain my excitement. "You will never believe what's happened."

"Did you hear from Juilliard again?"

"No, it's better than that."

I sprinted out of the room to grab the test, holding it behind my back.

Kat frowned. "Better?"

I smiled as I held up the pregnancy test.

"Pregnant? Girl, who's pregnant?"

"I am."

Her eyes widened. "You are? What?"

I nodded and sat on the couch. "Yeah, I realized today I hadn't had my period in a while, and when I thought about it, I remembered it was right before one of the last times with Danny."

Kat collapsed down next to me in shock. "It's D's?"

"Of course, it's his. Who else's would it be?"

"No, I know." She waved her hand. "I'm sorry, girl. You caught me off guard. Pregnant? Wow. So, what are you going to do?"

"I'm going to have it."

"Gabby, how are you going to do that? A single mother and all that..."

I shrugged. "I don't know. I'll figure it out, but I'm not giving up this baby. No way."

"Gabby—"

"No!" I jumped off the couch, interrupting the lecture sure to come. "I don't care what you think or what you say. I want this baby. I *need* this baby."

"Okay, honey." She stood and put her hands on my shoulders. "It's okay. I understand. I only want what's best for you. If this is what you want, then okay. Let's do it. I'll help with whatever you need."

"Really?"

"Of course. You're my girl!" She pulled me into a hug.

"Thanks."

Kat gave my shoulders another squeeze, before releasing me. "So, what do you want me to do?"

"I could use help telling Danny."

Her smile fell, and she sighed. "Honey, this isn't going to bring D back, you need to realize that. He's gone."

"I know."

She raised one brow. "Do you?"

"Of course, but he still deserves to know. It *is* his child."

"All right." She took a deep breath. "I'll help you put something out on Facebook, or we can try to text people who can get in touch with him, but only if you promise not to break down if you don't hear from him."

"I promise."

"Okay, let's do it. So, have you thought about names yet?"

"Oh, I already know what the name will be, regardless if it's a boy or a girl."

"Really? What?"

I beamed. "Danny."

Chapter 29

~ Gabrielle ~
Present Day

Even weeks after my reconciliation with Danny, I was still in a state of disbelief mixed with cautious optimism. Never in a million years would I have ever guessed we would be in the same room again, especially with his newfound fame, let alone back together. I never would have believed he still loved me, as I him, and that he wanted me in his life. After learning the truth, I was leery and a little reluctant to admit everything was perfect, but it was hard not to since, for once, all felt right in the world. After moving my belongings from the guestroom, we'd sat down with Dani and explained what we could to her, and the final piece to us becoming a family unit fell into place. Everything was coming together as I'd dreamed, but never dared to wish for, fearing the pain of holding out hope for something so hopeless.

Now I had to get my head around the sheer size of Danny's wealth and stardom. Sure, I'd known he was successful, but I never understood what that amounted to. When he revealed the staggering dollar amounts in all his accounts, I could only gape. He seemed so much the same guy as in the past, with nothing more than worn jeans and threadbare t-shirts, that it was crazy to think how much his life had changed. Overnight, I went from having to count my pennies to not having to give them a second thought. It was a little overwhelming.

Another thing I was uncomfortable with was the attention. Everywhere he went, people stared, or approached asking for autographs, wanting to talk to him or touch him. He took everything in stride—even though the hype sometimes drove him crazy—but he appreciated his fan base and tolerated it. Relieved Dani and I weren't the ones they all wanted to be around, I kept us out of the spotlight and away from the crowds, and thankfully, his fans didn't care. If the focus continued to avoid us, then it wouldn't be so bad.

Walking into the kitchen with Dani in tow, I turned on the small television hanging on the wall by the refrigerator, as I tried to decide what to make for lunch. I dug in the fridge, the newscasters' voices just noise in the background until Dani squealed.

"That's you, Mommy!"

I popped my head around the door and frowned. "What's me?"

She pointed at the show. "You were on the TV."

My frown deepened as I turned my attention to the news. A reporter was finishing a story on Danny, showing a video of him performing, followed by footage of him walking through the airport with swarms of cameras surrounding him.

"There is little known about this new lady in DOA's life, but we have reports indicating she has in fact moved in with him, and they have a daughter together. Many believe the woman may be the love of his life, Gabrielle Wells, whom DOA has mentioned in the past, saying she's in every one of his songs, which is interesting when you consider some of his lyrics. We'll stay on top of this story and report what we find out. For Your Entertainment News, this is Amanda Geddings. Back to you, Carol."

I stood stock-still in the middle of the kitchen, unable to believe my ears. Stay on top of this story? Report back? Why? How was I news? I stared at Dani.

"They showed a picture of me?"

"Yeah, of you and Daddy."

I couldn't remember any time being out with him and having our picture taken. Unease settled over me when I realized how easy it was to take a photo of me and plaster it all over the place without me being aware. He'd warned me, but I never believed it would come to this, that our relationship would be a story on the news. Dani hadn't been with us, thank God. The last thing I wanted was to have her photo splashed everywhere, but that was probably only a matter of time.

I tried not to let the unwanted attention bother me, even though it made me feel tense and uneasy, hoping the misplaced fascination with me would blow over. Maybe if I didn't make a big deal about things, we would become old news and blend into the background once again.

That didn't happen, as only a few days later, while reading the paper in the morning with my coffee, I came across another story about us, and this one gave me pause.

The piece confirmed I lived with Danny and we had a daughter of the same name. It highlighted our past, recounting our time together in high school before separating and now reconciling six years later. There were specific details about my dancing for Ms. Greiger's in the city, proclaiming me an accomplished ballet dancer with dreams of going to Juilliard, only for my plans to change drastically; most likely due to my unplanned pregnancy, they ventured.

Quotes from unnamed sources discussed how many had wondered how someone like me, a woman pure and wholesome, could be with a man like Danny. Continuing in the same tone, the article speculated how a mother of a young girl could allow her child to be around the negative influence of Danny, his music, and his known drug abuse, even if he was the father. The author speculated that perhaps my intentions were less than innocent, only looking to cash in because someone of my conservative nature would never be attracted to Danny's harsh and vulgar interpretation of life. Many opined that money and fame stood behind this sudden reconciliation.

My mouth dropped open from shock, and the more I read, the angrier I got. Who were they to comment on what I thought or how I felt? How did they know why I was with Danny, when I had never said two words to any of these people? Who were these unnamed sources who thought they knew us so well?

The constant projection of Danny into such a dark light made me sick, everyone assuming that whatever he talked about in his songs must reflect his personal life. If he sang about being a maniacal murderer, it didn't mean he was one, or would be one day; similar to an actor playing a murderer in a movie didn't mean he would actually kill somebody in real life. The whole "angel lured in by the devil" storyline was getting annoying.

I sat stewing over the article, not hearing when Danny walked into the kitchen.

"Morning, baby."

I jerked up and shut the paper, shoving it to the side. "Good morning."

Reaching into the cabinet for a mug, he frowned at my reaction. "You okay?"

"What? Oh, yeah. I'm fine. Great." I cringed at my overly cheerful tone. "Uh, what do you have planned for the day?"

He placed the cup on the counter and stood on the opposite side of the island. "What's going on?"

"Nothing's going on."

"Then why are you all jumpy?" He glanced down at the newspaper. "What was in there?"

"Nothing."

He reached for it and watched as my eyes widened. "Then you won't mind if I take it with me to read?"

I slouched with a groan. "Fine. There was an article I didn't appreciate."

"About?" He opened the paper, searching for the story in question.

"You and me."

His gaze flicked up and passed over my face before he lowered his elbows to the countertop, the sleeves of his black shirt straining against the bulge of his biceps. I watched him, waiting for any signs of anger or disgust as he read to himself.

He finished and refolded the paper, going back to his coffee with no reaction.

"You have nothing to say?"

He shrugged. "Nothing that hasn't been said before."

I walked around to his side. "Danny, how can the things they say about you not bother you?"

"It doesn't." When I continued to stare at him like he was crazy, he leaned against the counter. "Look, there's nothing I can say or do to get everyone to like me or say nice things. So, I don't try, and I don't let it bother me. They're paid to write their opinions, and that's what they do, regardless of whether they're right or not."

"But they're saying I'm with you because of your money! Or that you're a bad influence for Dani."

"And they'll continue to say those things."

"I don't…how can you…you're not going to…" I broke off, not knowing what to say, not understanding how he wasn't as upset about this as I was.

"Look." He put his mug down and reached out, wrapping a hand around my nape to tug me closer. "People are always going to say something, and the majority of the time, it isn't going to be positive. We're in the limelight now, whether we want to be or not, and you can't let it get to you. You and I, we know what the real story is, and that's all that matters. Now, if you agree with whatever it is they're saying, then we have a different problem, but as long as you and I are on the same page, then that's all that counts."

"But you could say something and maybe change—"

"You can't change people's opinions about me or us, baby," he said.

"But…" I sighed. He was right. Even if I corrected one person's misconceptions, there would be another in line right behind them. "It makes me mad, the things they say, especially about you."

He smiled. "And that's one of the things I love about you. You're my strongest defender. Nobody wants to mess with you once you're riled up."

I smirked and swatted at him. "Stop it, I'm serious."

He tightened his arms and pulled me against his chest, touching his lips to my forehead. "I'm serious too. I love that you want to defend me, but there's nothing we can do. It's just the way it is."

"Well, it sucks. And I don't like when they bring Dani or me into the picture. It's none of their business."

"It sucks, and it's not right, but we can't stop it." He leaned back and his eyes softened. "This is the way it's going to be, baby. If you don't want to be a part of this, then you need to walk away now. That's the only way to separate yourself from this. Even then, it will never be one-hundred-percent because of Dani."

I hesitated. I didn't like it, and I really didn't like exposing Dani to it. Would it always be this way? Or would the fuss die down? I'd just gotten Danny back in my life, and now had the family I'd wished for. Was I going to walk away from everything because of something out of our control? It had to subside at some point. We weren't that exciting.

I took a deep breath. "I don't want to leave. I'll figure out a way to deal with it."

He heard my uncertainty and raised a brow. "You sure?"

I forced a smile. "Yes."

He gave a dramatic swipe at his brow. "Phew! I was going to have to write a letter to the editor if you said you were leaving me." He hooked his arm around my neck and pulled me in for a quick kiss. "Don't let it get to you, G. We're bigger than that."

"I know, I know."

~ *Danny* ~

I kissed her again, this time lingering longer on her soft lips, loving the way she melted in my arms, before grabbing my mug and walking out of the kitchen. Little did she realize, this was the least of our worries. I didn't give a shit what the press said about me, and I hoped with time, she would get there too. Sure, it bothered me whenever they brought up her or Dani, but like I told her, the media would print whatever they wanted, regardless of what I did or said. Half the time, trying to prevent them from writing anything only made things worse, so why waste the effort. I learned to let the negativity slide off my back without a second thought, and I found a way to profit from the attention they slathered on me.

No, what we needed to worry about was much, much worse. I hoped nothing would come from the latest development, but I refused to be unprepared, just in case.

Terrell was out of jail.

I longed for the past to stay in the past, but as much as I wished for it, I recognized the pipe dream for what it was and ordered extra security for Dani and Gabrielle. I wasn't going to take any fucking chances this time around, since I now possessed the resources to protect those I loved. They would have to go over my dead body and an army of bulked up bodyguards before laying a finger on my girls. It wasn't going to happen. Not this time.

I stopped as I crossed through the family room to gaze out the picture window overlooking the in-ground pool lining the edge of the large cement patio before transitioning into rolling waves of grass, stretching out as far as I could see. A perimeter fence bordered the entire property, and security cameras caught every movement, which should make me feel safe, but it didn't. Yanked back into the past, I found myself fighting the urge to glance over my shoulder, wondering what waited around the corner to pounce out at me. I'd let myself believe in the false security that came with money, even though I always feared my past would show its ugly face again. I didn't want Gabrielle involved in the thick of things once more, but I refused to send her away. She was safer here in my house than outside of it, but I couldn't keep her chained inside, as much as I wanted to. I'd made a promise to her that I wouldn't keep things from her, and I wouldn't. I just needed to be sure, know the whole story, and then I'd tell her. If I told her false information, she'd panic and run off with Dani somewhere I couldn't protect them, and I couldn't let that happen.

No, she couldn't know anything until I had the whole report. Maybe we'd get lucky this time, and the past would move on rather than lurk in the shadows, plotting revenge, the promise made all those years ago going unfulfilled. But I didn't think we'd be so fortunate. I hadn't forgotten, and I knew Terrell hadn't either.

Chapter 30

~ Danny ~

"Stop!" I yanked off my headphones. "Cut it."

Dollar leaned down and spoke into the mic on the other side of the glass. "What's the matter, D?"

I collapsed in a chair and scrubbed my hands over my face. I was tired and felt like crap. It weighed me down, preventing me from finding my groove and resulting in recorded garbage.

I glanced around at all the eyes on me and waved my hand. "I'm sorry. We have to call it a day. Everyone go home."

I ignored the murmured rumblings of protest and was thankful when the room cleared out, leaving Dollar and Big T behind.

Big T sat in the chair next to me. "What's going on with you, man?"

"I can't sleep. It's fucking killing me."

Dollar raised one brow as he propped a hip on the table. "You mean you ain't getting sleep now that you got your girl back in your bed."

I smirked. "Nah, I mean I can't fucking sleep. Simple as that. Nothing to do with G."

He sneered. "Right man, like she ain't fucking with your head at all."

I leaned back and scowled. "What's that fucking mean?"

"Come on, man. You telling me her showing up out of the blue with your kid, and now you all playing house together, hasn't fucked with your head at all?" He shook his head. "It ain't right, man. It ain't right."

"We're not *playing* house, Dollar. This is the real shit. Hell, I plan on marrying her."

His eyebrows shot up. "Marry her?"

"That's awesome," Big T said in stark contrast to Dollar's alarm.

"Yeah, why wouldn't I? I love her, and I want to be with her. I want my family. I'm not letting her out of my sight again."

"You can't fucking marry her, D," he said adamantly.

"Why the fuck not?"

"Think about it!" He poked his temple with his finger. "This will ruin your career. You think your fans want to see you as a married man? With a family? You can't have both, man. It don't work like that."

I shot out of my chair with my arms spread wide. "I don't care what they think I should be. My professional and personal lives are completely separate. One has nothing to do with the other. Nobody can tell me how I should live my life, including you."

"Is that right? My opinion don't mean shit?"

"You're not giving me your opinion, and you know it. You're telling me what I can and can't do."

"As your manager and best friend, I'm just looking out for what's best for you and your career, man. That's it, and she ain't it."

"You know, now that I think about it, you've never been a fan of G and me, Dollar. Why is that?" I crossed my arms across my chest. "Why don't you tell me the real story, man?"

Dollar huffed with a lazy swipe of his hand in my direction. "I don't know what you talking about, man."

"No, I want to know." I stood over him, glaring. "Give it to me, Dollar. Be straight with me for once. Tell me what's really on your fucking mind."

"Hey, hey, guys." Big T tried to step between us, the tension rising to a palpable level in the small room.

"No, Dollar's got something he wants to say, and I want to hear it." I stared around Big T, my eyes never leaving Dollar's.

Dollar appeared pensive for a second before shaking his head and standing. "You know, you're right. I never liked the girl. She done nothing but fuck up your life, and I had to go around cleaning up behind you."

"What? She's been nothing but a fucking godsend in my life. I'd be in jail,

or dead, if not for her, and we wouldn't even be here. You fucking know it!"
I yelled as I pointed at Dollar.

"Nah, man. You wouldn't be here today if it wasn't for *me*, not her."

"You? You?" My voice rose, and I wanted to pull my hair out. "How the
fuck is all this your doing?"

"Who helped you separate yourself from her and the fucked-up situation
with Terrell, so you could focus and leave town? Me." Dollar jabbed his finger
into his chest for emphasis. "Who got you a ticket to LA and connected with
a label? Me. Who kept this whole fucking kid thing at bay, so you could
concentrate on being the superstar you became overnight and were destined
to be, just like I told you? Me. That's motherfucking who," he said, spitting
out the last words as he glared at me.

"Oh, man," Big T muttered. "No, you didn't, man…"

I froze, staring in disbelief at who I considered one of my best friends in
the world.

"You…" I broke off and swallowed hard. "You knew about Dani?"

"Yeah. I got the fucking pathetic texts she and Kat wrote, and I kept them
from you so you wouldn't come running back here and fuck up all your
chances. I hid all the whiny ass shit they put online. You had the world at
your fucking feet, D, and someone had to keep you focused on *that*, and not
some whore with a bastard."

All the blood drained from my face as anger roared through me. I saw
nothing but red, a bull charging a waving flag; the flag being Dollar, and only
giving him a pounding would take the rage away. I lunged around Big T and
gripped Dollar by the collar, shoving him out of the studio and against the
brick wall in the hallway. He stumbled, but somehow regained his footing,
and braced himself when I launched myself again. Despite being taller than
me and with a longer reach, it didn't help him, as I was stronger, thicker, and
had my fury as fuel.

Big T tried to pull me off him, but I was too quick and hauled Dollar
up, tossing him halfway up the stairs before chasing after him. Throwing
my body at his, we crashed through the door, landing in a heap on the floor
outside the kitchen, wrestling as we both struggled to gain the upper hand.

As we rolled around, hitting each other amid curses and grunts as fists
connected with skin, I heard Gabrielle scream.

"Danny!"

Big T attempted to separate us again, but his footing tangled between our flailing legs and he went tumbling. Gaining control, I jumped to my feet and yanked Dollar up by the front of his shirt, causing the fabric to rip and buttons to pop off. I shoved him toward the door and pointed.

"Get the fuck out of my house! I never want to see your motherfucking face again!"

Dollar's breath was ragged and hard as he wiped blood from his lip with the back of his hand. He straightened his ruined shirt before glancing between Gabrielle and me.

"Fine. It's your life, if you want to throw it all away for nothing." He threw a bitter glance in her direction, where she stood plastered against the wall, her eyes wide with terror and disbelief. He walked backward to the door. "She's nothin', D. Nothin'. You remember that."

"You're wrong," I said, my chest heaving. "She's everything, and she's what I want. I *can* have it all, you motherfucking asshole."

All three of us watched Dollar leave out the back door without another glance. Silence fell over the room and nobody moved for a few seconds before Big T picked himself up off the floor.

"Danny?" Gabrielle's voice trembled.

I stared at the empty space in front of me, my brain refusing to comprehend what had happened; that one of the people I trusted with my life had stabbed me in the back. I wondered what else he'd done that I was unaware of, and then I decided I didn't want to find out.

"Not now, G." I pushed past her and stormed upstairs.

~ *Gabrielle* ~

The slamming of our bedroom door reverberated throughout the house.

I turned to Big T. "What was that about?"

He let out a long breath as he lowered himself into a nearby chair and wiped sweat from his brow. "You, sweetie. You."

"Me? What about me?"

"You need to talk to D about it. It ain't pretty, that's for sure."

I rushed up the stairs and stepped into our bedroom. The room was empty, but I followed the sound of the shower running. His outline was visible through the frosted glass doors as he stood with his hands braced against the smoke-colored tiled wall, the water rushing over him.

"What's going on, Danny? What was that about?"

He didn't answer as he remained in the same position, the lines of his body tight and tense. Eventually, he turned off the water. Running a towel over his head and wrapping it around his waist, where it slung low, he stepped out of the shower, leaning against the long, gray marble counter.

He refused to meet my eyes as he passed a hand over his hair, causing droplets to spray the mirror behind him, his knuckles still red from where his fist had connected with Dollar's face, before he cleared his throat. "I know why you thought I should know about Dani."

"You mean my texts?"

He nodded. "Yeah. Dollar got them. He kept them from me."

"What? Why would he do that?"

"Uh, well…he seems to think we shouldn't be together. That I couldn't have all this," he said as he waved his hands, "if I had you as well."

"Why would he think that? It doesn't make sense."

He continued to study the ground. "I know, I don't get it either, but he's always been telling me to get you out of the picture, for one reason or another."

"I don't understand what I ever did to him to make him not like me."

"You didn't do anything; he's just an asshole." He shook his head again. "He was so adamant about getting me away from you, after the whole thing with Terrell…"

"He was the one who told you to dump me at the club?"

He glanced up, an angry red scratch following the line of one brow. "He and I agreed on that, and I told you why." He stepped forward and cupped my face, gazing deep into my eyes. "But you've got to believe me, baby. I would have been on the first plane back here had I known you were pregnant. Fuck Terrell, or whatever else."

"Do you agree with him?"

"Hell, no. I *can* have it all. Just like I told him downstairs; I can, and I will. There's no way I'm letting you go anywhere."

"Is it always going to be like this?"

He frowned. "What do you mean?"

"Are we always going to have people coming between us?" I shook my head. "Me, coming between you and your friends…"

"No." He pulled me in against him and wrapped his arms around me. "Someone who does that is not my friend. Forget it, G."

"I'm sorry, Danny." I rested my head against his bare shoulder, feeling the moist heat from his shower against my cheek. Dollar had been a part of his life for so long that this deception was a huge blow for him.

"Hey." He nudged his shoulder to get me to raise my head as he turned to look in the mirror. "You and me, we're going out tonight, so go get ready."

"Out?"

"Yep." He smiled at my reflection as he ran a comb through his hair. "Wear something hot to torture me, so I won't be able to keep my hands off you."

I studied him, not following at first why he would want to go out since he hated being in public, when I caught on. He wanted to forget what happened, and if he sat around the house, he wouldn't be able to put the events out of his mind. I might be glad Dollar was out of the picture, especially after finding out he was the one who'd kept my pregnancy from Danny, but I still recognized it as a huge loss for him. I loved him and hated to see him hurting, and because I realized what he was after—an escape—I took matters into my own hands.

I closed the bathroom door and gave a small smile when he frowned at me in the mirror. "I have a better idea."

He raised one brow. "Oh yeah? What's that?"

Reaching down, I unhooked the towel at his waist, letting it fall to the floor. "Why don't you turn around and I'll show you?"

His other eyebrow joined the first and he turned. "I might like the sound of this."

I grinned in agreement. "Oh, I think you will." I pushed him on the shoulder so he perched on the edge of the counter. I stepped between his thighs, dragging my nails over taut muscles and through coarse hair before taking him in my hand and caressing him. Leaning in, I nuzzled his neck, breathing in the spicy scent of his shower gel, before placing an open-mouthed kiss right below his ear. "Just sit there and relax. Can you handle that?"

"Baby, I'll do whatever you want me to if you keep that up. Pun intended."

He nodded down to his now full erection in my hands.

Trailing my lips over his hard pecs and running my tongue along the ridges of his abs, I licked and kissed my way down as I dropped to my knees. I knelt before him and, glancing up, found his eyes hot on mine, his pupils appearing large beneath lowered lashes, as I took him in my mouth.

He groaned low in his throat and watched as I swallowed him as deep as I could. Releasing him, I licked up his length and one of his hands tangled in my hair.

"Fuck, baby," he growled. "That feels so good."

Sucking, I twirled my tongue across the crown, and he moaned in appreciation, his hips giving a slight twitch as he fought the urge to thrust. I gripped him, working him with both my mouth and my hand, and soon he was shuddering.

His hold on me tightened. "God, baby. I'm so close."

I picked up the pace of my strokes and he cursed.

"You've got to be fucking kidding me!"

Before I could ask what was wrong, Dani's voice came from inside our bedroom.

"Daddy? Daddy, where are you?" She came closer to the closed bathroom door.

"Do *not* open the door," he gritted.

There was a quiet pause before Dani said, "What?"

"I said, do not open the door." He sounded in pain and didn't bother to cover his agony.

I released him from my mouth and stared up at him in disbelief at the horrible timing, before breaking into silent giggles, which only made me snort.

"It's not fucking funny," he muttered, even though there was a wide grin on his face. "You're not the one who has to walk around with blue balls."

"Daddy?"

"I'll see what she wants." I kissed him and waited for him to wrap the towel around his waist again, angling his back to hide the obvious tenting in the front. I sniggered again, and he turned his head to glower at me.

I opened the door a crack. "What do you need, sweetie?"

Dani danced in place as she tried to see around me. "Where's Daddy?"

"He's busy, honey. What do you need?"

"Well…" she hemmed and hawed. "It's just that…"

He cursed under his breath and strode over, gently shoving me out of the way so he could stand behind the door, revealing only his top half.

"What is it, baby?"

"Oh!" Her eyes lit up at the sight of him and she beamed. "Um, the DVD player in the movie room won't work."

"Did you ask Teddy?"

She shook her head. "He's not here."

He sighed. "All right, I'll be down in a sec. Give me ten minutes."

"Okay." She dashed out, mission accomplished.

"Say thank you, young lady," I called out.

"Thank you," she yelled over her shoulder.

I grinned at Danny. "So, this is what you want, huh?" I wrapped my arms around his waist. "Kids coming in and interrupting at the most inopportune times? Boring family stuff like watching a DVD, most likely a cartoon?"

He returned the smile and pulled me in for a kiss. "Absolutely."

"If only the world saw this side of DOA." My tone was teasing, but I realized I was serious. This is what I wanted the world to see. Maybe if they saw this side of him, all the negative commentary would stop, and the constant feeling that all eyes were on Dani and me would go away. But he wouldn't, so it would continue.

I smacked my lips against his again and turned to walk out of the bathroom.

"Where do you think you're going?" He grabbed one of my arms.

"Oh." I glanced over my shoulder. "Downstairs?"

"I don't think so. I think you're going to lock the bedroom door and get right back here. I'm not done with you."

"Lock the door, huh? You don't think she will give you ten minutes?"

"I'm not taking any chances this time."

He dropped his towel again.

Later, I walked into the movie room and took the time undetected to observe Dani and her father snuggling on the couch. I wished he would show this side of himself to the world and prove everyone wrong, so we weren't the only ones who knew how he was behind closed doors. It would help so much, erase so much of the negativity around him—and us, as a family—but he refused to do so. He was an amazing father, regardless of what anybody said. Yes, he had a rough side to him, a gruffness that came off as callous and harsh, but he cared, he loved us and would do anything for us; of that, I had no doubt. But all the baggage trailing behind him made everything so hard, made me question if I could do this, even with as much as I loved him.

His head turned, and he spotted me standing in the doorway. Our gazes held as he ran a hand over Dani's hair, a small smile curving his lips, and my heart melted.

"Get in here, Mom. Why should I be the only one tortured by two brats singing about building a snowman?"

"Daddy, shush!" Dani scolded.

I laughed and sat on the other side of him. He wrapped his other arm around me and pulled me down to kiss my forehead.

"I wouldn't give this up for the world," he whispered in my ear, and I believed him.

Chapter 31

~ Gabrielle ~

"Come on, Dani." I grabbed my purse from the table and walked around the corner, where Danny sat on the couch watching television. "We're going to go."

He glanced up and muted the sound. "Are you sure?"

"Yeah. We haven't seen Kat in a while, so it will be good to catch up with her. Besides, you'll be locked away in the studio all night, so you won't even notice we're gone. We'll be back before you show your face again."

He crossed the room and pulled me against him. "That's not true. I'll know you're gone the whole time, and I'll worry until you're back safe and sound."

I squeezed him tight. "Nothing to worry about, especially with all the extra security."

"I worry about you, baby. You can't fault me for that."

I gave him a quick kiss on his lips. "You're right, I can't. I love you."

"I love you too. Hurry back." He turned when Dani came around the corner. "Come give your old man a hug, baby girl." She smiled as she launched herself into his arms and laughed when he gave her a loud smacking kiss. "I love you, baby."

"I love you too, Daddy."

He shoved his hands in his pockets like it was killing him to let us leave the house, but he didn't try to stop us. "Have fun with Kat." He watched us walk out, and when I glanced over my shoulder, he gave a little wave. "Hurry back."

After loading Dani into the backseat of my car, a new Cadillac CTS Sports Wagon—which Danny insisted on buying to replace my old beater despite my protests, claiming I needed to think about Dani's safety rather than my pride—I drove down the driveway with my security detail in tow. I chuckled about how Danny believed he'd slipped it by me. One day, one car followed me, the next day, two, and both stuffed with men. I wasn't sure what prompted him to make the change, but I'd stopped questioning him or protesting the protection, especially after strangers had approached me while shopping. People recognized me, much to my dismay, and I was never sure how they would react when they did. The last time, to my horror, when an older woman yelled at me about raising a young girl with the devil, I was thankful my security had jumped in to pull the screeching woman away from me. I'd been so shocked by her outrage that I hadn't been able to turn away, frozen in place by her anger.

Danny must have had a good reason to ask for a couple more guards on my detail, and I assumed the motive behind the increase was due to extra publicity around us. I didn't like it, but understood it came with being a part of Danny's life. Moreover, I wanted all the protection I could get for Dani's sake. As long as she was safe, that was all that mattered.

~ *Danny* ~

"D!" Big T came rushing into the studio.

I turned off the beat I was messing with. "What?"

"Did G already take off with Dani?"

"Yeah, they left a little while ago." I frowned, taking in T's concerned expression. "Why? What's going on?"

"I just got the information you were asking for. About Terrell."

I shot up out of my chair. "And?"

"He's back, hanging in the old hood, and people are saying he's dissing you, blaming you for everything because you disrespected him." He shook his head. "I don't know, D. I don't think we should assume it's safe. We need to warn everyone that he's hanging around. Especially G."

"Fuck." Apparently, Terrell held grudges, and for a very long time. I sighed and hung my head. "I need to let G know."

I grabbed my phone off the counter and dialed.

~ *Gabrielle* ~

The car phone rang, and Kat's name and number appeared on the in-dash display.

"Hey girl, what's up?" I answered. "We're on our way."

"Oh, good. I'm running a little late, but let yourself in. I'll be there in a jiffy."

"Okay, sounds good." A beep sounded through the speakers. I glanced down and Danny's cell number blinked on the screen. "Sorry. Danny's trying to call."

"I'll let you go."

"Oh, it's fine. He's probably calling to tell me he misses us already. I'll call him back when we get to your place."

Kat giggled. "You two are silly."

I smiled. It was nice to feel wanted and loved. "Anyway, we're almost there. We're looking forward to girl time together."

"Me too!" she squealed. "I'll see you soon!"

I hung up and a few minutes later, we pulled into Kat's complex. I walked over to the lead car of my security detail where they were parked on the street.

"She's not here yet, but we're just going to go in," I told the head of my security team, Joe.

"Okay. We'll be right here if you need us."

"Thanks, Joe. I hope you guys don't get too bored hanging out here all night." I always felt guilty that they spent their time watching my less than exciting life. "You should go get something to eat and come back."

"We'll be okay, Gabby. This is what we do. You enjoy yourself and let us know when you're ready to go."

Using my key in the front door, I ushered Dani inside. "Make yourself at home, kiddo, but don't touch anything."

"I know, Mom." She headed to the couch and hopped up. "You tell me every time."

"I tell you every time, because every time, you pick up something you're not supposed to."

She worked at the buckle on one of her shoes and rolled her eyes, letting the shoe drop to the floor.

I threw my purse on the table and pulled out my cell phone. Danny had called again and sent a text message. I frowned, wondering what could be the emergency, when a noise caught my attention. I turned toward the hallway at the same time a silhouette emerged from the guest room. When the shadow became solid, the blood drained from my face and spots clouded my vision, my cell phone slipping out of my grasp.

He shouldn't be here. Why was he here? How did he get in here? He was supposed to be in jail, not standing here in front of me. My mind whirled, trying to make sense of what my eyes were showing me.

He couldn't be here, not when Dani was with me. I wanted her nowhere near him. Somehow, through the fear racing through me, locking me in place, the thought of my daughter propelled me into action.

"Run, Dani!" I shoved her toward the door.

She hesitated, and that slight pause cost her. I pushed her again, but she tripped over her sandal on the floor and hit the deck.

Terrell strolled over to stand in front of the door with a sneer on his face. "You ain't going nowhere."

Tall and thin, with an evil glint in his eye, nothing about him had changed. He'd lived hard and aged, but he looked the same; even gave me the same leering smile as he had in the past. "Hello there, sugar. Long time, no see. I've missed you."

I found my voice as I reached down and shoved Dani behind my legs. "What do you want?"

He glanced down and smiled at Dani, who peeked out from around me. "Well, hello. You must be little D. You look just like your daddy."

"Don't talk to her," I snapped at him, catching him by surprise. "You leave her out of this!"

"Well, well. Aren't you the little protective momma? I like that, I like that."

I breathed hard and my gaze followed him as he wandered around the room, like he was out for a Sunday stroll, and when he turned at a wall, I didn't miss the gun stuffed in the back of his pants. "Please, just leave us alone," I begged, hoping to reach his compassionate side, if he even had one.

He pretended to think it over. "I could do that." He saw my eyes dart around the room, searching for something to use as a weapon, or a way out. "Don't bother trying anything." He smiled and patted his gun. "I won't hesitate to use this."

He paced again and rubbed his chin with his long fingers, as if he was contemplating something. "You see, the way I see it, sweetie. You owe me."

"Why do I owe you?"

"Well, first you took my boy from me."

"I didn't take him from you. He didn't want to be a part of anything you represented."

"True, true," he agreed. "At first, yes, but he would have come around."

I scoffed. "You wish. He despised what you stood for."

He lunged at me, his stale breath hot on my cheek, thrusting me back to the night in front of the dance studio. My throat tightened and my head swam.

"He would have come around!" he yelled.

We eyed one another, both of us breathing hard for different reasons—me, because of fear, and him, because of rage—before he inhaled and leaned away.

He cleared his throat and paced again. When there was space between us, my muscles relaxed, but only a fraction.

"Secondly, you and I, we didn't finish what we started."

My stomach churned. I dreaded where this was going. "We didn't start anything."

"Oh yes, we did, honey. You and I, we gonna finish." Terrell peered down at Dani and smiled again. "And she gonna watch."

"You won't get anywhere." I tried to put conviction into my voice, even though I wanted to curl up into a ball. "Kat will be home any minute now, and I have a whole security detail right outside the door. One word from me and you're dead man."

He shook his head again, like I was a sad little girl. "We won't be going out that way." He nodded toward the back bedroom of the apartment. "We going out that way. They won't even see us."

I swallowed hard. If we went with him, who knew how long it would be before anyone noticed we were missing. I glanced down at Dani and tried to think of an escape, but my mind was empty. I had nothing. All my hopes of getting away depended on going out the front door, but he was going to make us climb out a window and go straight into the woods that lined the back of the apartment complex.

He pulled the gun from his pants and pointed it at Dani, should there be any thoughts on my part of trying anything. "Let's go."

Dani cried out and gripped my legs. I pulled her into my arms, her little body shaking with fright. "Please don't point that at her."

"Any funny business and she's…poof."

"You're sick." When he lifted the gun again, I held up my hands. "Okay, okay. We're going."

I willed myself not to let the tears fall as I led the way out of the apartment. I had no idea what lay ahead for Dani and me, but one thing I knew for sure. The nightmare was only beginning.

Chapter 32

~ Danny ~

I walked into the kitchen when my cell phone rang. When I saw it was Joe's number, I didn't like the unease that settled in my stomach.

"What?"

"D, I think we've got a problem."

I stopped cold in my tracks. "What do you mean, 'a problem'? Where's G?"

He cleared his throat. "That's the problem. We don't know. She's not here."

"What do you mean, she's not there?"

"I don't know." He let out a sound of exasperation. "We saw her go in, and then Kat came running out later, saying they weren't in there."

Icy fear froze my heart. My warning to her had been too late. "I'm on my way."

Big T walked in at that moment. "What's going on?"

I glanced at him as I raced toward the garage. "G and Dani are missing." I put the phone back to my ear. "She and my kid better be alive, or you're going to wish you'd never met me!" I ended the call.

Big T was right behind me. "Did you tell her about—?"

"I tried." I jumped into the Hummer and waited as Big T climbed into the passenger side. "I called her a few times, left her a message, even texted her, but she didn't get back with me. Fuck!" I slammed my hand on the steering wheel and tore down the driveway, my security right behind me.

"We will find them, D," T said.

"We better. Get my piece and make sure it's loaded."

"D," he protested, but stopped when I pierced him with a look that said I wasn't fucking taking no for an answer. "Fine, fine, but you should let the team do the dirty work. Not you. You're no good to anybody behind bars. There's too much at stake now."

"And look where that got us. Even with them, he still got to her. What the fuck!" I slammed my hand against the steering wheel again, ignoring the pain that seared my palm.

Heavy silence fell in the SUV before I broke it again. "I can't lose them, T. I just can't." My voice cracked, and I turned toward the window.

"You won't, man. You won't. We'll find them and get them back to you, I promise."

Despite Big T's promise, I didn't believe I would be lucky twice, and had an ugly feeling this time when I found Gabrielle, she wasn't going to be unconscious. She was going to be dead.

* * *

We rushed into Kat's home. She jumped up from where she'd curled into a ball on the couch when we came through the door.

"Did you find them?" she cried. Her tear-streaked face held an ash gray pallor, and her eyes threatened to overflow again.

"No," I answered. "You hear anything?"

"Oh God." She held a shaky hand over her mouth. "No. Nothing." She cradled a little sandal to her chest. "What happened to them?"

I snatched the shoe from her and squeezed it in my hand as I closed my eyes against the sharp pain in my heart. I forced myself to take a deep breath and shoved it in my pocket, praying this wasn't my last glimpse of my little girl.

I peered up at Big T. "Where would he take them?"

Teddy shrugged his big shoulders as Kat asked, "Who?"

"Terrell," I answered. I glanced at Joe, who had stepped inside the door. "Anything out there?"

"Nothing."

Kat held up her hand. "Wait, how do you know Terrell is involved with this? I thought he was still in jail."

"No, he's out." I pulled out my gun and undid the safety.

Her wide eyes watched me. "D, you're not going to shoot him, are you?"

"I might."

"Perhaps we should call the cops?"

"No! No cops. They'll just fuck everything up, and who knows what will happen to Gabby and Dani then. No," I repeated, when they appeared ready to interrupt. "I'm doing this on my own. It's all because of me, anyway."

Big T and Kat both protested, but stopped when my cell phone rang. I snatched it out of my pocket and studied the display. "I don't recognize the number," I told them, but answered anyway. "Yeah?"

Silence crept across the line before hard breathing.

"I can hear you. Who the fuck is this?"

"Danny." Her weak voice was barely audible.

"Gabrielle!" My skin flushed cold, mixed with fear and relief. "G, baby, where are you?"

"Danny, you have to find her," she sobbed, her voice cutting off at the end.

"Baby, you need to tell me where you are. Tell me where you are."

"Dance…"

"Come on, baby." I squeezed my eyes shut, silently urging her to tell me where she was. "Hold on, don't pass out on me. Where are you? Please tell me where to find you."

"Ballet…dance…" The line fell silent.

"G? Gabrielle? Dammit, G, don't you go quiet on me!" Fresh waves of terror swamped me as visions of her bleeding out somewhere filled my mind. I glanced at Big T and Kat, who were both eyeing me with concern. I shook my head as I fought the surge of emotions washing over me. I wanted to cry like a little girl while ranting and raving like a mad man out of control. "She went quiet," I told them. "Gabby?"

"What did she say, D?" Big T asked.

"I don't know…something about dance…ballet…that's it." I paced, refusing to put the phone down, my last lifeline to the love of my life and my baby girl.

"Dance?" Kat frowned. "What does that mean?"

Big T's eyes widened. "He went back, D. He went back to where this all started."

I stared at T before I understood what he was saying. "Shit! He took her back to the ballet studio."

I sprinted out the door with everyone on my heels.

Jumping in my vehicle, I placed my gun on the console between the seats, within quick reach. When Big T was in, I raced back to the old hood. It was where everything had started, and now where everything was going to end.

Twenty minutes later, I screeched to a halt on the street outside of the old studio. The building was dark, with no signs of anyone, but I jumped out and ran to the front door, finding it locked.

Big T came up behind me. "Anything?"

Cupping my hands on the window, I tried to see in. "I don't know. I can't fucking see a thing." I turned when Joe came rushing around the corner. "What's up?"

"The back door is broken," he said, and we all took off running down the alley.

When I got there, I pushed ahead of the rest of the guys. "Let me through."

I stepped into the dark studio and listened, but all I heard was the heavy breathing of the group behind me. I moved, waiting for Terrell to show his face, but was blinded when the lights poured on from overhead, causing everyone to groan.

"What the fuck?" I glared over my shoulder.

"Sorry," one guard mumbled.

Once my eyes adjusted, I saw the studio was the same, with mirrored walls in the long, narrow room. I glanced around, looking for anything, when I spotted the trail of blood leading into the waiting area. My heart caught in my throat.

I rushed over and found Gabrielle slumped on the floor with the phone by her hand.

"Gabrielle!" I cradled her head in my lap. "Wake up, baby. I'm here. I've got G!" I yelled to the others. "Find my baby girl, goddamnit!"

I ran my hands over her face, trying to find the source of her bleeding, which was from a nasty cut on her head. He'd bound her ankles, and the skin at her wrists was bloody and torn, evidence she'd fought hard against the binding and somehow got her hands free, so she could drag herself across the floor to the phone that sat on the desk in the tiny waiting area.

"Gabrielle, baby, please wake up." I ran my hands over her hair, and when I got too close to her cut, she frowned and moaned. "Gabby, wake up, baby. I'm here. Wake up."

It took a moment for her to get her eyes open and focus on me, but when she did, she tried to sit up. "Danny!" Her voice was hoarse.

"Take it easy, baby. Take it easy."

She held her head in her hands while I worked to unbind her ankles. "Did you find Dani?"

At that moment, one of the security guards came back into the room. "Find her?"

"No, she's not here. Neither is he."

She clutched my shirt and forced my eyes to hers. "You came here without looking for Dani? You have to find her!" Her breaths hitched.

"Hey, hey." I shushed her and pried my shirt out of her tight grip. "We're going to, baby. We're going to."

"No! You don't understand!" She shook her head and tears spilled down her face. "He's going to hurt her. He didn't want me, Danny. He wanted her. Nothing can happen to her!"

"Did he say where he was taking her?" Gabrielle was close to losing it, bordering on hysterical, which only fed my precarious hold on my anxiety, but I somehow remained composed. "Baby, you need to tell me everything you can remember. Calm down, baby. Please. You need to tell me what you know."

"Uh…" She took gasping breaths, struggling to recall anything. "I don't know!"

"Come on. You can remember. He must have said something."

Everyone gathered around, waiting for her to recollect something. She took several deep breaths before trying again. "Uh, he said something about making a point and going someplace that meant something." She struggled for more, and when nothing came to her, panic took over again and she grabbed at me. "I can't remember anything!"

"Okay, okay. You did good." I rubbed her back. "Making a point, and a place that meant something." I frowned at Big T. "Mean anything to you?"

He puzzled it over before shaking his head. "I don't know, D."

"Making a point...meant something." I willed my brain to put the pieces together. I had to, for the sake of my daughter. There was no way I would let Terrell take her away from me.

"Is there a place around here that meant something to you guys?" Joe asked.

"Well, G used to dance here," I said. "Wait!" I straightened and turned back to Gabrielle. "Did he say making a point, or going to the point?"

"Uh. I don't know."

My eyes met Big T's, who had caught on and was nodding his head. "It's got to be Lighter Park. G and I used to go there all the time and sit at the point. It's got to be that." I grabbed her arm. "Can you stand, baby?"

With a new fire lit under her, she jumped up without my help, but stumbled, and I reached out a hand to hold her steady. "We've got to get there, Danny. Let's go!" She tugged on my grip, eager to leave.

We rushed out the front door and piled in the cars. Big T climbed in the back as Gabrielle sat in the passenger seat.

I sped toward the park where Gabrielle and I had spent most of our time together. I wasn't sure what Terrell was trying to pull, but he was making a fucking production; a little trip down memory lane, intending this to be the last one for all of us.

I held my hand up over the seat. "Hand me that towel back there, T." When Big T handed it over, I gave it to Gabrielle. "Hold this to your head to stop the bleeding, baby."

She lifted her head and stared at me, her eyes filled with utter sadness and fear that gripped my soul and ripped it out. "Please get there, Danny." A big tear trailed down her cheek before she grabbed the towel from me and pressed it to her temple.

"I will, baby, and I will get our baby girl back. I promise you."

Chapter 33

~ Gabrielle ~

The caravan of SUVs raced over the bridge and the expansive park loomed ahead. Thanks to Danny's contributions, the entire area glowed with lights, but there was so much ground to cover that I worried we wouldn't get to Dani in time.

Danny parked, and after Big T slid out of the back, he put a hand on my arm as I opened my door.

"Please stay here. I don't want to worry about you *and* Dani. It will be easier if you stay here."

"But I want to find her," I protested. "She's my baby. I can't sit here and do nothing."

"Please, baby. She's my baby too, but I need you stay here so I can concentrate on bringing this fucker down."

I swallowed and remained silent, before sagging against the seat and nodding. "Okay."

"Lock the car and if anything happens, hit the emergency button on the OnStar."

He jumped out, and my gaze followed him as he raced over to the group to distribute orders. They all took off in multiple directions before I realized I no longer saw anyone from where I sat alone in the parking lot. I glanced around at the park in front of me; a place that held so many good memories, now being replaced with horrible ones. Nothing could happen to Dani.

Nothing. If anything did, I would die.

I tried not to let the panic creeping in at the edges envelope me, and evened my breath to prevent hyperventilation, but it was becoming difficult to ward off, especially with each minute that passed with no sign of Dani. I shook my head, trying to shake out the jumbled confusion of my racing mind, and when I did, something caught my attention. I peered out the side window and spotted the gazebo in the distance. Or rather, where the gazebo should have been, the area now dark and forgotten. No one had gone in that direction, and I stared into the blackness, every fiber in my being telling me my daughter was there.

Throwing the towel down, the overhead light came on when I pulled on the door handle, and a flash of silver glinted from Danny's pistol where it sat on the console, forgotten and left behind in his rush. I reached down and lifted it, the cool metal a sure, sturdy weight in my hand. I had never fired a weapon before, but I wouldn't hesitate to shoot when it came to Dani's safety. Not at all.

I tightened my grasp on the grip and shoved the door open, stepping into the night. A brisk wind stirred up my hair as I started toward the gazebo, shoving the pistol into the waistband at the small of my back, but I felt nothing. Not the chill in the air, not the pain in my wrists, or in my head. I didn't feel the sting of my cuts or the ache in my ankles. I felt nothing but cold determination.

~ *Danny* ~

In the middle of the expansive fields, I grouped with Big T, Joe, and a few of the other bodyguards. Everyone panted hard from tearing through the park, trying to locate Dani.

"Anything?" I asked as I sucked in a breath.

"Nothing," Joe said.

"Fuck!" I turned around, my eyes straining to pierce through the darkness to find my baby, who must be scared out of her mind. I was too, not knowing where she was and what Terrell was saying to her, doing to her. I made myself stop before I went crazy, not letting my thoughts go astray and imagining Terrell's hands on my baby girl. If I did, the horror would paralyze me.

I spun in an agitated arch again and turned back when a shadow in the distance caught my eye. The gazebo. I'd forgotten about it in my haste, since the structure was invisible, the bright lights that lit the structure dark. My feet were moving in its direction before I even realized it.

"Where are you going, D?" Big T was right behind me, his breathing labored as he struggled to keep up.

"The gazebo," I shouted over my shoulder, digging deep to make my legs carry me faster than I'd ever ran before in my life. "The asshole is there with her."

I raced up the path and stopped when I reached the center of the structure. Darkness surrounded me, and I walked around, taking shallow breaths, trying to hear any telling signs. A crunching sound broke the silence when I stepped on glass. Terrell had killed all the lights by shattering the bulbs.

The sounds of multiple feet pounding the ground echoed as everyone caught up, and I waved my hand to hush them.

"Come on, Terrell. Let's quit the game," I called out, so certain the prick was hiding somewhere nearby, watching me. "I'm here, what you wanted." I continued to walk out of the gazebo toward the water.

I took one step at a time, waiting for a hint to where Terrell remained hunkered down. Nothing except giant shadows of trees lined the jagged water line, but I somehow knew this was where he waited.

I glanced behind me and found my crew covering me about ten feet back, but well within striking distance. Nobody would hesitate to use force if needed.

"Terrell, come on. This is stupid. I didn't realize you were one to hide like a pussy."

A soft chuckle came out of the darkness to my right. I turned as he emerged from the black shadows. Alone.

I fought not to let the panic show on my face as my brain screamed out for my daughter. "Where's my girl?"

Terrell gave a nonchalant shrug. "Maybe I know, maybe I don't. I can't remember a lot of things these days." He chuckled as he tapped his temple with his finger.

I took a step toward him with my hands up. "Let her go, Terrell. You've got me, and that's what you want."

Anger glinted in his eyes. "How the fuck do you know what I want?"

"That's what this has always been about. You and me. Not Gabby, and not my baby girl. You and me." I held out my arms at my sides. "Well, here I am, motherfucker. Let's finish this."

"It's far from finished, my man. This is just the beginning. I start with your little girl, then I move to your woman." He leered at me, his posture smug and tight. He might have aged while in prison, thinned out, but he was still angry, and that anger outlined his whole body. "I'm going to make you watch me kill everything that means anything to you, and then you'll be begging me to kill you."

Even as a cold chill ran through me, I refused to show any fear. As soon as Terrell believed he had the upper hand, it was over. Until then, I needed to keep him guessing on what I would do, which wouldn't be anything other than talk, as I didn't have my piece on me, but he didn't need to know that.

"What's the point?" I asked. "Just kill me; that's what you want, anyway. Why all this fucking drama?"

He shook his head, like I was a sad piece of shit. "It's all about family, man. How many times do I have to tell your sorry ass? It's all about family, and this here is your precious little family. You shunned mine. You thought you were better than all of us, so I'm going to kill yours."

This fucker's crazy. I tried to figure out what my next move should be. Any movement from anyone, and Terrell wouldn't hesitate to pull the trigger. As long as he was away from Dani and Gabrielle, that's all that mattered. I'd keep him talking for years, if that's what it took.

Out of the corner of my eye, I spotted a shadow moving behind the trees at Terrell's back, the outline too thin to be any of the guys. So that only meant it could be one person—Gabrielle.

Damn her. What the fuck is she trying to do? Get herself killed? But she was looking for our daughter, so I needed to keep Terrell's attention on me.

"I didn't shun your family, Terrell. It wasn't for me. It was for you and I've nothing against that; that's your choice, but it wasn't for me. You knew that. You knew I was a fucking loner, and that wasn't my thing."

Terrell shook his head. "No, man. You said we ain't good enough."

"I never said that."

"You turned your back on me, on us. On the help we gave you."

I shook my head. "No, man. It's what I had to do to get out of here. You know that."

"I don't fucking know that. We all could have gone with you. We could have made it big as a family, but no. You turned your back on us."

"I couldn't take everyone, Terrell!" I poked my chest. "I barely got myself out of here, let alone everyone else. I couldn't save everyone."

He pointed at me. "You turned your back on us. You didn't even try to help anyone but yourself."

"Terrell—"

"No! There's nothing you can say to change my mind." He glared. "This is how it's gonna be. Dollar might be asking me to do his dirty work again, but I'm glad to be doing it this time."

My head spun. Doing Dollar's dirty work? Again? What did that even mean? But I couldn't question any of it because Terrell was heading back to the trees. I saw Joe move and waved my hand, holding him off. No one could jump in on this. Anyone else, and I lost my girls for sure. If I wanted this over with for good, then it was up to me to finish Terrell off, once and for all.

~ *Gabrielle* ~

I rushed up the path, trying to be as quiet as possible. I wanted no one to see me, prepared to reach out and grab Dani once Terrell came out with her. But as I watched from my hiding spot, my heart stopped when he emerged without her.

Where was she? What had he done with her?

Hidden in the cover of the trees, I listened as he and Danny went back and forth. In the past, I would have panicked and raced out to stop Danny as he offered himself up, believing I couldn't live without him. It wasn't that I didn't feel a trickle of fear now for his safety, but there was someone more important, more innocent, than him or me. I had to find our daughter; nothing else mattered, and because of that, I needed the distraction he provided.

I kept my ear out for Danny's voice to keep apprised on how things were going with him and Terrell as I crept low, looking for any sign of Dani. I treaded as lightly as possible, trying not to make any sound from the brush on the ground, the lapping of the water providing cover noise.

"Where are you going?" Danny yelled at Terrell, which made me stop in my tracks. I paused, holding my breath, waiting to hear what came next.

"I ain't going nowhere," he replied. "I ain't afraid of your white ass."

"Well, then get back here, you fucker," Danny taunted him. "Why you walking away from me then?"

I had little time, either before things between them escalated, or before Terrell came back around the trees. In about twenty more steps, I would be out in the open, exposed and out of the tree line. It also meant there was no other place nearby where Dani might be. My heart pounded harder, and a fresh layer of cold sweat broke out over my skin. I refused to believe I was too late. I couldn't be. There would be no purpose to my life without my baby.

I stopped, straining my eyes to see anything, when I spotted a faint white mass resting under a big pine tree. As I crept closer, it became clear it was a small person on her side with her knees pulled up to her chest.

I plunged underneath, a cry of relief escaping me. "Dani! Oh my God, Dani!"

He had tied her to the trunk and blindfolded her. "Mommy!"

"I've got you, baby. I've got you!" I wept as I tried to figure out how to untie her little wrists. I was so busy trying to find something to cut the rope with, that I didn't register the sounds of someone crashing through the branches until I heard Danny yell.

"Gabrielle! Dani! Get the fuck out of there!"

"I can't! She's tied up and I'm not leaving her."

As Terrell thrust through the last of the limbs, pointing his gun at me, I planted myself in front of Dani and faced him.

"Get away from her, bitch," he snarled.

"No." I raised my gun and pointed it at him. "You get away from her, and you get away from me, you dirty piece of shit."

"Gabrielle!" Danny emerged from the trees, but then stopped in his tracks and held up one hand. "G, put the gun down."

"No." I didn't take my eyes off Terrell and his smug grin. "No, I won't let him continue to do this to us."

Terrell chuckled with a casual glance over his shoulder. "It's all right, D. It's not like the little priss is gonna pull the trigger. She'll hurt herself before she hurts—"

A loud bang interrupted him, shock passing over his face before he dropped his gaze from me to the bullet hole in his chest. He stumbled to the right before crumbling down to the ground, a gurgling noise coming from him…and then there was nothing.

~ *Danny* ~

I ignored Terrell and the others filing in behind me, and stepped toward Gabrielle, keeping my eyes trained on her. She was ghastly white, and her entire body shook as every emotion overtook her. She kept a death grip on the gun as she stared in disbelief at Terrell's body a few feet away.

I laid my hand on hers and pushed the pistol down to her side. "It's okay, baby. Look at me." I waited until her wild eyes found mine, her breaths coming in short, hard pants. "It's okay. I'm here. Give me the gun, baby."

Her gaze flew to Terrell again and back. "I killed him."

"Yes, you did. Give me the gun, baby."

She let go, and I held on to her as her knees gave out. Lowering us to the ground, I wrapped myself around her as she trembled violently. I continued to cradle her, while leaning over to kiss Dani's forehead as she bawled.

"It's okay, baby. We've got you. You're safe," I said, trying to keep a hold on my emotions even though my eyes watered. "Someone get over here with a knife to cut some rope."

Gabrielle sobbed as she draped herself around Dani, while I embraced them both, finally letting my tears fall. My family was in my arms and they were safe, and that's all I ever wanted.

Chapter 34

~ Danny ~

We returned home early the next morning, after a long night at the police station and the hospital, both Dani and Gabrielle getting attention to their injuries. Gabrielle had said little, only answering the questions the detectives, or the doctors, had asked her. I was afraid to push her, afraid of forcing her over whatever edge she was teetering.

I carried a sleeping Dani to her room, and Gabrielle and I both tucked her into bed after stripping off her clothes. She'd passed out in the car on the way home, exhaustion ruling over any fear she might have still been experiencing. I was thankful for the blindfold that had prevented her from witnessing her mother killing Terrell, but there was no doubt nightmares lurked in her mind from the experience that we would have to work through. Even I would not be immune to having them.

After checking on Dani one last time, cracking her door open and leaving the hallway light on, I stepped into our bedroom. I'd expected to hear the shower running and Gabrielle trying to wash off the night, but instead, I found her sitting on the end of the bed, staring at the floor.

I sat next to her and put an arm around her shoulder. "How are you holding up?"

She jerked, like she just realized I was there, and shoved to her feet. Her hair was a tangled mess, with blood matted from the cut on her head. Dirt covered her face, and her eyes were bloodshot. "Did you know?"

I frowned. "Know what?"

"About Terrell?" Her voice rose. "Did you know about Terrell and not tell me?"

"I did, and I tried to tell you."

"When?" She ran a shaky hand through her hair. "When did you try to tell me, Danny?"

"Gabrielle, honey. Let's not get worked up—"

"Don't tell me what to do!"

I stopped and gaped at her when she screeched at me.

"I'm sick and tired of you always thinking you know what's best for me."

"I don't. I swear, I don't."

She didn't hear me. "Every time, look where that's gotten us." She paced away from me and shoved her hair out of her face again. "Is it ever going to end, Danny?" She spun back. "Huh? Is it ever going to end, or are there more skeletons in your closet that we'll have to deal with?"

I reached out to touch her arm, but she backed away. "I'm sorry. I don't know what else to say but I'm sorry."

"You can't, can you?"

"What?"

"You can't promise this won't happen again. Who else, Danny? Who else have you pissed off enough that they are going to try to kill your daughter?"

I clenched my jaw. "No one."

"No one? Can you promise that?" She shoved my shoulder. "Can you?"

"No!" I took a deep breath and blew it out my nose. "No, I can't, but I don't think—"

She rushed past me. "I don't care what you think. I want a promise!"

Gabrielle disappeared into the walk-in closet, and soon, the sound of materials moving around carried out. I stood in the doorway, the scene in front of me filling me with alarm. "What are you doing?"

She knelt on the floor, stuffing clothes into a bag. "I can't do this. I can't live like this. I can't live your life. I thought I could, but I can't. I can't handle the spotlight, the attention, and I can't handle always wondering if Dani is safe."

"Gabrielle, please." I grabbed her arms and turned her toward me. "We can work through this. You're upset about what happened—"

She pushed me away. "Of course, I'm upset! I killed someone, Danny! I shot him! I will never forget this. Hell, I may go to jail because of this." Her eyes watered. "This is so messed up."

Remorse and guilt surged through me, and I wished I could turn back time so I was pulling the trigger and not her. But most of all, there was shame. Shame that she'd done my dirty work for me, and would suffer because of it.

"I know, baby, I know, and it guts me that you had to. It was self-defense, and I know they'll see it that way. You don't need to worry about that." I reached out a hand, but then let it drop. "But let's not make any rash decisions tonight because of this. Let's just go to sleep and we'll talk about it tomorrow."

She shook her head. "No. I need to get away from you right now."

My eyes widened, and I stepped back, deep hurt causing every bone in my body to ache, my throat to tighten, and my head to throb. "You need to get away...from me?"

"I can't think straight when I'm around you!" The tears spilled over and she covered her face with her hands. "Danny, I'm crazy about you. You know that. I love you with every fiber of my being, but...but...I can't deal with this." She paused and took a deep breath. "I just need to get away. I'm taking Dani and we're getting out of here. Please don't stop me. I'll be in contact."

She hurried past me out of the closet, dragging the suitcase behind her. I wanted to give chase, beg her to stay, but it would do no good. She asked for space, and I would give it to her, even though it almost killed me and left me breathless. Besides, what could I say to change anything? Nothing. Everything she'd said had been right. I couldn't promise their absolute safety, and I'd done nothing to change anything, letting my stupid pride get in the way. But I refused to live without my girls in my life, so if she needed time, then she'd have it. But in the meantime, I would give her everything she'd asked for. I would find a way to fulfill the promise she wanted so she'd come back.

She *had* to come back.

~ *Gabrielle* ~

I stretched out on the bed in the hotel room Dani and I were sharing with Kat. Her apartment held too many bad memories, and neither of us wanted to go back there for the time being. Kat was even considering finding a new place, but she'd deal with that later. We'd holed ourselves up at a nice establishment for two weeks and pampered ourselves on Danny's money. It was the least he could do, in my opinion.

Exhaustion was a heavy weight on me; sleep a distant friend. Every time I closed my eyes, I relived that horrible night, from the absolute terror of trying to find Dani to the gut-clenching moment when I'd pulled the trigger. Once I'd gotten past the horror of what I'd done and the emotional aftermath, there was no regret because God knows Terrell was certainly going to kill us, there was no doubt about that. I would have to live with this decision for the rest of my life—one I would make again, if faced with the same situation—and I hoped no legal repercussions came from it.

I didn't blame Danny for what happened. The situation with Terrell had always had a life of its own, and he'd done everything possible to get us away from it. But I blamed him for not trying to change other things; like showing the world what a kind, loving father he was, and stop all the negative commentaries and ridiculous accusations the press threw at us, but he refused to do so. It was a waste of his time, according to him.

And Dollar. He had to do something about Dollar. The Danny I knew and loved would never just sit back and let others threaten his loved ones. The Danny I knew and loved would do everything in his power to protect us.

I sighed. I had hoped the time away from him would make the answers clearer, but it hadn't. If anything, after two weeks, everything was cloudier. I was in a no-win situation. I couldn't live with Danny, and I couldn't live without him. I missed him so much I ached, but being with him meant having to deal with things I didn't want to. Every day, Dani asked when we were going home to see Daddy, and every time, I had to ignore the deep sadness in her blue eyes when I didn't answer.

I glanced down at my cell phone where it sat next to me on the bed. Kat had brought it with her, having found it under the table in her apartment. Still to be cleared were the notifications that Danny had called and left a voicemail, as well as texted. I had yet to listen to his message or read the texts, but I knew what they were—his warning that Terrell was out there. He'd tried to tell me, had kept that promise. He'd also respected my wishes of leaving me alone, as he hadn't contacted me since I'd stormed out of the house. He was giving me the time I'd asked for, even though it had to be driving him crazy.

The door opened, and Kat and Dani walked in.

"We're back," Kat announced.

"What did you find?"

Dani held up bags of chips and candy bars. "This!"

"Oh! That looks like a very healthy snack." I reached out and snatched a bag of potato chips. "I think these are mine."

Dani giggled as she dropped everything on the bed, except for a bag of cheese balls. "Can I watch TV?"

"Sure, baby."

She planted herself in the connecting living room and turned on the television. Kat set a bottle of water on the nightstand next to me, and then sat on the other bed.

"She asked me if she could use my phone," Kat told me, giving me a knowing look.

"I know, I know. I should let her talk to him."

"You need to do something, Gabrielle. You can't stay here forever."

I tossed the greasy chips aside, whatever appetite I'd had, lost. "I just don't know what to do."

Kat sat back against the headboard and plucked a pretzel out of the bag she was holding. "What do you want?"

"I want Dani to be safe."

"And you don't think she will be with Danny?"

"I thought so, but as long as we're in the spotlight, I don't see how she can be. Even if it isn't someone from Danny's past, there are plenty of people out there who feel it's their place to 'protect' Dani and me, and he won't do anything about it."

"What do you expect him to do?"

"I don't know. *Something*!" I ignored Kat's slanted look. "Tell people to shut up; anything more than nothing."

"Now, you didn't ask my opinion or anything, but I think he's doing about as much as he can."

"Of course, you do." I scrubbed my face in frustration. "Sometimes I wish we could go back to the way we were. Danny not famous, and it's just me and him. Before the incident in front of the ballet studio, when everything between us was perfect."

"Now, you don't believe that silliness, do you?"

I scowled. "What do you mean 'silliness'? It's true."

"If that was the case, there'd be no Dani. And you really want Danny to suffer the way he did? He's made so much of himself, and you'd want to take that away from him?"

I cursed myself for my selfish wish. Kat was right. Danny's life had been rough for him; and, not that it wasn't rough now, but it was different, and it was a better life for him.

"Of course not."

"You knew being with him would be tough, given his new life, but you still went for it. And why?"

"Because I'm an idiot."

"No, because you love him, and he loves you. You guys were meant for each other. I've always believed that."

"I'm scared," I whispered.

"And you have every right to be, with what happened, but that doesn't mean you should walk away from him and what you guys have. You have a wonderful family. Don't break it up because there are things in Danny's life he has no control over. He's trying. You know he is."

I did, but somewhere along the way, I'd forgotten it.

"Give him a chance to make this right."

"Yeah, but what? He can't promise me something he has no control over."

"Hey!" Dani's voice carried in from the other room. "It's Daddy."

"What do you mean, honey?" Kat asked as she scooted off the bed toward the living room with me in tow.

Dani pointed at the TV, where a news anchor was reading a story about Danny, his picture hanging in the upper right-hand corner of the screen.

"In Entertainment news this evening, we have a statement from the rapper, DOA."

The screen shifted, and text filled the display.

"To everyone who believes my private life is your business, it isn't. To everyone who believes it's their place to tell Gabrielle and me how to live our lives and raise our daughter, it isn't. Gabrielle and Dani are my life, but they're my private life, and I refuse to share them with my professional life. I'm sorry if this is difficult for some to understand, but I refuse to allow them to fall under the same scrutiny as my music.

Many people have a difficult time believing I could be a good father, and to them I say, I don't care. As long as I know I am, and Gabrielle believes I am, that's all that matters. But Gabrielle wanted me to do one thing, and I'm going to do it only because she asked it of me. I'm going to share a private moment with you in hopes that it will serve as proof that I am being the best father I know how to be."

A video started, taken by someone's cell phone, most likely Big T's, because I had never seen it before. Music played in the background, and Danny held Dani in his arms. They both sang along at the top of their lungs, dancing with each other, and the happiness in both their eyes was unmistakable. Gone were the walls, gone were the hard edges, and all of Danny's true emotions were on display.

"Oh, girl." Kat put a hand over her mouth and her eyes filled. "That is the sweetest thing I've ever seen."

"That's me!" Dani pointed at the screen with a big grin on her face.

The screen went back to the text and the end of Danny's statement.

"I understand everyone is curious and interested because you're my fans, but please give us the privacy and respect we deserve. Thank you."

My eyes overflowed. I'd asked Danny to do something, and he did. He'd bared himself to the world, showed his softer side, and I couldn't have asked for anything more. He had always promised he would do whatever I wanted, would give me whatever I needed, and he'd come through again. Why I ever doubted that—doubted him—I had no idea. But what I did know was I would not lose my family again.

Turning away from the television, I headed back into the bedroom.

"Where you going?" Kat asked.

I grabbed the suitcase and started packing. "Back where I belong, where Dani belongs. Back with Danny."

Chapter 35

~ *Danny* ~

I sat in the dark living room, nursing two fingers of whiskey. My house was empty, silent; the way I wanted it, but I'd never been so alone. My heart ached, and a constant dull pain throbbed behind my eyes.

I missed my girls.

I'd promised to give Gabrielle time, even though it was a struggle not to pick up the phone and call her, or drive over to the hotel that had showed up on my credit card. I wanted to give her the time she needed, but the wait was killing me. She had to come back because she wanted to, not because I begged her.

I swirled the glass and contemplated a sip. I shouldn't be drinking, I didn't want to give in to the addiction I fought against daily, but I was finding it hard to care anymore. I had nothing, so what did it matter.

Two weeks had passed and still no word from her. I'd tried to do what I could, worked on a statement with my publicist, saying all the things she'd wanted me to say. I had no idea when it would air, or if she would see it, and I was unconvinced it would work. If it had, she'd be here by now, right?

I'd even tried to find Dollar, but so far, I'd come up empty-handed. It still hurt, knowing someone I'd trusted with my life had done those things out of sheer greed. I felt sick any time I thought about it and had moved quickly to remove Dollar's name from everything, refusing to be associated with him anymore, and cut off his earnings from my music. I hoped never to cross paths with him again, and if we did…well, he should be ready for paybacks. Gabrielle was right. We weren't safe if Dollar was walking around feeling jilted. If he'd stooped to the level of working with Terrell, then who knew what else he would do.

All I could do now was wait. Wait and see if I'd lost everything, or had all I'd ever wanted. I could do nothing else, *wanted* to do nothing else. All I could do was sit in the dark, in my large, deserted house, and wait.

The back door opened and closed, but I remained where I was, figuring it was Big T coming to check on me. There was silence before a light flew on in the kitchen, followed by the scamper of feet.

"Daddy?"

Dropping my drink on the table next to me, I shot out of the chair. Dani spotted me, a huge grin breaking out on her face, and my heart almost burst. I knelt, and she threw herself at me, wrapping her arms around my neck. I stood as I hugged her tight, closing my eyes and inhaling her sweet scent.

"Hey, baby," I said.

"I missed you, Daddy!"

"I missed you too, sweetheart. So much." I turned at the sound of foot-steps behind me and caught Gabrielle's eye. "Hey."

She gave me a timid smile. Reaching out, Gabrielle rubbed Dani's back. "Honey, can you give Daddy and me a moment, please?"

She leaned back in my arms and kissed my cheek. "Come upstairs and play when you're done?"

I smiled. "There's nothing else I'd rather do."

I set her down, and she ran up the back stairway. Turning, I shoved my hands into my pockets. "How are you?"

"I'm okay. You?"

I shrugged. "Okay."

Uncomfortable silence fell between us, neither one knowing where to start. I wanted to pull her into my arms and tell her how much I missed her, how much I needed her, and how much I loved her, but I couldn't. She had to make the first move, letting me know where we stood.

So, I remained quiet, waiting for her to begin. She let out a sigh, walked over to a chair in front of the island, and sat down.

"I owe you an apology."

"You owe *me* an apology? Why?"

"For running out like I did. I was just so scared, so confused, so…sick and tired of worrying about…everything."

"You don't need to apologize. It's understandable—"

"I blamed you." She noticed my flinch at the sting of her words and took a deep breath before continuing. "It was your fault we were in the spotlight, and bad things being said about me. It was your fault everyone continued to rip you apart and you wouldn't do anything about it. It was your fault Terrell just would not go away."

I nodded as I sat in the seat next to her, hunched over like she'd punched me in the gut, because everything she said was true. It *was* my fault. "I understand—"

"No, you don't." She grabbed my hand with hers. "I blamed you, but in reality, you weren't the one I should be blaming. None of this was your doing. You didn't ask for anyone's opinion about what you do outside of your music. You didn't ask for anyone's approval for how you live your life and who you have in it. You didn't ask Terrell to threaten me or Dani." Giving my hand a squeeze, she smiled at me. "You're the last person I should blame, because all this happened because you did the *right* thing. You got away from Terrell and everything he stood for. You got away from your father and became an outstanding one yourself, despite what you grew up with. You made yourself into someone successful. You became who you wanted to be, and you should be so proud of that. I am. You're a wonderful person, an even better father, and I lost sight of that. Can you forgive me?"

I took a deep breath, moved by her words. She was the only person in my life who'd ever truly believed in me and really saw me for who I was. I loved her more than I ever thought possible.

"Baby, there's nothing to forgive you for. You had a lot thrown at you, even in the past, and I don't blame you for getting overwhelmed with it all. I had years to get used to it, but you only had a few months before everyone was all over you. Then throw the shit in there with Terrell…" I shook my head. "It *is* my fault. This is *my* past following me around, not yours. I tried to get away from it, but I guess…" I dropped my hand to my lap, not knowing what more to say. "All I can promise is to try. To always try to make things right. I won't give up until you're happy. That's all that matters, baby."

"I know, and thank you for doing that."

"For doing what?"

"For the statement. I saw it tonight."

I ducked my head, embarrassed. "You liked it?"

She leaned forward and put her arms around my neck. "I loved it. It was perfect."

"I'm sure some dick out there will have something to say about it."

"Let them." She gave me a gentle shake. "You know why?"

"Why?"

"Because someone wise once told me, it doesn't matter what anyone else says, as long as we know what the real story is."

I chuckled. "Sounds like a smart person."

"The smartest." She leaned in and touched her lips to mine. "I love you, Danny Anderson."

"I love you too, my GE."

"Always."

"Always," I promised.

Epilogue

~ Danny ~

Sitting in the gazebo at our park, after a night of reliving our first date, including dinner at the same small Italian restaurant, Gabrielle and I sat on the bench bearing our names, gazing out over the water. We had made ourselves come back to this place to create new memories rather than let the recent bad ones take the specialness away from us. To do so would let Terrell win, and we refused to let that happen, even if we averted our eyes from the line of trees where it all had gone down.

Questions still lingered and legal things remained, but they'd filed no charges; the ruling being Gabrielle acted in self-defense. We were slowly putting everything behind us and working on healing emotionally.

I squeezed her hand before releasing it and draped an arm around her shoulders, pulling her closer. I couldn't stop touching her or Dani, especially when I thought about how close I'd come to losing them both.

"So, I've got a question for you…" I started.

"What's that?"

"How do you feel about having another baby?"

She smiled. "You want to have another baby?"

"I want to have another baby with *you*. I want to be there from the beginning this time."

She studied me, and I didn't miss the glow of love in her eyes before lowering her head to my shoulder. "I would like that very much."

I rested my head on top of hers. We sat, enjoying the peaceful surroundings for a moment, before I stood with a hand out. "Come here."

She let me pull her up and we walked to the water line. A strong breeze flipped her hair around her face and hugged her strapless red summer dress closer to her body. I tucked my hands into the pockets of my gray slacks, and she hooked her arm through mine as we took in the city skyline in the distance. I cleared my throat.

"The first time I brought you out here, I somehow knew I wanted you in my life forever. No matter what. That what we had was real. Special, even." I turned and held her hands. "Even to this day, I'm in awe you were willing to see past all the shit in my life and just be with me, the *real* me, no matter what was going on, no matter what anyone else said. Especially considering all the shit that went down. When I think about how close I came to losing you two; first with Terrell, and then afterward…" I stopped and cleared my throat against the emotions constricting it.

She reached out and touched her finger to my lips. "But you didn't."

"I wouldn't have been able to handle it, G. I can't lose you and I can't lose Dani." She tried to speak again, but I kept talking. "Let me get this out."

She nodded as I paused and took a deep breath.

"You two are my life. I never believed someone would love me, or that I even deserved to be loved. I certainly never believed I could love anyone more than life itself. I didn't believe I could ever have a family filled with love and happiness and all that cheesy shit. That's not what I knew, but you showed me not only that I can be loved, but I can return that love and have the family I always dreamed about. And I thank you for that."

I gave her a small smile, which she returned as her eyes flooded with tears. I caught her mouth, briefly tangling my tongue with hers, before pulling back and resting my forehead against hers. Dusk was settling around us, the light of the day making the slow transition to night as the lights of the city burned in the background.

"You are my life, Gabrielle," I continued in a low voice. "Even when we weren't together, you were still in my head and my heart every day. You're the reason I'm a success, the reason I went to rehab, got clean, and the reason I'm still standing here today. I've always promised you always, and that's what I want, what I want to give you." I straightened so I could gaze into her eyes.

"Marry me."

She gasped and her eyes widened. "Marry…? Danny, are you serious?"

"I've never been more serious in my life."

"Omigod!" She threw her arms around my neck. "Yes!"

I took her mouth with mine. When we separated, we smiled as I took her hand in mine.

"Well, I guess I need to get you a ring."

"I don't need one."

"What the hell do you take me for?" I chuckled and reached into a pocket. "I'm not that white-trash."

I opened the small box facing her, and her eyes widened as she took in the ring. "It's probably a little bigger than what you would have picked out, but I designed it, and it will look awesome on you."

"A little bigger?" she said, short of breath. "Danny, it's huge. I can't wear that. It's too much."

I pulled out the large emerald-cut diamond surrounded by rubies and aquamarines, reminiscent of the necklace I'd given her for our first Christmas, which hung around her neck. "You can too wear it." I put the ring on her finger and held it up to catch the light as I grinned. "Like I said, you can wear the hell out of that thing."

"It's beautiful."

"Nothing's as beautiful as you, but it will do."

I kissed her again, and this time when I pulled back, we were both breathless. Grabbing her hand, I turned her toward the car. "Let's go get started on a little brother or sister for Dani."

* * * * *

About the Author

Rhonda owes her love of reading to her mother who would read to her each night before bed and sometimes give into her pleads for more than one chapter. These days, if Rhonda doesn't have a book in her hands, it feels like something is missing. While romance is her true passion, Rhonda enjoys reading multiple genres.

Born in California, but transplanted to the Midwest, Rhonda is warm weather girl to the bone (even years later, winter and her are not on speaking terms), and loves nothing more than a balmy, summer evening. She and her husband are diehard fans of pretty much all sports. Rhonda was a life-long dancer before her body told her she needed to come down off her toes and wrap it up. She also loves all animals--especially moose. She is a proud member of Romance Writers of America.

Rhonda loves to hear from readers, so please visit her website at http://www.rhondashaw.com. You can also find her on Facebook at Rhonda Shaw, Author and Twitter at @AuthorRShaw. Make sure to sign up for her newsletter to receive updates about upcoming titles and their release dates.

Other Titles by Rhonda Shaw

<u>Men of the Show Series</u>

The Changeup (Book 1)
The Ace (Book 2)
Caught (Book 3)

www.ingramcontent.com/pod-product-compliance
Lightning Source LLC
Chambersburg PA
CBHW050025180626
46810CB00002B/584